THE FINAL BORN

The Final Born

By Mason Monteith

Copyright © 2024 by Mason Monteith

Contact Info: *authormasonmonteith@gmail.com*

Chapter Header and Dividers by: Etheric Tales

Cover Design by: Miriam Schwardt @miriamschwardt_designs

Hardcover Design by: @Okaykois

Map by: Saumya Singh @Saumyasvision/Inkarnate

Race Design by: Senrouk @senrouk_arts

ISBN: 979-8-9899032-1-4 (hardcover) 979-8-9899032-0-7 (paperback) 979-8-9899032-4-5 (ebook)

First edition: May 2024

10 9 8 7 6 5 4 3 2

MASON MONTEITH

THE FINAL BORN

SHARDS OF MAGICK

SIGN UP FOR MY AUTHOR NEWSLETTER

Be the first to learn about Mason Monteith's new releases and receive exclusive content for both readers and writers!

WWW.MASONMONTEITH.COM

CONTENTS

Dedicated to everyone who has challenged the box others put you
in.
Never let the perspective of others define you – and keep charging
forward towards your dreams.

THE FINAL BORN is a gritty and violent Ancient-Greek-inspired fantasy novel with elements that may be triggering for some readers, including but not limited to: depictions of and references to death, depression, bullying, trauma, animal death, and physical harm. Please be mindful of these and other possible triggers.

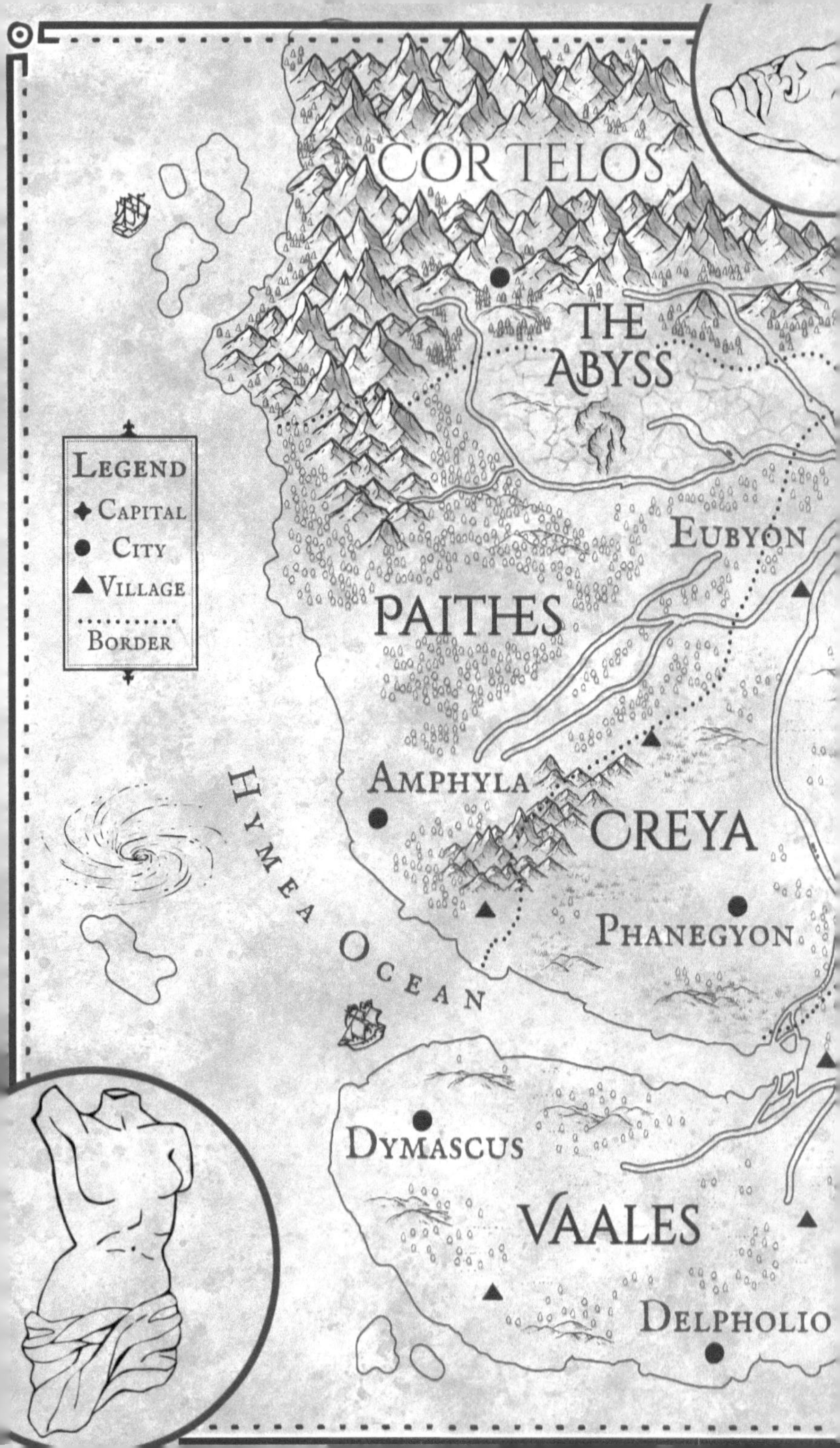

COR TELOS
THE ABYSS
EUBYON
PAITHES
CREYA
AMPHYLA
PHANEGYON
HYMEA OCEAN
DYMASCUS
VAALES
DELPHOLIO
LEGEND
CAPITAL
CITY
VILLAGE
BORDER

MYTHDE
PILAVIA
THE BORYDA SEA
CAPITAL
LYREAS
MYRMEZE BAY
RYZAKE
ISLAND OF ARYNTH
SHARDS OF ARYNTH
THE EMPIRE OF
VALYSA

THE RACES OF VASYLA

HUMANS

The humans of Vasyla are one of the more common people found here. The most common appearance of a human in Vasyla is fair, copper, or deep umber skin tones. Heather or Dark brown hair, and emerald eyes are all the more common looks found in humans - though the royal lineage of the empire is known for its fair skin, white hair, and ocean-blue eyes.

While humans have the weakest connection to Magick of all peoples, they have the highest affinity with controlled magicks with very few naturally containing the ability to handle wild magicks. since magick is outlawed within the empire, with the exception of water magicks, it is hard to say whether or not this statistic has changed over the years.

Humans take up two of the four Houses of the Emperor's Council. House Nephus and House Teresi both currently have human head Lords and Ladies.

S K O R V I A N S

The Skorvis or Skorvians are a desert-dwelling people known for their medicines and healing capabilities. Not only do they excel in healing magic, but they are also known for having the ability to create the deadliest poisons from their metastoma.

Most Skorvis in the Vasylian Empire stay within the capital city for trade or take up residence within the southern territories due to a preference for a warm climate - though there are some who are known to travel north to learn about rare poisonous plants of the northern territories.

The Skorvis people are best known for trade overseas, as the siren's call has little to no effect on male or female Skorvians.

VOLTUANS

Gypsborn or Voltuans are a people akin to vultures. Thought to have evolved from primitive birds like how humans are assumed to have come from apes. Birds are sacred in Vasyla, as they are seen as messengers of the Aspects. Because of the sacred nature of birds due to the religious state of the empire, Voltuans are also considered holy despite being a regular people. It has gotten to the point where knights will avoid any disturbance involving a Voltuan, in fear of upsetting the One in all their Aspects. Most Voltuans stick to their own communities but there are a few who are outwardly social. It is more common to find friendly Voltuans within the lower district of the capital city Lyreas than it is to find any in the upper districts.

THERE ARE VERY FEW VOLTUANS WITHIN THE CHURCH

CENTAUR

Besides humans, Centaurs are the second most common people within Vasyla. Half-horse half-human people said to come from the mountains. Most notable is the sheer amount of them in the Northern Territory of Cor Telos, The district currently run by House Florakys.

Centaurs tend to be tall, standing at seven feet or taller, but there are cases of half-centaurs who usually end up far smaller than their usual sizing. They are best known for their edge in combat - and most of Vasyla's armies are made up of the centaur of the north.

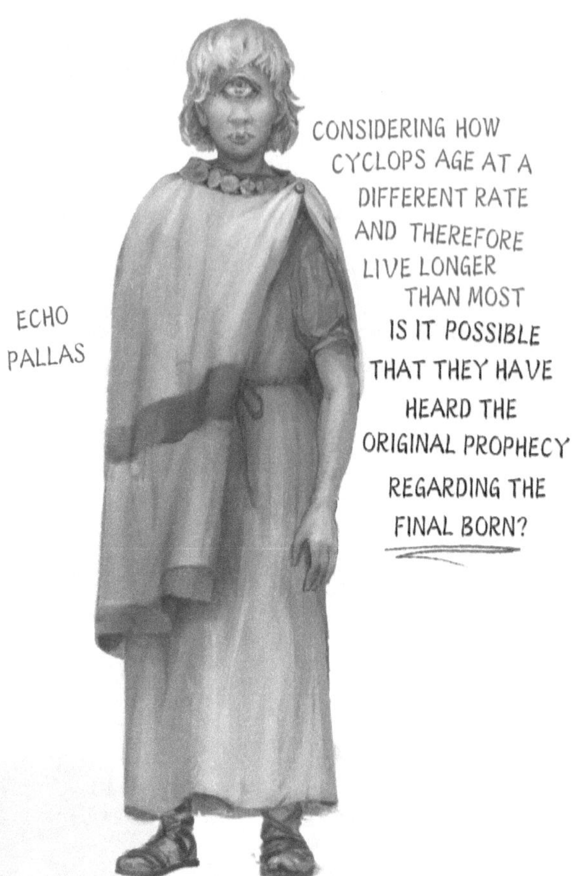

CYCLOPS

Cyclops are the most unique people of Vasyla, as they do not age at the same rate as others. A twenty-five-year-old Cyclops may be at the same educational stage as other races but they still have the look and size of a child.

Cyclops do not begin to grow to their full height until they pass the age of eighty and they don't stop growing until they die. The largest recorded height of a Cyclops was nearly fifteen feet tall and died at 532. The average Cyclops only lives to be 380, so it is extremely rare.

O P H I O P H O R

Ophiophor are not as much a people as they are a curse. From the descendants of the dragon slayers of the island of Arynth - when the dragons that once ravaged the island and its shards for riches were finally wiped out they left a curse upon their killers. Any descendant of dragon killer blood would be cursed to bear the bodies of incomplete dragons - or serpents. Seen as a sin against dragonkind, serpents are not even worth than more animalistic form of a dragon, the lesser drake.

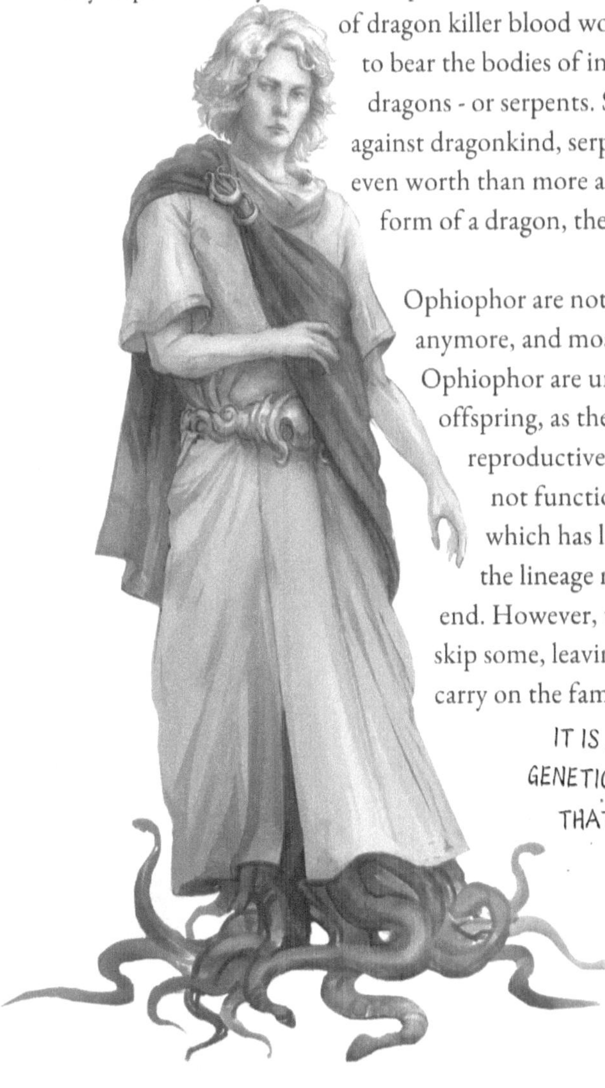

Ophiophor are not common anymore, and most who are Ophiophor are unable to bear offspring, as their reproductive system does not function normally which has led to most of the lineage meeting its end. However, this curse does skip some, leaving siblings to carry on the family bloodline.

IT IS ESSENTIALLY A GENETIC DEAD END LIKE THAT OF A MULE

PRONUNCIATION GUIDE

Peoples and Places:

Vasylia: *vas·see·lé·a*

Vasylian: *vas·see·li·an*

Vasylite: *vas·sil·lite*

Lyreas: *lie·rē·ə*

Paithes: *pə·th·es*

Creya: *krā·ya*

Vaales: *vāl·es*

Cor Telos: *kȯr tell·ōs*

Arynth: *er·rin(t)·thē*

Pilavia: *pil·lā·vē·ə*

Races:

Human: *hyu·man*
Skorvian: *scór·vi·an*
Voltuan: *vōl·tu·an*
Centaur: *sen·tór*
Cyclops: *sī·kläps*
Ophiophor: *ō·fē·o·for*

Names:

Calypso Pallas: *ka·lip·so pal·las*
Ophelya Nephus: *o·feel·ee·a nef·us*
Leandre Elias: *lé·an·dré ee·lie·as*
Oryon Pallas: *o·rie·ən pal·las*
Harkyn Florakys: *har·kin flór·é·kis*
Deakon Pallas: *dee·kən pal·las*
Hectyr Pallas: *hec·tuyr pal·las*
Avalon Pallas: *av·ə·lahn pal·las*
Adonys Pallas: *ə·do·nis pal·las*
Kyril Pallas: *kir·əl pal·las*
Echo Pallas: *e·kō pal·las*
Zagora: *za·gór·ra*
Iago: *ee·ah·go*

The Cycle of Traditions

Kryptym, 1057 AH (Anno Harmonia)
As winter approaches, Dragons and Wyverns return to their dens — signaling the cold winds and rain of autumn in The Empire of Vasyla. The Vasylian's turn their focus to the Fertility Aspect as they pray for bountiful harvests before the bitter cold kills any remaining growth. Joy fills the air as the festival begins this season. The Zodiac of Kryptym is the Vulture. Bringing with it death and rebirth in the image of autumn.
The Festival of Halved Souls is near...

1

TWO SIDES OF THE SAME COIN
CALYPSO

Calypso Pallas never considered herself a very trusting person. As a Pallas, she was a royal scion — descended from generations of bloodshed and misery until it reached her. Standing on the streets of the Vasylian Empire capital city, it was to no one's surprise as to why.

As people passed the robust young woman many glared or cursed under their breath as they hurried by. Calypso ducked her head as she backed up closer to the alley. Further, out of sight, she watched those who passed by with envy — she stood out amongst the crowds with her ashy blonde hair, hazel eyes, and milky white skin from being sheltered many days away from the sun. Most people within the empire looked vastly different from her. Many humans had copper or heather-colored hair, and emerald or amber eyes — and that was just the humans. The rare sight of a scorpion-like Skorvian to the common centaur roaming the streets — nothing looked alike to a Pallas royal. Then again, neither did Calypso.

Without the ocean-blue eyes and gleaming white hair of the royal lineage, Calypso knew her appearance was off-putting for many. She was similar to the other royals but with key differences. Like a piece of silver in a bag filled with gold — perhaps it held value, but it was easily overlooked by the shimmer of the higher value coin.

Yet this difference in appearance was not the reason she was disliked by most of her people. Born under the star of the White Tern, Calypso was thought to be an ill omen. It had been many moons since the last royal was born under that star, and they were remembered with a grim story.

Taking a deep breath, Calypso put up her hood and strode out into the sea of people. *I have a mission to complete*, she thought to herself. *And that means no time to sulk about myself.*

The brick roads were packed with people of all kinds, yet despite the heat radiating through crowded areas of those rushing to and fro, the cool air of the harvest season kept the peace in the city. Cal quietly thanks the Wind Aspect under her breath for keeping the day cool — if she had to break up one more fight in the streets she might not be able to keep her level head. And that was something she could not afford.

Not with the eyes of the empire already waiting for her to slip up. One mistake and it was all over for her.

The streets were crowded as people were hurrying to prepare for the upcoming festival, and shopkeepers hurried to raise prices with the sudden prospects of foolish tourists in the area. Stalls were filled with an overabundance of ridiculously priced products: from vibrant bolts of silks and fabrics to the baker's olive cheese breads, which filled the air with its savory and tangy scent. Calypso smiled. Relishing the nice scent in the air as she passed the baker's stall, however, she doesn't dare stop for fear of how sour that interaction could go should she be identified.

Resting her hand on the hilt of her sword she relaxed slightly; *I'd much prefer to have kept my spear on hand... but it would be much more obvious of me to carry such an ornate weapon around. Besides, an iron machaira blade is much more common to see in the city. It is better to blend in with it.*

Calypso made her way past the busy markets and down the streets towards the outer ring of the great Capital City — to the Lower District. This was where her goal would be completed. Then she could return to the Citadel. *Hopefully, I can make it back in time for training.*

As she reached the Lower District of the capital city, she grinned. Though it was not as vibrant or as joyful as the Upper District, this place was just... better. Many here had it rough, they were harsh and aggressive to anyone who treated them with disrespect or even looked at them wrong. At the same time, they showed unending kindness to those who treated them the same. It was as Calypso wished it could be back at the Citadel.

Walking over a bridge, she spotted a small gondola being rowed down the river beneath her. Calypso clenched her jaw as the person on it squinted at her, as though they were trying to recall her face — but as soon as they recognized her they didn't shout or sneer, instead, they smiled and waved. Less people recognized her here, at least — not as Princess Calypso. They had much more important things to do than memorize the faces of all seven royal scions. After all, only one would become emperor, and their power was still kept in check by the court. The Lower District kept their attention on the Lords and Ladies who guided the emperor — as there was no stronger influence over the rule of an empire than those who whispered in the leader's ear. Calypso let out a relieved sigh before waving back.

He may recognize me for what the Lower District knows of me, but he does not know of my true identity. Calypso reminded herself as she dipped her head at the man. Continuing to make her way onward. She didn't have time for idle chat and neither did he.

Down here, I am just Cal — not Calypso.

So why do I still feel so anxious? This is supposed to be my safe place.

She shook her head as though it would ward off the ill mood that hung over her like a thick fog, continuing down the eerie streets. The Lower District had been made dark by the shadows cast by the large buildings uphill in the upper-class ring of the city, and darker still due to the bridges spanning rivers and between second-level streets for those of the Lower District to walk beneath.

Calypso finally stopped in front of a beat-up-looking brick building — it was a tavern. It was only midday but the place was already bustling with business by the sounds of loud cheering and clamoring of glasses being slammed down onto tables. Cal shoved her way into the building and everyone went quiet as they turned to see who entered. It was so quiet one could hear a feather fall as the patrons stared at the intruder.

As they stared, almost as though they were waiting for something, Cal met their gaze unwavering. She pulled an object out of her bag, the fang of a lesser dragon. As they saw the object, they let out booming cheers as they raised their half-empty glasses to her.

The man behind the bar let out a cackle — which came out as more of a squawk as Cal made her way over with the fang. He was a Voltuan — the bird-like people who were known for their devout belief in the All-Aspects. Because of the importance of birds in Vasyla as they were known for being messengers of the Aspects, Voltuans in turn were treated with the highest of respects... for the most part. It was odd to find one running a tavern and working with mercenaries, but here he was. Iago the Voltuan, in all of his scrawny feathered glory. His graying feathers were already ruffled as he saw the object which Cal held, this made her laugh.

"Surprised I made it back?" Cal asked as she dropped the fang onto the lower end of the bar. This end was made for humans and other races of a shorter stature. Iago grimaced as he lifted it with a rag and wiped the spot on the counter down.

"It's not that, I was hoping the knights would listen to our request for once... But a job done is a job done. Excellent work as always Cal." He rolled the tooth around in the cloth, it was as hefty as his taloned hand. "How come this was all you brought back?" he asked as he held a magnifying glass up to it.

"It had ravaged the wildlife of the area for a while, I figured it best to leave the body and allow the scavengers to have it."

Well, that and I couldn't haul it back to the Citadel last night before bringing it here, but Iago doesn't need to know that.

"So the knights still won't respond to any of your requests?" Cal asked as she laid her sword on the chair beside her. She leaned against the bar.

"Of course, they won't!" piped up a centaur holding a glass of wine in each hand, "It's the festival soon — they don't care about us down here right now!"

"Or ever," added a small Cyclops woman, everyone took a huge chug of wine in response. Calypso rolled her eyes at that. The knights were supposed to be a figure of hope and comfort for those in the city. *I would make a much better knight.*

"It's a good thing you're around Cal, it has been difficult with the sudden rise in beasts coming near hunting territory."

This was it. This was the light that could be seen at the end of the tunnel. Cal was a hero, with far more possibility than she ever had as the accursed Princess Calypso. With a title nobody was even sure could be hers. As Cal saw the joy and cheer of the warriors and mercenaries of the Lower District, she felt a small seed of hope sprout within her. Perhaps this was it, this was how her life could be fixed. By slowly winning over the people with her strength. Or was it just wishful thinking? After all, none of the people in the tavern knew she was a royal scion.

Cal dipped her head in response to the praise, making them laugh. Iago squawked, "See? She even has manners like a royal! Our Cal here could blend in anywhere!"

Yet there it was, always following her everywhere. Calypso was very lucky those of the Lower District didn't care much for the royal scions, or they might have figured it out by now.

If they found out who she was, would they despise her for the curse? Or would they accept her as a warrior?

Is there a way I could prove myself to the people of Vasyla so I could survive? Or was it just a pitiful desperate dream?

"Here's your pay —" Iago dropped a small pouch of coins onto the bar, Cal opened it. Silver Cryss coins. He scratched his neck and shifted from foot to foot. "Eh, sorry it couldn't be more. You know things have been getting rough in these parts."

The tavern patrons glanced over to watch and a few shook their heads, glaring at the small bag and Iago. He lowered his head in shame.

"It isn't a problem, the lesser dragon was an easy kill, so the pay is equivalent. Besides —" She took the pouch and shoved it back towards him. "I believe *I* owed *you* after a night of seemingly infinitely wine coming my way."

The patrons went back to their conversations and wine, and Iago let out a relieved sigh. There had been no such night, but she didn't want to take his money — or embarrass him.

"You're a blessing from the Aspects, Cal."

"A blessing?" Cal forced a laugh. "I doubt that very much."

Placing her sword back onto her belt, Cal stood up. "I need to get going now, I'll try to be back sometime this week to check for any new requests."

"Can't let the blade go rust now, can ya?!" A centaur cheered as she walked past.

"You know it," Cal said as she pushed the door open. She said her goodbyes and shut the door. Letting out a sigh.

It was time to go back to the Citadel. *So why do I not want to go?* Cal began to make her way out of the Lower District but found herself taking a different path. Within twenty minutes, the town square had come into sight. The middle ground between the upper and Lower Districts, and the entrance to the abandoned Colosseum. Although, abandoned — it was still used, it just wasn't particularly active at the moment as during the festival coming up, it was seen as a disrespect to focus on glory in battle rather than thanks to the Aspects. When the challenge for the crown began though... It would be a different story.

Calypso looked around, it wasn't too busy here... well it was.

But it wouldn't hurt to sit down and rest for a while, would it? Returning to the Citadel right away wasn't necessary, I would be far too early to train anyway.

Calypso pulled at her hood, making sure enough of her face was covered before going to sit at a slab bench near the baker's market. She smiled slightly at the chance of a moment's peace within the city, as moments like these did not come often. Cal relaxed as she watched passersby from the quiet edge of the city center. The sound of water flowing through the fountain made the sounds of loud crowds bearable.

Cal watched as two children hurried between others as they played in the busy street, an elderly woman chatting with a middle-aged shopkeeper, a group of water magick users hurried to get back to the piers, and finally, the gleam of armor shining in the sunlight caught her eye. Calypso couldn't help but stare. Not because she was charmed by its wearer, but because all she daydreams of was herself striding down the streets with them. Helping to keep the peace in the Vasyla Empire's cities, as they *should* be doing better. She frowned at them as she recalled Iago's wounded pride at having to ask the knights for help. It took a great deal to get anyone from the Lower Districts to ask them for help, yet still, they didn't give it.

If I became a knight, a good one for all... Would that be accepted?

Cal sighed and waited another moment before she began to get up to continue back to the Citadel. As she stood the winds blew through the streets pushing at her, and she laughed halfheartedly.

Even the winds don't want me to return.

She may have wanted to stay, but she knew there would be repercussions for her actions if she continued to stay out too long without her guard there.

It was only after the knights had passed that the sounds of a man and woman arguing nearby reached her ears. Others pass by the pair, casting concerned glances at the woman but not stopping to intervene. The man seemed sluggish, his words slurring together and unable to focus his eyes as he shouted obscurities at her. Drunk this early? Though many had started to drink by this hour, it was odd to see someone already drunk.

Cal watched the man, his brows furrowed and his nose crinkled in disgust at the woman as he grabbed at her arm. She shouted in surprise and struggled to pull away, looking around for help. Cal didn't hesitate as she stepped forward.

"I suggest you step away," Cal said as she stopped by them, the man dizzily wobbled about as he gripped the woman for support.

"You should — you should keep your nose to yourself — " His words were a mumbling mess as he spoke. Calypso stepped between him and the woman and pulled his arm away from hers, shoving him away. He stumbled back and caught himself by grabbing the wall. He glared up at her.

"I don't wanna hit a girl," He slurred his words, "but you're making — making me do this —" He reared back to punch her and threw a sloppy punch. Calypso ducked beneath it with ease, nose curling at the stench of booze. His fist didn't even touch the top of her cloak. The man looked down and saw her face from beneath the cloak.

"Wait... you're —"

Before he could finish, she raised her fists into a defensive position. Quickly she jabbed him in the gut and threw another under his jaw. He fell back into the baskets of the nearest market stall. Angering the shopkeeper. They yelled at him to get out but he didn't move. He was out cold. Calypso scoffed before turning to the woman.

"You should go ahead and get out of here, the knights should find him... eventually," Cal said as she began to turn away.

The woman dipped her head quickly, "Thank you! Thank you a million times over, I don't know what would've happened if —"

The woman lifted her head and looked up at Calypso's face beneath the hood. As her eyes went wide, Cal grit her teeth.

The woman gasped, "You're —"

"*Princess Calypso!*"

Cal frowned as the call of a young knight rang out around the fountain, she turned to see he was making his way over and the crowd had parted to allow him through. She glanced back at the woman and shook her head. The woman backed away, pointing with shaky hands.

"You can try to change, you can dress like a commoner and act like one too, but a demon dressed like a human is still a demon!"

A demon? Now that is a new one.

The crowd began muttering amongst themselves as the word spread around like a wave in the ocean.

"Demon?! Who said a demon is here?"

"No, it's a royal scion!"

"Which one is it?"

"I heard someone say Calypso!"

Cal lifted her hood of the cloak up and sighed at the woman.

"By the Aspects... It is Princess Calypso!"

"How dare she show her face here!"

"Someone should call for the knights!"

"Get out of here," was all Cal muttered to the woman before slipping past her into the nearest alley. Her skin crawled as she felt the woman's gaze piercing her back as she slipped away. Feeling relief only once she turned a corner behind a building and fell out of her sight. The sound of clanking light armor and footsteps echo behind her and Cal quickly prepared for an ambush.

"Princess Cal-"

As the person rounded the corner, Cal grabbed them. Shoving them to the wall. Covering their mouth with the palm of her hand so they could stop calling her name. As she looked him over though, she groaned before backing away.

"Really?"

It was Leandre, her knight. He was different looking from the other human knights, with his warm skin tone, prominent, narrow gray eyes, wavy, ashy-brown hair, and distinctive large nose and high cheekbones. But this wasn't exactly what made him stand out. No, it was due to the fact that he was far shorter than the average human in Vasyla, standing just a few hairs taller than Calypso, who stood at 5'7. He wasn't all that intimidating either and seemed more... introverted than ominous. He was more comparable to a lost puppy than a knight — but that was mostly Cal's opinion of him.

"Leandre!" Calypso sighed as she quickly stepped away. "Sorry, I didn't recognize it was you when I grabbed you. I didn't hurt you, did I?"

As Leandre dusted himself off, he shook his head. "You startled me, but I'm ok." His eyes were narrowed as he looked at her. Was he annoyed?

"What have I said about using my name and title in public?" As Cal stepped away he quickly dipped his head in apology. "You're my personal guard for crying out loud! I would think you of all people would know better than that."

"You looked like you were in trouble, Princess —" He stopped himself, "Er —Cal."

"Well, saying that only made it worse!"

Leandre frowned and lowered his gaze, as Calypso looked at his solemn expression she relaxed slightly. It wasn't like he had ill intentions... Everyone else might but he didn't.

"I thought I had another hour before I had to go back to the Citadel."

Leandre sighed, "Well..."

"What happened?" She asked.

"I had forgotten about preparations for tomorrow's festivities when I told you that," Leandre answered, hardly able to meet her gaze. "It is better for you to stay in the Citadel before more guests begin arriving."

Calypso clenched a fist at her side, angry. Not quite at Leandre's forgetfulness, but at her own.

"Fine."

At least that means Ophelya will be arriving in the capital soon.

Leandre brightened up slightly, "We're going back?"

"Sadly, we have to," Calypso answered begrudgingly. "Hopefully, Emperor Oryon doesn't push me into coming to the festival opening."

You would think he would be thankful when I didn't show my face in public... Yet still... he probably would want all the royal scions at this event in particular.

Calypso sighed, It was almost enough to make her hideout in her room until the event ended, but she knew she couldn't keep avoiding it.

After all, fate *is* absolute, is it not?

Calypso turned to look down the alley, beginning to make her way to the quickest path back to the Citadel.

"Let's begin heading back."

2
THE LIFE OF A HOLLOW KNIGHT
LEANDRE

For Leandre, training with Cal had once been something fun and lighthearted. It began when Cal saw Leandre during his training to become her guard. Leandre had been a foolish child — he was quite the show-off and loved the attention Calypso gave him. This led to her wanting to be trained as well. So he taught her in secret, as the royal scions were only permitted to receive strictly regulated training to prevent anyone from having an advantage against the rest. They could continue their training alone, but to get outside help and an advantage? That was unfair. Of course, that didn't mean they didn't go around this rule, but it was a matter of if you were caught or not.

When this began, that was one of Leandre's earliest memories, the rest of it was stuck in a fog of confusion and shards of recollection.

And now, Calypso wanted to become a knight.

Leandre couldn't stop thinking of how hard it was just to leave the Citadel to find Cal. As soon as he had reached the gates, the other guards stopped him to ask why he wasn't with the princess — when they discovered that she escaped his sight they laughed. Their mocking never ceased as he tried to push past, and that's when the fighting began.

It's not like they would tell anyone, seeing that they lost...

"Come on, we have plenty of time for a few more bouts!" Cal said loudly, pulling Leandre out of his thoughts.

Leandre grit his teeth as he glanced around anxiously. The knights' training area might have been empty, but for how long? When would one of them return? Usually, they would take their training to the caves by the shores but it was too late in the day to make the trip there and back in time. Her speaking so loud was careless and needlessly risky. His face flushed as he recalled his own mistake calling her in public earlier.

I allowed my emotions to get the better of me when I finally found her. Surely that's not such a crime... right?

His heart faltered a bit as he remembered Cal's angry expression as she shoved him against the wall in the alley. He shook his head as he looked back over at her. She wiped the sweat from her brow and eagerly await the next bout.

This is too dangerous — if she were ever found receiving extra training that no other royal scion got... it would be seen as preferential treatment. She would be ahead of the others by twisted means They could have my head for this...

But then again...
They could have hers if she is without it.

Leandre handed Calypso a spear after a moment, silently praying to the Aspects that the training area remained clear while they still used it.

"This round, you take the spear, and I will be using the machaira."

The curved blade would be difficult to face with a spear, as it could hook and catch her weapon if used correctly, but it also meant she would be more well-rounded for tough situations in combat.

As soon as Leandre got into a defensive position Calypso charged. She deflected Leandre's defensive moves with ease. She was a robust woman, but many didn't realize how much of her build was muscle as her attacks were quite difficult for Leandre to deflect — But still, after several bouts between the pair she was beginning to wear down.

Leandre's eyes landed on her right leg, she was favoring it and putting less pressure down as she moved forward to strike. Leandre took this advantage, ducking towards her right side and hitting it with the hilt of his blade. It was enough to topple her, but not enough for permanent damage. Cal landed on the ground and rolled to avoid too much direct force. She sat up with her nose scrunched in disgust.

"That was a dirty move for a knight," Cal growled.

Leandre laughed, "Knights will not be the only thing you face."

She grimaced in pain and gripped her spear for support, Leandre's eyes widened.

"I didn't mean to hurt you, are you alright?" He began to lean down to help her up, but before he could react Cal swept the floor with the spear and knocked him off his feet. Leandre looked up to see Cal at her feet, her spear pointing at his chest. Leandre felt his face flush as she smiled down at him. Eyes glistened with excitement at her victory.

"Call it a draw?" Leandre said, putting his hands up.

Calypso laughed heartily, "Alright fine, you look like you could use it." A wide grin spread across her face when she extended a hand to help him up. As they stood, Leandre feels the aching in his body from all the workouts of training suddenly stopping. "It's about time to retire for the day." He said as he looked at the setting sun. She nodded and tried to control her ragged breathing as she took her spear back to the weapons rack.

"Why were you favoring your leg?" Leandre asked, "Don't tell me you went out again."

She didn't look at him as he placed his weapon away as well. Her cheery demeanor was suddenly gone.

"Cal, you can't keep going out like you're a knight." He sighed. She turned away.

"How else will I be able to become a knight if I can't build a reputation?"

"Because of your other reputation, and what is expected of you as a royal!"

"You mean to die?" She said, turning to glare at him.

"It isn't guaranteed that you will lose the challenge to your siblings, that is why we are training."

"No," she said as she started to walk away. "That is why you think we are training, I have no interest in even attempting to survive that bloodbath of a challenge. I will find a way out of it."

"What other choice do you have?!" Leandre said angrily, "I can't defend you from them, so you must survive it."

"If I became ruler, the people would call for my head," She laughed, "After all, I'm cursed remember?"

Leandre's face was flushed as he followed her back into the Citadel's looming hallways of pillars and paintings. *What else can I do for her? I train her to survive, but her plan is dangerous! But how I can defend her when I can't even make a decision for my own future...*

If only she never chose me as her knight.

Leandre frowned, guilt was written all over his face for even having bitter thoughts against Calypso. Yet still, he felt useless.

Without my memories, every move I make feels like a shot in the dark or a fool's errand. Like I would make one wrong choice because I lack the precognition to make the intelligent one. Is there more I should be doing for her as a knight? It's not like I can just take out the competition and if I did — I wouldn't make it one step out of the capital. Then I'm no use to myself or Cal.

Leandre watched the servants they passed on the way back to Cal's room for the night. Not one of them looked at her directly — quickly averting their gaze or changing to an awkward pace to get away from her. Yet Cal continued striding forward like nothing was wrong as the servants hurried away to work, no doubt hurrying for final preparations for the festival's opening soon, but still.

"I wish we had been able to train longer." Cal muttered once servants were out of earshot, "We had planned to this evening anyways."

"Of course, we had, Princess," Leandre agreed, "But the plan was for much earlier than it is now — and you need to sleep before tomorrow's events."

She rolled her eyes, "I already told you that you don't have to call me princess, nobody else does." Leandre sighed before she continued speaking. "Anyways we may have time for extra training in the morning if I get up early enough... Or we could try to catch Ophelya on her way here."

He smiled, *it would be nice if the three of us could have a moment alone like we used to. But right now I couldn't focus on that.*

Leandre cast a glance around the halls, nobody was nearby. He took a few strides faster to catch up to and walk beside Calypso. *This is my chance.*

"Princess —"

Cal cast an annoyed look at him, making him quickly straighten up his stance.

"- Er... Calypso — you know I'm not against teaching you to defend yourself — but this? Battle training? You are aware of what the others will think if they find out —"

"Find out about what?"

Leandre clenched a fist at his side as he turned to see three shapes appear from one of the rooms down the hall.

It was Kyril, the fifth child of the emperor, and one of Cal's six other half-siblings. Despite being further down the totem pole of children under the emperor, Kyril was a rather cocky man. All because his scheming mother, a concubine, was able to convince Emperor Oryon to name their son after the tenth emperor of Vasyla.

"Why should you care?" Calypso retorted sharply. Leandre stood to attention and took a step behind Calypso — where knights should be — as Kyril glided across the marble flooring to stand in front of them with his own guards behind him. *Two* guards.

"You know, I have been hearing strange rumors of odd behavior amongst some of our siblings... most notably of you." He said snidely as he glanced at Cal. "I am surprised to hear you are training, all things considered."

Leandre frowned at his implications as his guard stifled a laugh.

"What is that supposed to mean?" Leandre asked through clenched teeth. He knew it was out of turn for him to speak to a scion so casually, but so was Kyril.

He put his hands up and stepped back, "Whoa, no need to get aggressive. I only mean it must be tiring for someone of her size to swing a sword — besides, I thought you didn't care about fighting to rule?"

Fighting to rule. That's right. The challenge. Everyone knows that once the Emperor passes it will be time for the half-siblings to begin a competition of survival to see who will defeat all others to rule. The Challenge of Cressyda. All stemming from the greed of a younger sibling with powerful magick who covet the throne her brother was meant to fill. Over a millennium ago now. The Vasyla Empire is the only country known to have such a barbaric tradition

— yet somehow the empire was considered the strongest in terms of government, with the emperor and his... or her court.

"Who said I do care?"

"You're right, why even try? You are the youngest, after all."

Leandre glanced at Cal, noticing her trying to force her shoulders to relax but finding it excruciatingly hard. *I would too*, He thought to himself as he looked at the smug expression on Kyril's face. He continued speaking after a moment.

"I only think you should be more careful, after all, if anything more gets out about how unruly some of the emperor's children are the people might have more problems, especially with that prophecy looming over your head."

"When are you going to realize that I don't care?" Cal lied.

Kyril shrugged and began to continue past Cal and Leandre, calling back over his shoulder as he did.

"I would suggest you spend the rest of your day preparing for tomorrow's festivities, after all, we don't want you arriving late and exhausted now do we?"

Leandre spun around, bristling at Kyril but Cal shook her head at him as their footsteps echoed throughout the halls.

They continued down the hall in silence, until they finally stopped in front of her room.

"I'm fine from here, Leandre," she said as he opened the door for her. Glancing inside Leandre spotted a dress, fine jewelry, and a mask that had been all neatly laid out. Most likely prepared for the festival the next day.

"Do you need me to call your servant?" He asked.

She shook her head, "No, I'll be fine." She glared inside, "It looks like the emperor will be expecting my attendance tomorrow anyway…"

Leandre nodded before taking up his position next to the doorway. The other guards could at least be trusted in guarding her room at night, but he still kept the first watch.

He slowly began to lean against the pillar before shaking his head and standing up. He may be tired, but he had to stay alert. If she had another guard, he would be able to take shifts protecting her. As her only guard — it all fell to him. Patrolling guards passed him and said nothing.

I can't stand this. The fog in my head, my inability to make a choice, and this bitter feeling I felt towards Calypso. Was it her fault I was here? Or had my foggy recollections been wrong?

How can I tell what in my head is real and what is not?

3
LIVING IN A SHADOW
OPHELYA

People tend to say many a word, but most often those words are hollow and carried little to no meaning so instead of listening to these empty words — Ophelya preferred to watch people. Their actions, movements, and gestures almost always said the opposite of what their words did.

It started when she was little. Her older sister, Maeve, had made a game of it. To ignore people's words and watch their movements and actions instead. To watch if they seemed open or closed off. If they were angry, anxious, or happy. If they were enjoying the conversation or if they were stuck in it or hated it.

If Ophelya made the correct calculation as to what the person's true feelings were without focusing on their words, her sister would reward her. If not, she wouldn't get angry or irritated as their parents did — No, Maeve would push her in the right direction and quietly guide her to try again with someone else.

This odd little bonding moment... This little game of theirs might seem strange, but it's because of that little game that Ophelya had survived this long. It's how she outlived even her sister. It's how she became the sole heiress to a title she did not desire.

Ophelya couldn't help but recall this silly little game as she watched her parents interact. The three of them were inside a carriage on its way to the capital. Her parents didn't even sit side by side, instead opting to be across from one another. Ophelya sat next to her father with her mother across from them both.

The air in the small cart was chilly as the windows had been left open, and the conversations were long and drawn out. Her father wouldn't stop speaking, continuously rubbing his hand over his neck before making wild motions with his hands to go with his words. Meanwhile, her mother chimed in where she could. When she wasn't speaking, however, her lips were pursed tight, and her arms crossed tight against her chest.

So many empty words floated across the air between them. Yet the body language of those within the cart said the real story. Though anyone with half a brain could see that, at least that is what Ophelya believed. The journey had taken them weeks, so of course tensions were high as they neared the end of the treacherous roads.

Of course, Father would be afraid to let her get a word in, Ophelya thought to herself as she watched through narrowed eyes. *For if she did get many it would be to chide and badger him over what to say and what not to say in front of the courts.* She sighed. *Then, of course, he will fail to heed any of her lectures when the time would come for the court meeting while everyone was in the capital.*

This would be one of the first meetings she would be allowed to attend, the one coming up during their visit to the festival. Ophelya's parents weren't getting any younger, and she was coming to the age typical to inherit the position — which of course *terrified* them.

"Ophelya," her mother called — she stifled a sigh as she turned her gaze from the window to her mother. Her sepia brown skin was beginning to look ashy from the colder temperatures outside, her narrow eyes a deep hazel green, her cheekbones high set, she had a prominent jawline and her curly coiled hair was done up so tight that you could see if a single hair were to fall out of place. Ophelya gulped as she looked at her mother. The pair looked almost exactly alike, down to the dark circles beneath their eyes.

I can only hope that it's only skin deep, and not her attitude that I would inherit.

"Yes, mother?" she asked with a sickeningly sweet tone, one that kept most people from finding annoyance with her. Of course, her mother still would, but at least she tried.

Her mother scoffed, "Be sure you remember your goals while you are with us during our meeting."

"Of course, I will," she answered quickly, praying to the Aspects, every single one of them, that her mother would stop there and turn the conversation back to her father. But perhaps the response was too quick.

"There it is, that quick and bold attitude again, exactly like your sister Maeve." She rolled her eyes and held her arms even closer to her chest. "If you don't lose that intense attitude, you'll never snag yourself a royal."

Listen to her, snag a royal. Thankfully she never spoke like this out in public, but if she did... *I couldn't even imagine the consequences.*

Her father let out a quiet sigh of relief as he relaxed in his seat, clearly happy with his wife's change in target. Ophelya struggled not to roll her eyes at him.

"Let's hope my words mean something to you. You can't keep wasting time outside of the court, or did you want to end up like your sister? Dead before achieving anything worthy of the name?"

Ophelya clenched a fist beneath her open palm, *how dare she bring up her like that? Maeve's death was a tragedy yet still, she acts as though it was deserved just because Maeve wasn't afraid to speak her opinion.*

Her mother began gnawing at her fingernails anxiously when the Citadel appeared close. They would be stopping any minute now.

"You've heard the rumors," she continued anxiously. "Cultists — within the capital no less! Not to mention the rumors of the emperor's failing health! At this rate, the Challenge of Cressyda might begin moons earlier than we originally thought!" Her eyes quickly pinned Ophelya in her seat. "That means you will have to secure a relationship with the strongest of the royals to ensure a proposal once they are crowned emperor."

"Or *empress*," her father chimed in, making her mother roll her eyes.

"Yes, yes, or empress. It doesn't matter as long as you manage to achieve something worthy of the Nephus family name."

If I were to become the empress of the next ruler, my parents would no longer be lord or lady, but their places would be more secure as the lesser houses would struggle to be allowed to become the new lord or lady of the land.

Was that really all she wanted? To do nothing in a cozy position? *It wasn't what I wanted.*

The cart finally stopped, and Ophelya finally could breathe.

As she got out, she looked to the Citadel. Built on the hilltop of the capital city, the Citadel is a large ominous structure, with polished pillars and ornate engravings upon every spiraling tower, or block of a room. There were many lush gardens and walkways surrounding it leading to the guest houses along the side as well — this was where each Lord or Lady of the Court was granted their own place to stay during events.

As her parents got out of the cart the servants began getting the luggage off of the carriage. Her mother glared at one younger servant — he was already quite shaky and anxious looking and her gaze didn't help. As they struggled to grab a piece of luggage, they noticed her eyes upon them, making them drop something in fear. And so it began.

While Ophelya's mother spoke angrily at the servants, she spotted two familiar figures near the Citadel entrance. Both are roughly the same size — a curvy woman with long dirty blonde hair and a distinctly shorter knight beside her. Ophelya grinned.

Cal and Leandre were already ready — so it was time to go. As she began to walk away, she froze as her mother clicked her tongue.

"And just where do you think you are going?"

Holding her hands together in front of her, Ophelya looked up through her lashes and softened her gaze. "To see the shore, today will be the only day I have time to see the ports of the capital as after this I intend to focus on my studies intensely."

Her mother narrowed her eyes, clearly not believing a word out of her daughter's mouth.

"She can see the shore while we are here... surely," her father responded. His voice softened as his wife turned her piercing gaze at him. "Afterward, she will be busy with all the work she needs to learn about the running of the court."

She opened her mouth to respond, but before all hell broke loose the foolish servant dropped another container.

Her mother groaned as the servant looked over with wide eyes.

"Fine, I suppose it will be easier to get set up in our guest housing without you underfoot."

Ophelya smiled big, her mother's jaded words bouncing off like sand as she quickly turned and began making her way to the Citadel entrance. Sandals clicking on the brick roads.

I have to get to the shores quickly, Cal and Leandre are already on their way there!

The smell of saltwater and grainy sand on the cold autumn air reached Ophelya long before she reached the shores of the Vasylian capital city of Lyreas. The sun was still high in the sky, and many of the crews working the docks nearby were taking breaks below deck to save their skins — most likely playing cards too before their captains could whip them back to work.

Ophelya jumped from the docks to the beach as she made her way towards the less inhabited end of the shores. Large stony outcrops and coves could be seen in the distance. Very few people actually went to the coves, as rumors of sirens and other beasts calling it home scared them off. Of course, those rumors were of the trio's making, but it worked nonetheless.

As Ophelya slowly made her way towards the cove, she looked out over the sea and smiled as the winds blew on her face. Away from her parent's eyes, she almost felt should could sing.

The ocean has been there for many of my happiest memories, it makes me wish I didn't have to return to our home.

Home. The Southern territory of Vaales. The land was under the watchful eye of the Nephus family. As the current holders of the position on the court, they ruled that shard of the empire in the name of Emperor Oryon. Just as God was split into shards and called the Aspects, the lands of Vasyla had been too.

The land I would supposedly inherit. Ophelya shook her head as though to ward off thoughts of home. *I am here now, and that is what matters.*

She began to hurry towards the cove, and as she neared the entrance laughter could be heard from inside. She peered inside to see both Leandre and Calypso. They were sitting by a shoddily made fire made of gathered sticks and such — with a pile of driftwood that was too wet thrown off to the side. As soon as they turned and saw

Ophelya peering inside they were both on their feet and hurrying over.

"Ophelya!" Calypso shouted gleefully as she pulled her friend into a big hug. Ophelya was almost lifted off the ground by her shorter friend as she hugged her back. Leandre only gave an awkward wave as Ophelya saw him over Cal's shoulder.

"It's good to see you again, Ophelya," Leandre said as the pair separated. Ophelya smiled.

"It is wonderful to be back," she said as she made her way to the fire. "The journey here was awfully long though!"

Calypso laughs, "And here I was beginning to think you'd always hated being in the capital!"

"Well of course I hate the capital with all the royal riff-raff, but the shores are my favorite place to be along with you two." She turned to Calypso, "So what is new? Have you been doing well on your little side quests in the lower district?"

"You knew?!" Leandre asked, astounded. Cal laughs.

"Yes, she mentioned it in her last letter, I didn't mention it to you because well... I expected that reaction."

That's right, the three of them were very lucky to have been able to send letters between themselves without being caught. However, because of the secrecy needed, it took months for the letters to arrive.

Cal pulled something out of her bag, "Here, I kept an extra fang from the lesser dragon to show you."

"That is the fifth time you've pulled that out since we got here!" Leandre scoffed.

Cal handed Ophelya the fang as Leandre laughed and rolled his eyes, it was rather impressive in size — especially for a lesser dragon. Ophelya glanced at Cal — she had quite a proud expression on her face.

The two began bickering over the fang, yet even Leandre looked proud as he chided her for her boldness for going out again.

It is wonderful that she can have small victories like this one, Ophelya thought to herself.

She smiled at her two friends. *My mother may have ideas of grandeur and a tremendous marriage to secure her fate — but the fate that I wanted was within the cove with me, and I would do anything to create a future where I could keep those close to me safe. Even if I had to change the world myself.*

I will not have another event like what happened to my sister.

4
THE FESTIVAL OF HALVED SOULS
LEANDRE

Surrounded by fools dressed in gilded gold and silk, Leandre followed Calypso into the great hall. His skin itched as he glared around at everyone else within the pillared room. He kept his posture straight as he scanned his surroundings, a bitter expression on his face.

"Chin up, Leandre," Cal said quietly. "You look too gloomy."

He grit his teeth as he smiled, "I hate these things."

"You and me both," She laughed.

Leandre sighed as he followed her. *I understand why she hates these things... but it's different for me.*

It's a reminder that I don't belong here.

A reminder that I have nowhere else to call my own.

These are not my people, and they never would be.

He frowned at Calypso's ignorance on the subject but immediately averted his gaze from her.

It's not like it's her fault I'm here...

Not that I can remember anyway.

A small side of Leandre still felt as though Calypso was key in his being brought here, but without the memory to back that up, he could never be certain.

All around them were many rich lavishly dressed people — not many people from the lower class were included tonight, as the opening night of the festival within the Citadel was for the aristocrats, the lords, and the ladies of the empire. Leandre's position here was to view each and every one of them as a threat and to contain any that would arise. This is his job, life, and his path. It was one he never had any choice in.

Many people around them wore gowns or cloaks covered in feathers — of course, they weren't real feathers. They were mock feathers. Birds were seen as messengers to the Aspects — to harm one would be seen as a battle cry against God in all their aspects. Yet to be seen as a messenger to God? That was a luxury few could afford, as only skilled merchants could craft mock feathers from odd materials such as silks, fabrics, or even ropes. Leandre struggled to not curl his nose at the sight.

Just because you can afford an expensive outfit doesn't mean you would be seen as a messenger to the Aspects. It was quite a ridiculous trend, especially when you considered Voltuans lived within the empire. A bird-like race among people trying to mimic birds for a trend? It was odd indeed. Though even more odd was how revered the race was. Voltuans were like anyone else, but because of the respect for birds in the empire, they were seen as holy as well.

Great large tables with foods and refreshments of the highest caliber were set up, with a large space for the dancing and chattering crowds in the center. At the far end of the hall, people were still coming in, opposite of it was the emperor's seat — yet it was still empty. Leandre frowned at this, glancing at Cal. She seemed to have noticed as she looked past the throne but didn't really react, then again, she had gotten better at hiding her emotions in the past few years.

"Are you fine Cal — Princess Calypso?" Leandre quickly corrected himself as others nearby gave him an odd look. Cal didn't seem to notice them as she turned to look at him.

"I'll be fine," she replied with a half-smile. "Don't worry, we won't be staying too long. I know you want to be here as little as I do."

He doesn't respond. He looked expectantly at her as though she would say more, but instead, she gave a reassuring smile before she led the way to the refreshments table.

Leandre bowed his head to her and glanced away, face flushed at her bright smile at him. *Hopefully, nobody notices us interacting too much.*

She had enough to worry about with the future promised to her by the stupid traditions of the empire. It wasn't her fault.

"Things should be starting soon enough," Calypso said as the pair stopped by the table. They both looked up to the emperor's seat again, but still no sign of him.

The emperor had never been late to this festival... other festivals and events yes, but this one? The Festival of Halved Souls? Never.

Everyone in the great hall had a mask on, and each mask covered half of the person's face — on theme with the soul split festival. Leandre's mask covered the right side of his face, the same as Cal's mask.

Leandre paused by the table as he noticed a servant who worked there didn't have a mask on. All of the others nearby already wore one.

He scoffed, *really? You had one job.* He made his way over to them, quickly whispering in their ear for them to hurry out of sight and get one from the servant's hall. Before a lord or lady decided it was a fun day to mess with those below them. As Leandre stood up straight after he told them, their face turned red as they looked around and recognized. Probably too overworked to have noticed. The servant then scurried out of the great hall in search of one. Turning back to Cal, Leandre huffed as he saw her laughing at his behavior.

"What?" he asked quickly.

"Nothing," She said. Taking in a breath to stop laughing. "It's just funny how prim and proper you really are." Cal motioned to his perfect posture after correcting the servant. His face flushed red as Cal's gaze moved beyond him to something else. He followed her eyes until he spotted her target — but by then Cal was already making her way over.

It was a young woman, not much older than Leandre. Her thick curls were braided back into a bun with a few stragglers left around her face. She wore golden makeup and a mask that covered the left side of her face. Her outfit did not reflect her status as it was a rather modest garb — but her stance could tell you immediately that she was someone worth knowing. She was smiling. Focused on observing those around her more than the conversation in front of her.

Modestly stunning, and observant? That was Ophelya all right.

"Good evening Lady Nephus," Cal said as they stopped in front of the tall young woman. "It's been a while since I last saw you," she added, the choked laughter in her voice apparent. Ophelya turned away from the older couple she stood by, her parents, and curtsied when she saw Cal.

"Princess Calypso, how marvelous it is to see you attending a festival once more."

As her parents looked at Cal and her guard they scoffed and turned their attention elsewhere. That was house Nephus alright. One of the five houses that ruled the court of the emperor.

"I am surprised you showed up, Cal." Lady Nephus said under her breath as her parents walked away.

"Well... I didn't *want* to, Ophelya," she said in response. "The emperor left this outfit with a note... If I didn't attend —"

"Then you would be on tighter reins," she said with a sigh. "I am lucky I get to at least pick my own clothing for this."

Even though they were friends, Leandre noticed how closed off Cal became when in public with her. Ophelya was stunning by Vasylian beauty standards. She was beautiful, but more importantly, she was a kindhearted soul — well, once you got past her cold exterior. She was like a ray of sunshine inside and out, with her always radiant sepia-colored skin, cloudy blown-out umber-colored hair, and her calculative yet bright smile that could light up a room. She was taller than the average young woman of the Vasylian Empire, standing a few inches taller than Leandre, and she was built like a whip but had an even-tempered attitude. She was by all means gorgeous, but so was Calypso. Cal was built like a statue of a goddess, yet she had the personality of a warrior, and she was as gorgeous as one would be depicted as well, but without the white hair and blue eyes of a royal, she was overlooked easily.

Even if she were not pretty, I wish more people would take the chance to get to know her. Leandre thought to himself sadly as he looked away from her so as to not be caught staring.

Ophelya dipped her head at him, "Good evening, Leandre." Her lips pursed together to not laugh as glanced between the pair.

He dipped his head in return but held his tongue on naturally returning her greeting as he felt the eyes of the crowd watching them. It may be safe enough for Cal to speak with Ophelya, but Leandre joining in? It would only cause them more problems than needed.

Calypso let out a giggle, and as they looked at her she put her hands up.

"Sorry, it's just funny seeing you both act so formal in public," she whispers as she glances around.

Leandre half-smiled. She was right, it was funny. It felt like interacting with different people when they were at events and such. Leandre found both of them to be much more likable in a more casual setting when they could take the masks off, both figuratively and literally.

"Princess Calypso, I believe you are needed elsewhere." Ophelya nodded her head towards something, the emperor had suddenly appeared on the throne. A large space had been cleared at the end of the great hall and six figures stood before the emperor.

With that Calypso began to make her way over, they watched her as she went. Pushing her way through the crowd to reach her half-siblings and stand before the emperor.

"Has she been ok?" Ophelya whispered.

Leandre shrugged, "She's been... getting better at hiding how she feels." he said. *She's not the only one*, Leandre thought to himself as he stood close enough to notice the slight puffiness under Ophelya's eyes.

She sighed and nodded towards Cal, "I think you should get closer, just in case. I'll be up shortly as well."

He dipped his head one last time before he pushed his way through to stand at the edge of the crowd. He could see Calypso standing next to her six half-siblings, lined up from oldest to youngest. Deakon stood to the far right, as the oldest, not to mention the tallest being a half-centaur. He still had the looks of a regular centaur, but was much smaller than the average adult male, standing at 6'5. Next to him in order were Hectyr, Avalon and Adonys, Kyril, and Echo. The only odd ones out by appearances were Deakon and Echo, the latter of whom was a Cyclops. Echo looked as though she could be the youngest — but then again, she would age differently. Other than that Avalon and Adonys being twins made them stand out as it was nearly impossible to tell them apart.

Calypso stood at the end of this lineup, the youngest being twenty years old. The last child of the emperor. The youngest. The final born to the Pallas family.

I've been told I was the youngest of my family like her... but I cannot recall by whom or why that matters anymore.

The emperor had a pleased look on his face as he looked at his children, but as anyone looked at Calypso it was easy to tell she would rather be anywhere else.

The emperor slowly lifted the glass given to him by a servant moments prior as he began to speak.

"Here is to the late Empress, my first wife, Elayne Florakys, to whom this festival is held after."

Held after? The festival was not created for her.

As everyone around cheered, people clutched a hand over their chest or cooed in admiration. After all, to them, this is where Emperor Oryon met his 'other half', at the Festival of Halved Souls. The festival of tradition where many other princes and princesses met their supposed soul mates. A tradition held in the myth that people split apart as the Aspects did, but for mortals, it was expected that you would find your other half to live your life with. This was a myth of the celebration of the final seasons of the year — and it came long before he met Elayne.

Leandre scoffed at the emperor's words. *It is ironic that the emperor should meet his other half, his first wife, only to meet several other women he also deemed worthy to become his concubines.* If the emperor were to be split to meet his soulmates, he must have been shattered into too many pieces — much like the Aspects.

Perhaps he saw himself as one?

As a shard of God?

I pray not though.

This was just the first event of the festival. The first of many. The festival lasted a few months, but at least it meant Ophelya could be around more for Calypso's sake.

As the emperor continued to speak Leandre could hardly focus on his words, instead, his attention was caught by listening to the jeers of those around as they curled their noses at the sight of Cal.

"Why do they even allow her up there?" One whispered.

"If it were up to me, it wouldn't even live up to the challenge day."

"Something needs to be done," a centaur remarked louder than the rest. "Before —"

"Something needs to be done about what, Lord Florakys?" Emperor Oryon called out, directing attention to the one who loudly interrupted his speech.

Leandre clenched his teeth as he turned and spotted him, Lord Harkyn Florakys, brother to the late Empress, uncle of Deakon Pallas. Despite having relations with the royal family, he still ruled as a lord of his territory. Supposedly, because he had the position before his sister married the emperor, but still it seemed odd. He ruled over one of five kingdoms within the Vasyla Empire. Each of the members of the royal council also watched over a kingdom in the empire, and Harkyn was the worst of them.

The Empire of Vasyla was divided into four territories occupied by four houses. House Nephus occupies the southern territory of Vaales, House Florakys occupies the northern territory of Cor Telos,

House Teresi occupies the central territory of Creya, and finally, House Nao occupies the western territory of Paithes Each house lord rules on the court of the Emperor, who oversees most matters of the Empire. Or at least, he should. The two were supposed to work together. The court though, did more now that the emperor was slowing down.

"You are aware of the myth of those born under the time of the white tern," he began, glancing around at the crowd. "So why must we even tempt fate by allowing it here?"

It. Leandre tried to relax his shoulders as he listened to those disrespectful words. *This is why I hate the people within the capital. They only think of themselves. They claim to be religious and working for the will of The Aspects – then pull stunts like this. Hypocrites.*

"Are you questioning my decisions, Lord Harkyn?" The emperor asked.

Lord Harkyn bowed his head, "Of course not, Your Majesty, only expressing my profound concern for our people."

The Emperor frowned but said nothing more on the matter, instead turning back to face all seven of his children. Calypso froze up as his gaze landed on her. He defended her from the public, just barely, yet when he looked at her it was hard to say how he felt about his youngest child.

Did he hate her? All because of the Vasylian Zodiac she was born under?

Or does he despise the people for believing in the myth behind it?

The emperor may love his children, but even he was not an open or affectionate person. The only one to see that side of him was Empress Elayne Florakys, and she had long since passed away.

Leandre looked at Deakon. He was not the most unique looking out of all of the royal scions. He doesn't even look much like the emperor, taking much more after his mother — especially the centaur part. He was far taller than Leandre, with striking white hair and fair skin, he had very round features and a large distinct nose, he stood proud and yet wasn't at all intimidating. Even though he was a centaur — which were normally quite large and intimidating — Deakon was by far the most loved by the people out of the seven of them.

But does he have what it would take to rule?

Deakon glanced over and their eyes met for a moment, Leandre quickly looked away as he gave a friendly smile. As he looked away from his eyes Leandre noticed his hands, clenched into fists at his sides — yet nobody else seemed to notice. Strange... Wasn't he known for his calm behavior and attitude?

He doesn't seem like a killer, but...

Will there come a day I have to defend Calypso from him?

Leandre quickly looked ahead to realize the Emperor had said something else, the rest of the Emperor's children bowed as he held up his cup, and everyone cheered. Leandre didn't join in as clapping echoed around him. Instead beginning to step away as he almost crashed into Ophelya.

"Were you there the whole time?" he whispered, and she nodded.

"You're pretty oblivious for a royal knight," she said with a smile.

Leandre chuckled quietly, "And you're pretty sneaky for an heiress."

Ophelya laughed before glancing past him at the emperor. She frowned, "The Emperor is getting old, Leandre, I've heard the rumors of his health, and tonight only confirmed that. You do realize the day is coming soon —"

"I know," he interrupted. Ophelya lowered her gaze.

The pair went silent for a moment, as clamor went on around them, it felt like they were stuck in a bubble of doom and gloom.

"We can't keep avoiding the subject, Leandre, we need to make a plan to save Cal or else..." She glanced around.

Or else she will die. Neither of them said those words, but they hung heavy in the air like the decorative tapestries around the great hall.

"I'm not sure what we can do if someone else becomes ruler." She said with a sigh.

She has a point, without Cal — I would be sent to a different position and that was if I was even trusted as guardian to a 'cursed' royal. Not to mention Ophelya's future was to receive a position she did not desire, she had her whole life planned before her sister died, and now... If Cal would die too I knew that would have an awful effect on her.

As the emperor neared the end of his speech he was cut off as he erupted into a coughing fit too great to continue speaking. The crowd watched closely as he coughed, servants quickly surrounded him to care for him as he did but he pushed them away. In that short moment, Leandre spotted blood dripping from his lips, but he was quickly covered by another servant as they began helping him up and guiding him away from the event.

Leandre looked at Ophelya with wide eyes, she sighed deeply.

"Did you see —"

Before he could continue speaking music began to echo in the hall. A harp, a lute, and many other instruments create the elegant harmony that begins the first dance of this festival. The emperor's children would be expected to find a partner quickly and make their way to the dance floor, but Cal would rejoin her two allies instead. She already was disliked by the people, and dancing wouldn't solve that.

Leandre looked to the emperor, expecting a disapproving look at her inability to join in the dance, but instead, he was being guided away by servants. He looked exhausted.

He is supposed to be healthy... It was supposed to be just rumors... Even then, he hasn't seemed unhealthy. How is the sickness showing so obviously now of all times?

Ophelya's eyes slightly widened and Leandre turned — expecting to see Cal joining them, but instead, he was met with the second eldest of the Pallas family.

He sighed, *Hectyr*.

Ophelya quickly bowed in respect of the prince and Leandre dipped his head. He hardly noticed Leandre hanging back in the shadows, instead focusing on Ophelya.

"Good evening Prince Hectyr," she greeted in a forced cheery tone.

"Lady Ophelya," he greeted her, he looked as though he had more to say but it took a while to continue. Leandre furrowed his brows at Hectyr, resting his hand on his sword hilt.

He was not likely to attack Ophelya, he was far too weak but still... *Better to be safe.*

He didn't seem like any of the other royals. His posture was quite awful. He was quite tall, yet as he slouched over to speak with Ophelya he was her height. If he would stand properly though, he would be almost too tall compared to the men of the empire. Perhaps even taller than Deakon, or at the very least at his height. He had tightly coiled curly gray-blond hair which was almost white and wore a dress-like cloak that dragged onto the floor hiding his feet — it would make him a difficult dance partner indeed. Out of all of Cal's half-siblings, Leandre found Hectyr to be the strangest of them. He wasn't even raised in the Citadel his whole life like the rest of the royal scions either.

The silence began to grow awkward so Leandre spoke up.

"Were you going to join your siblings on the dance floor, Your Highness?" he asked with a bow.

"I was about to —" Before he could properly respond, Calypso appeared.

As she stopped beside Ophelya, Hectyr's gaze turned toward her and he smiled awkwardly. She flinched at his gaze. His icy blue eyes look off with the darkened circles so poorly hidden by makeup underneath his eyes.

"Princess Calypso," he said, dipping his head at her.

"Prince Hectyr," she responded curtly. Her eyes couldn't quite meet his, so she looked to Leandre. He frowned and slightly shrugged in response.

He must have noticed this, as with a glance between the trio Prince Hectyr began to back up. He glanced back to Ophelya. "It was great to see you again, Lady Ophelya. I'm going to turn in for the day, er- it was nice seeing you."

With that he awkwardly slithered away, they watched him for a moment until he fell out of sight.

"What did he want?" Cal asked.

Leandre sighed and looked at Ophelya with a knowing smirk. She glared at him before turning her attention to Cal.

"He just wanted to ask me to join him for the first dance... I think," she chuckled slightly, trying to make light of the situation. However, it is easy to tell she was fearful of her mother catching onto the situation.

"Why would he want to dance with Ophelya?" She asked. "One of my few allies? Anyways, I thought that Hectyr was uninterested in the challenge?"

Leandre frowned at Cal, she was on edge and it was no wonder as to why. She and all of her half-siblings just had front-row seats to see their doom begin before them. The emperor left The Festival of Halved Souls due to his health, everyone knew this didn't spell positive news.

Ophelya sighed, "I think all of your siblings are interested in ruling, no matter how they may act now, it will change once the challenge begins."

"Ophelya —" Leandre began to interject.

"It's the truth, Leandre, and we need to be ready for that."

Cal lowered her voice and glanced around before speaking. "Does he really want to find a way to deal with me first, when there is more challenge in the others?"

"I highly doubt that is the case, Cal," Ophelya interjected. "Hectyr hasn't been within the Citadel as long as the others — he is the least likely to be out for blood."

Leandre huffed, "I can't wait for this whole festival thing to blow over so there is time for us to rest."

Ophelya laughed, this time it was real, "Yes, I am excited. My parents will be busy trying to curry favor with the other Lords and Ladies, so we should have time to visit more away from prying eyes."

Leandre felt an aching feeling for that time to come faster — *The few good times I can recall within the Citadel are when the three of us were together.* From nights sneaking outside of the Citadel to frequent visits to the rocky coves by the shores of the capital.

My memory may be hazy, but I'll never forget those treasured moments. Those rare times when I can leave behind my rank and forget about the box I fit into here in the Citadel.

Ophelya suddenly spoke up, "Speaking of that, we need to start making plans for the challenge, I think I have a few —"

"Ophelya, not here," Calypso said quickly, casting an anxious look around herself. Her happy demeanor suddenly disappeared.

This again. The trio had spent years trying to find a way. Some secret hidden in history books or some missing link to allow Calypso to leave the challenge unscathed. But now... Desperation was beginning to sink in as nothing came to light.

"Then when? Where?" Ophelya asked, a little louder, making Cal look down at the floor. This was the only way to get her to even consider her words. "We will not have many chances to have the three of us together."

"What are you thinking, Cal?" he asked quietly.

She sighed, "I think that I am ready to leave."

Ophelya frowned, but dipped her head, "I understand... My apologies... Goodnight Cal."

As Cal began to make her way to an exit, Leandre glanced back at Ophelya and frowned.

"I'll try to speak to her about it again soon," he said quickly. "Will you be alright?"

She nodded, "I will be fine, you can go after her."

Dipping his head, Leandre turned to follow Calypso, leaving Ophelya by herself.

As he followed her through the crowds he struggled not to cough from the intense perfumes and colognes used by the rich people in the hall. He was eager to leave as well, but not if it meant that Cal was upset. As they walked down the hallways, Leandre spotted Prince Deakon nearby as well, his two guards seemed to be pulling him away from the festival as he fought them. Leandre quickly blocked Cal.

"We need to stop for a moment."

"Why, we're almost —" She stopped as soon as she saw Deakon. He yelled and argued with his guards until finally they pulled him into his room and shut the door.

"What was that about?" Calypso asked, looking at Leandre. He slowly shrugged, while her eyes were still glued to where Deakon had been moments ago.

First the emperor, and now this?

"It's not a good sign."

They continued down the halls in silence, as they passed the door that led to Deakon's wing the shouting was faint. Once they finally reached the hallways and got far enough away, Cal began to speak.

"You do not need to follow me to my room, Leandre, I will be fine."

He sighed, "But Hectyr —"

"Hectyr isn't foolish enough to kill me before the competition begins." She retorted. "If you're here to continue Ophelya's conversation, you can drop it now."

"Calypso,' Leandre said sternly, "We need to start making plans if you are to —"

She spun around to face him, eyes blazing with emotion as she interrupted. "If I'm to survive? I have no interest in killing my half-siblings to gain a crown nobody wants me to have. Maybe when I was eighteen I would have loved to plan a future where I could live, but now... perhaps that's nothing more than a dream." she blinked quickly and took a step away from him. "Besides, if anyone had to make a plan it's me, not you or Ophelya!"

"You have a plan then?"

She took a step back as though she had only just realized she had been shouting, and she crossed her arms. "I'm sorry Leandre, just... drop it, please."

Leandre watched as she continued down the hall, but didn't bother following her. He was only a knight, if anyone saw him overstepping his bounds once more he could be killed. *Then who would protect Cal? Without her... I would be free, but without her would the freedom granted be worth having?* His time was short, something had to be done but he could feel the reins placed upon him by his role now tightening with every move made.

Why can't I make the right choice in anything?

5

SERVICE OF THE BLADE
CALYPSO

Ever since she had been little, Calypso wanted to be a warrior. One that fought for her people and was loved like the knights she saw within the Citadel. Of course, back then she didn't fully understand why the people hated her, so she wanted to serve them. Now... Now she believed that if she could prove herself useful in some way, if she could show that she had no desire to rule, maybe then whichever of her half-siblings ended up on the throne may spare her. That was just wishful thinking, as what ruler would accept a threat so readily? Better yet, could they? Now with the emperor falling ill, she had no more time to try to slowly ease into this plan. To slowly convince the empire that she could fight for it — just not as the empress.

It was indeed wishful thinking, but to Calypso, it was a better plan than anything Leandre or Ophelya could come up with.

At least my idea would mean less danger to them, so that meant it would be easier... right? Leandre already couldn't do much, he would be risking his neck trying to help, not to mention Ophelya... with her parents and the expected role, she has enough on her plate without my own struggles.

"You want to train with the royal knights?"

The general of the knights stood before Calypso. Armor shining and not even the slightest bit worn, either he had put a lot of effort into its upkeep, or didn't do a whole lot to damage it in the first place.

Most knights in the capital didn't have much to do — seeing as the mages left didn't cause any trouble. So they had gotten lazy with most matters, but Calypso's goal was to be different. To bring the knights to a new light. Yet... Some training was needed.

The other knights behind the general cast awkward glances around. Training weapons were sprawled about as they had yet to clean up the training grounds since their last bout — which by the looks of it was hours ago since all of the knights seem energetic. Most of them were smack-talking one another, while others just sat and awaited the general's orders. They all looked wary of Calypso's presence. The clouds covered the sun as rain approached, casting a gloomy mood over the training yard — but even if it were sunny, the mood wouldn't shift enough in Calypso's favor. One woman wouldn't even look at her, and Cal noticed her hands were shaking as she cleaned her blade.

What do they think I'm going to do to them? They have no reason to fear me!

"And is your training with your advisor not enough? Are your guards not providing enough assistance during this?" The general glanced around for Leandre but he wasn't nearby. "The regulated training all royals receive isn't enough for you?"

Cal grits her teeth, "*He* has been, and my regulated training is good — but I need more training than that."

The general glanced back at his knight who shrugged or looked away quickly, unable to meet his gaze.

"If you are preparing for the challenge, I believe you should be speaking with your advisor and not —"

"That's not it," Cal interrupted him.

Now's the time.

You can't keep pushing this off!

She takes a deep breath before looking the general right in the eye. "I want to train to join the knights!"

The general's eyes go wide and the knights behind him go quiet.

"There isn't really any way you can become a knight-" he sputtered out after a moment. "Even if you survive the challenge, you'd be expected to rule, not fight among the knights."

"What if I don't want to be in the challenge?" Calypso retorted.

The general stepped back, "To not partake in the challenge isn't even an option for a royal scion. Even if you don't want to be a part of it, I can't see you out of all of Emperor Oryon's children being allowed to carry a blade in service of the next emperor."

He had a point, there were no cases of a royal scion letting a sibling live, or one getting away – at least none were ever recorded.

If being the first is what it took for her to live, so be it.

Yet Calypso wanted more than to survive. She wanted to fix her tarnished name.

"Emperor or *Empress*!" One of the knights called out, and someone nudged them immediately to make them stay quiet.

"Yeah right, like Avalon or Echo are going to win," another snarked back.

"Avalon is a devout believer and servant of the church! If you don't believe in her you don't believe in any of the divine Aspects!"

"Yes well," The general glared at the knights who were bickering. "Either way, I will not train you unless you have permission from the emperor, we haven't had a case like this ever work out, so I wouldn't bother."

"I already can fight far better than any of your knights here," Calypso claimed boldly. Many knights quickly straightened up as the general cast a glance over them.

"No offense, Your Highness," the general said through grit teeth, "but I highly doubt that. All of my men and women are highly trained individuals. While we may not be as brutal as the Vasylites, we are far more organized than they are."

Calypso couldn't help but scoff out loud at that claim. *If I could have chosen between the two — the Vasylites would bring more honor and glory to my name — but they only take those below seven for harsh training, and I had missed my mark by thirteen years.*

If only I could reveal the number of monsters I have been keeping clear from the edge of the city. But I had to keep that information to myself for now.

"How about a challenge?" A cocky knight proposed, making others snicker.

The general frowned, "Yes, perhaps a true show of what a knight will help you understand why we cannot accept you since reason won't." He stopped for a moment before glancing over the knights nearby. "Aneurin!" he called, making one of the quiet knights step forward. "You will face my best trainee knight in basic — swords and spears only. Do you accept this challenge?"

Calypso's heart raced as she dipped her head in acceptance. She was so excited that she had gleaned over the disrespect of a trainee being chosen to face her. Quickly, she stepped aside to grab a spear from the nearby weapon rack and stopped in the center of the training area. The weapons were shiny, expensive, and clearly hardly used. The ends were dulled and not sharp so as to not cause actual injury.

Odd, Leandre and I train using real weapons and the knights don't even do that much?

Calypso's mood faltered slightly as she looked at the spear.

Perhaps Leandre and I trained more like Vasylites?

Her opponent — Aneurin — saw the weapon she chose and grabbed an iron machaira. His hands shook as he grabbed the weapon off the rack. The curved blade would be difficult to face with a spear. *Then again, that would make it even more incredible if I win- No, when I win.*

It is a good thing Leandre and I trained on this the other day.

As the other knights ushered back quickly and the general stood watching, Aneurin approached her in the training clearing.

"Begin!"

It's only dangerous if I allow him close. Cal thought as she wielded her spear defensively as she faced him. He grabbed his weapon with his right hand, which means coming at him from the right side would be the best approach as swinging back with that sword type would prove difficult.

The trainee also took a more defensive stance until he saw how slow Cal was taking things. His eyes widened as he assumed she was fearful, and he began to take a more aggressive approach. You could see in his eyes that he was trying to visualize past training and references from manuals before he suddenly snapped out of it. He charged. Cal quickly ducked to his right. With a sick grin at the shock on his face, she smacked his leg with the side of the spear. Trainee armor wasn't the best, his leg buckled almost immediately. The trainee seemed horrified at the unexpected force behind the blow. Kicking his sword out of his hand — Cal pointed the spear down at his chest and stood by his head. The trainee took off his helmet and Cal almost laughed as she saw just how young the boy was.

I suppose we have been having fewer and fewer knights want to join the royal guard as more rumors about me spread, she thought bitterly.

The boy looked horrified as he looked up at her. Calypso looked up at the general as he was half smiling, impressed, yet in his eyes was a grim expression as he watched. He shook his head.

"Chatelet!"

The cocky knight who suggested the challenge grins as he steps forward. He stood several feet taller than Cal, as a centaur would.

First their weakest and now their strongest, huh?

"You will face him next, same rules."

Cal extended her hand to help the trainee up, but he quickly stood and rushed aside. She frowned at this but said nothing, turning to face her next opponent.

"Begin-"

Chatelet charged before he finished speaking and Cal immediately rolled aside, clutching the spear as she got to her feet. Spinning, she swept the floor attempting to catch him off balance as he missed but he jumped over the spear and slashed down with his own blade. It caught with her arm and despite the dullness of the weapon it drew blood. Gasps came from the other knights. Chatelet grinned and lightened up as he saw the red beads forming on her skin. The general opened his mouth to speak, but Cal moved quickly. Using Chatelet's moment of glorious distraction, she used the spear tip to catch his curved blade and pulled it out of his hands. It hit the floor with a loud clang.

Calypso smiled and dropped her own weapon.

"Might as well make this fair for you," she said, arms opened wide.

Loud laughter came from the other knights at his vain behavior. Even the general couldn't help but snort. Chatet turned toward her, enraged. He charged and Cal held up her fists in a defensive position.

"Chatelet! Enough! You cannot mark the seventh royal scion any further!" The general shouted. Though he didn't stop as he threw punch after punch at her — his aim was no longer to knock her down but to knock her dead. Cal dodged almost every single one of them, exchanging equally heavy blows and landing twice as many on him. Chatelet showed no signs of stopping and Cal's heart was racing.

Her eyes were wide and had a wild glow to them as her fangs were bared in a grin. This was it. This was what she enjoyed. The rush. The surge of emotions and adrenaline. She could die in combat or live with the glory of becoming a knight. This was why Calypso was a terrifying foe — she had nothing to lose and everything to gain.

She was getting too into the thrill of the fight, her eyes were glowing. There was no more laughter from the others as Chatelet fought like a raging bull and Calypso's excitement in battle became apparent. As Cal dodged and delivered concise blows to her opponent, all that filled her thoughts were memories of training with Leandre.

Dodge left, keep your arms in close, strike through your target, and...

As Chatelet reared up onto his back hooves, kicking at her with his front Cal rolled aside — electricity running through her veins as she jumped off the weapon rack and felt her fist collide directly with his face. As Cal landed on her feet, she looked down at her arm, a burning sensation singed from her fist to her shoulder. Grasping her arm she fell to her knees. Chatelet was on the ground knocked down as well.

Calypso looked at her arm, and after a moment she realized what had happened. What she had *allowed* to happen.

I let the rush of battle distract me.

I was so eager for the reward at the other end... I flew too close to the sun.

She had allowed her magick to show through. There were two facets of magick — wild magick and controlled magick. Wild magick is what Calypso had just cast — and it wore down the user's energy and could be used at unexpected times. Controlled magick required words or runes to create and had little to no effect on the user. Both were seen as barbaric — yet wild magick was seen more as that of beasts, and that was what Calypso just did.

"There! She used magick!" A knight screeched gleefully. "The rumors about her are correct!"

"How is that a good thing?!" A woman shouted, her voice shaky.

The knights quickly began hurriedly talking to themselves as the centaur opposing her slowly got to his feet, he stood like he was about to charge at her again but the general stepped in his way.

"I've seen enough of this."

Cal's arm was burning, yet she stopped her hand from clutching at it or itching at the singing burns from the lightning. Watching the reactions of the knights. Her opponent scoffed at her and slowly relaxed.

"Don't all royal scions have magick in them though?" One knight whispered.

"Yes, but they aren't supposed to use it anymore! It's outlawed *because* of them."

"No matter, it's not like she can do much else now that she let this slip."

The general glared at Chatelet.

"What? We must report this to the emperor immediately. He would want to know so we can have her ki-"

"Silence!" The general shouted at him, he waved his hand to send him back to the others before glancing back at Calypso. "She clearly has no control over any magick affinity she may have."

"But you saw me fight — even without that I would have won!" Calypso shouted.

"Be that as it may, I cannot have an out-of-control princess working as a knight."

"But I proved myself! I'm better than even your best knights! Leandre said —" Calypso quickly stops, but the damage is already done.

"Leandre is it? Is that the guard who keeps filling your head with such ideas?" the general smirked, "Sounds like someone needs to speak with him and remind him of his place."

"I don't believe you have any business in speaking with my personal guard of our conversations." Calypso held her head high, though her voice cracked.

"With all due respect, Your Highness, I have every right to as the presiding general over the Citadel's knights."

Calypso sighed, "Forget it. I'll find my own way then."

The General dipped his head as she turned away, and as she made her way back inside the clamor of chatter began.

"Do you think she was being genuine?" a woman asked.

A sword dropped and hit the ground with a loud clang, Chatalet laughed anxiously. "Even if she is being honest, remember the prophecy?! She could bring doom with her unintentionally, and if we trained her to be stronger…"

"Stronger? You're one to talk."

"Hey —"

"What are you thinking, general?"

Calypso pressed herself against the edge of the wall by the doorway, struggling to hear them as they spoke of her. The general loudly sighed.

"She does seem genuine, but none of them can escape the challenge — that would look appalling for whoever wins. Besides," he laughed, "She isn't exactly in shape to train anyways." After the others laughed, the general groaned loudly. "Now I must speak with the emperor of this… he should know."

Calypso clenched her fist at her side as she hurried up the stairs away from the knights' quarters, hurrying before the knights would come through and see her lingering. Hot tears of rage spilled down her cheeks. She curled her nose in disgust at the attitudes of the knights — even when beaten, they were still snide.

Chivalrous knights? *Yeah right.*

Though I am a bigger build than most, I could wield a sword and fight with the best of them. Even Leandre agreed I have better muscle and strength than him. Still, all people saw when they looked at me was the large and accursed princess, unfit to even try to change.

I just needed a way to prove myself, even a slight chance. Once they see how useful I really am. They'll change their tune… right? Yet they can't even give me that.

As always, the choices are made for me.

She stepped out from the stairwell into the halls of the Citadel, the great pillars suddenly seeming like prison bars as she ran.

What am I supposed to do now? Accept my fate? Die to one of six others as they fight for a throne? I won't even get to see who rules next.

I haven't had my magick go out of control like that in years since I stopped trying to learn it as a child — so why did it have to happen now?

How much time do I have left? The emperor grows older with each passing day — no — with each passing hour the challenge could begin. Life is short, and death is a certainty across time. Who knew how much time I could make use of before my fate became sealed in stone? Or is it already?

Why does the emperor even defend me, if my fate is absolute?

Rubbing the tears away from her cheeks, Cal choked down a sob as she passed a few servants. She stepped out from the halls and into a small enclosed area outdoors. It was a garden, though most of the plants were dead or dying. It was a very bleak sight. This was the garden of Florence Selous. Calypso's mother.

It is the most empty of the gardens in the Citadel. None of the servants kept up with it, and nobody forced them to. After all, this garden was not a gift from the Emperor, it was a suggested olive branch by an advisor — something to heal their relationship. That definitely went according to plan. Now that advisor is surely long forgotten.... or if it was a member of the court they'd probably deny it now. The garden is mostly stone pathways following dead plants or dirt left behind. Along with many moss-covered statues and a large ominous stone gazebo, with a massive statue taking up most of its space. Calypso usually didn't enter the garden at this time of year, but right now she didn't know of anywhere else to go. She passed by multiple other statues, one of them was built after her mother. Made in her likeness whenever she first became the emperor's final concubine, and it's how Calypso knew she looked more like her than him.

Walking down the stone path past the statue of her mother, Cal stared at the statue under the gazebo. The pillars were worn, and the gazebo and the statue looked to be the oldest structure in the garden. Calypso stopped in front of it and sat down, leaning her back against the statue as she struggled to slow her breathing. Rubbing the tears from her face she sniffled and hiccuped.

The emperor is getting old now. Which means I am closer to the end.

"Why can't I control a single thing in my life?" She wondered aloud as she looked up at the statue. Cal sighed, the sun was setting, though it was still mostly hidden behind clouds. Cold air swept across the garden, and it felt like it was going to rain soon. The smell of the salty water of the seas blew through the air. Calypso felt herself letting her emotions get the better of her, and she felt wild magick flowing through her veins once again.

"All of this because I was born within a certain time frame, all because I shared one thing with a woman from centuries ago. All because the zodiac of the White Tern —" She smashed her hand on the ground beside her, and the magick energy that was building up quickly exerted itself creating a pulse throughout the garden. Cal froze.

Suddenly a part of the statue broke and she fell back. She sat up, face flushed. The sound of stone dragging across the tile filled the air.

"What the —"

Calypso slowly got to her feet and turned around to see the statue moving.

Didn't I hear something break?

Glancing over the statue she found nothing that looked different. It's still a dramatic woman driving a sword through her own heart, only... *is it moving?*

She took a few steps back, the statue was moving!

The skies were going dark as night fell, and as the figure finally stopped moving she couldn't believe what she saw.

A stairway was hidden beneath the statue, and for some reason, it revealed itself to her. She glanced back to the Citadel and sighed.

Maybe it's time I made my own choices.

As she slowly made her way down the stairs, she heard the statue shifting behind her. The world went black and Calypso felt a chill go up her spine. Panic rose in her chest until suddenly a light appeared, and then another. And another. Small candles were suddenly lit and lit the way down the rest of the stairs and into a dark hallway. *Detection magick possibly? But that is impossible, nobody was here to hold the spell in place... right?*

As she followed the lights Cal couldn't help but feel anxious.

This has to be some form of magick going on, and almost all magicks have been outlawed since the last royal born under the same zodiac as me.

Calypso followed the lights down an eerie and ancient hallway. The architecture and design of the flooring and walls looked like something straight out of a history book, and as she went deeper inside, weapons could be seen scattered across the old floors. Kneeling down she picked up a sword. *This hilt design hasn't been used in over a century... What's going on here? Is this a tomb of some kind?*

Calypso huffed as she pushed herself back up to her feet, keeping the sword held tightly in her left hand as she continued through the tunnel. The air had grown thick, and the candlelight only seemed to light up as she got nearer to them.

All that laid before her was darkness.

Sweat began to form on her skin in the hot air of the cave-like halls. Wiping the sweat from her brow, Cal began to see the faint outline of an opening up ahead.

As she reached the opening a blinding light filled the room and she had to cover her eyes. Slowly, she lowered her arm as the light dimmed. Revealing a large almost empty room, spare for a few broken weapons lying around on the floors. The walls had odd markings worn into them that one would assume to be signs of aging. In the center of the room, there it sat. A full set of armor sprawled out — it looked completely different from the armor of today. While most knights wore silver or brass armor, higher-ranking knights who traveled the country to slay monsters wore the black knight's armor. A rare heavy armor set with the deepest of blacks engraved with fine golds and silvers which harmed the monsters who touched it, with the maroon color of the Vasylian flag showing in the strip of fabric tied to the waist and in the plume atop the helmet. Yet this armor that sat before Calypso was almost the opposite. Instead of black, it was a cream-colored metal... Could it be Aduinite? The material had become so sparse, that armor hadn't been made with it in centuries. Not to mention the plume was smaller, and the engraved designs had mock feathers instead of the country's symbolic flower- the Clematis. It even had wings on either side of the helmet.

This armor had to be ancient — and rare. Perhaps it had once been a great symbol for the people. *It has to be, as the feeling I get when I look at it is more intense than any emotion I have ever felt before.*

Could that kind of hope and determination really stand the test of time in an object alone?

As she kneeled down on the rough and worn flooring and began to look at the armor, she spotted something crawling out of it and leapt away. Quickly grabbing a broken blade from the ground and pointing it at the armor, she felt her heart race until she recognized the shape. It was a spider. More specifically a Dreamweaver, but why would it be here? Dreamweavers tend to stay in places where creatures sleep, named for their ability to gain magick energy from eating nightmares and spinning them into dreams instead. In fact, it wasn't uncommon for Cal to find them over her bed at night either. But here?

Was there someone living in this room? The other doorways that would continue deeper seemed to be filled with rubble, so all that really could show signs of someone being here was the armor.

Who is using such ancient armor in this day and age? Surely I would have heard of it somewhere —

That was it.

I'll show them, I'll show them all.

Cal shooed the spider away, it made a mad dash for the nearest wall as she began picking up the armor pieces and dusting them off.

Perhaps this is a sign, this is just the thing I need. A sign of hope, an ancient symbol of peace to prove myself as a knight. A symbol for a symbol, a prophecy to fight a prophecy... I would have to get to work immediately but... perhaps this prophecy of mine could be avoided. Did I have a future after all? Could fate be avoided?

Perhaps I am about to find out.

6

ENTER THE TARNISHED COURT

OPHELYA

Once again, Ophelya found herself thinking back to times spent with her sister when she entered that place. That den of snakes dressed in polished gold — their hearts beneath were tarnished and filthy, but outward appearances were all that really mattered here. As long as she kept her cool and played her part — the gullible newcomer to the court — Ophelya should have been safe.

This was the first official meeting of the court during the festival period — they often used the excuse of festivities to be able to gather everyone without hassle. After all, they were all in the capital so why not take advantage of that?

Ophelya was waiting on her parents, mostly on her father. He was the one who was the most actively included in the royal court. Her mother was as well, but not as much since she had married into the Nephus family. From a lower class at that.

Ophelya sat next to her, being told it would be a good experience to silently listen to how the royal court interacted and solved problems from the four kingdoms within the empire. The sad reality was she learned more about what not to do rather than what to do. Glancing at her mother, she noticed her tapping her fingers on her lap below the table as her father spoke. She sat disturbingly straight, and Ophelya could tell that her mother wasn't actually listening to him, but rather waiting for him to go silent so she could have a turn to speak.

Whenever she did get a word in, it usually caused chaos. This was only because she constantly contradicted others to boost her own appearance. Meanwhile, Lord Nephus kept his cool while speaking, well, for the most part. He cast anxious glances around, and the smile on his face didn't quite reach his eyes. As odd as both of her parents act though, they were not who Ophelya paid the most attention to.

There is one person, in particular, she kept her eyes on, and that was Lord Harkyn Florakys, Calypso's *'uncle'*. Though not actually related by blood. He still preferred to be considered the uncle of all the royal children. Though he clearly had favorites.

His word didn't carry the same weight in the court as it once did when his sister was alive — yet still, he was a powerful lord all the same. Ophelya watched the way he sat. Elbow on the counter and resting his head on his fist as his eyelids were half-shut. He barely tried to pay attention as her father, Lord Nephus spoke. He had little regard for what anyone was going to say once he had said his piece. Ophelya narrowed her eyes at him.

I wonder if he thinks by becoming close to the next to ruler he will have that power once more. But who does he think will win the competition once it begins?

When her father finally stood, the rest of the court did as well. Since he was the last to have anything to say, supposedly that meant they were finally free to go. Lady Nephus bit her lip as everyone else bowed and began to leave. She clearly had wanted to speak but never got the chance to. They had been discussing trade deals with Pilavia, the neighboring country that shared borders with Cor Telos — the northern territory. Since they had to go through Harkyn's domain, he held a lot of power in such deals, and her mother knew the points that needed to be made would not come from Lord Nephus. Ophelya would feel bad for her mother if she didn't already know what was coming next.

As everyone else left, her mother turned her attention toward her.

"What is this I hear about one of the royals approaching you during the festival?"

Her stomach turned but she did not show any emotional reaction to her words.

I wonder who told her. Who was watching so closely? Who even noticed our short interaction?

"I believe he was going to ask me to dance," she replied simply, pushing her chair in.

"Which one was it?"

"Hectyr," she said, not bothering to explain beyond that. He may have been nice, and he might not even be bad — but Ophelya knew that going for a royal scion was exactly what her mother had wanted.

And Ophelya was not going to play into her game.

Lady Nephus suddenly looked disinterested.

"Why didn't he ask you?" she asked anyway, making Ophelya clench her teeth. No matter what her next move was, she knew where this was going.

"I am not sure," Ophelya answered as she began to follow after her father, who was already out the door. *Even if I did find Hectyr attractive, I will not go for someone based on appearances alone — and he hasn't shown much action since he arrived at the Citadel... So it is difficult to formulate an opinion on him.*

"For such a harsh girl you lack the bluntness when needed, you should have taken that chance to lure one of them in — if not Adonys then Hectyr will have to do."

Lure one in. Quietly, she thanked the Aspects as Ophelya looked around the now-empty meeting room. Thankful that nobody else stayed around to hear her mother's crude words as she turned back to her.

I can't really tell her it was Cal who scared him away, that would be worse than just myself...

Before she could speak though, her mother continued.

"If you keep acting like you do, you'll scare off any suitors. Royal or not." She scoffed, "With that intense face of yours, you'll be lucky if even a lowly water mage wants to marry you."

But the thing is — I'm not interested in attracting suitors on false pretenses. I want to attract someone based on my own looks, however intimidating I may be, someone who doesn't flinch doesn't get angry at the woman who isn't easy to take, someone who isn't easily scared by appearances, and who will listen to my words better than you do.

But even these words Ophelya did not say aloud, for she was too tired to argue with her mother anymore. Instead, she dipped her head to Lady Nephus. "I'll keep this in mind next time the situation arises."

"I hope you'll do more than keep it in your head!" She began gnawing on her nails again now that nobody else was around, "Perhaps it's better this way, Hectyr isn't that good of an option for them all either way... But the emperor is even worse than I imagined he could be. He didn't even stay for the whole opening festival night!"

Ophelya didn't say anything in response, simply dipping her head making her mother huff.

She didn't even look at her again as she hurried after Lord Nephus, probably to complain to him about their daughter's behavior as well.

Once alone, Ophelya quietly let out a deep sigh.

Did my sister have to deal with this as well?

Or has it only gotten worse since she passed on?

This was the one thing she couldn't recall. It didn't matter though. *If only I had time to slip away and see Cal... she always knows how to cheer me up despite her own situation.*

Despite everything, she is a flower that bloomed in the dark, and I will not allow that flower to wither any further... A spouse is the last thing I need to look for right now — or even ever. That will happen when it was meant to be.

Right now, I need to plan.

Ophelya needed to find a way to keep Calypso alive, even if she didn't rule, she didn't want to face a future of losing more people close to her.

I don't think I could stand another moment of this dreary future ahead without her and Leandre at my side.

She shook her head. *I need some fresh air.* Perhaps that would help.

Ophelya began making her way outside and as she reached the gardens she breathed in the cool air and floral scents. The clematis flowers were in bloom as they grew in a winding style up the sides of pillars and arches. It was a refreshing sight.

As she began to stroll around the sound of a harsh whisper nearby filled her ears. Quickly she ducked behind a bush.

A loud gasp. "He did what?!"

"SHHH! Keep your voice down!" another responded. It was Lord Harkyn and one of the other lords. Ophelia knew Maeve never trusted those two. Recalling their times together in the Citadel, before she began leaving her with Cal and Leandre when she was busy — she would hide her younger sister behind her back whenever these two came around. There must be more reason for that.

Ophelya peered through the leaves in the bush to see that the pair were arguing.

"But if Deakon is suddenly bloodthirsty what does that mean? He is demanding the challenge begin now but why?!"

"We may know why, but it must never get out —" Harkyn said harshly. He glanced around him and Ophelya ducked even lower. "Are you sure this is a safe place to be speaking?" He asked. Hooves clicked as Lord Harkyn began to search his surroundings.

She needed to get out before he came in her direction. She held up her skirt and began creeping across the ground as she kneeled. The sounds of hooves stopped nearby — she glanced back. Lord Harkyn was close but wasn't looking in her direction. She struggled to keep her breathing quiet as she made her way towards the nearest entrance into the Citadel. She slipped behind the pillars and stood, running without looking back.

Deakon wants to begin the challenge now?! But Deakon isn't known for his aggression or impatience for that matter...

There had to be a reason he would suddenly be pushing for this. And it seemed like Lord Harkyn knew.

7

THE FIRST BANE
DEAKON

"You will never be what they want you to be. Hot and cold. Flame and frost. An aggravated envoy. A peaceful war seeker. You will inherit the light of your father, but you are not him. You are not flame. You are starlight, and you must grow above the rest."

Those are the words Deakon Pallas lived by. Day after day, night after night. The words of his mother — Elayne Florakys. He never completely understood what she had said until the emperor's health began to falter. He never even contemplated it much until then. *A peaceful war seeker?*

Peaceful but war-seeking?

How can I be both?

It was easy to look upon the prince and believe him to be peaceful. He was like starlight to look at. He looked kind. With soft facial features — a round nose, moon-eyed, and pale skinned. His hair was as white as his father's, though his centaur half had flecks of gray.

Deakon was unaware of his surroundings now, too wrapped up in thoughts of the past to recognize the present.

They want an ideal emperor. Strong yet weak. Kind yet cruel. Perfectly balanced.

He thought of the fire he felt in his veins at the festival's opening. He felt like he was burning. Like the stars his mother always compared him to. Yet the thoughts that riddled his head at that moment were like kindling to flame.

Mother always thought I stuck to the more peaceful side — but what if she was wrong?

What if I am my father?

"Your Highness?"

Deakon shook his head and looked at his surroundings. One of his guards stood in front of him, a concerned expression on their face. He had to look up to meet their gaze — as a fully grown whole centaur was far bigger than the eldest prince.

"Yes, Ermys?" He looked away from his guard to the room around them. It was a great room, with ornate statues, painted vases, and great stories depicted in carvings on the walls. A historical art gallery, yet nobody else was there. The place had been cleared for the first prince.

"It's just... Are you alright, Your Highness?"

Deakon wanted to grit his teeth and walk away. How many times now, had he told his guards to call him Deakon? Or at the very least — Prince Deakon? He had many guards over the years. Always changing as they moved on with their lives. Retirement, children — there were many reasons his guards would leave his service and be replaced. The one that bothered him the most though, was a month ago. Marriage. Something Deakon could not even contemplate until after the challenge. As it would be cruel, to allow the royal scions to marry only to put targets on more people's heads when the challenge began.

I am already thirty-four... almost thirty-five.

Is it... difficult for one to find someone past this point?

You can't even try until after the challenge. So why even mull it over?

If the emperor would have already died, I could start my life.

Deakon bit his tongue at such a thought, turning to his guard.

"I am fine, Ermys." He replied simply. Ermys had only been among his guards for less than a month. Why burden him with his troubles? "What makes you ask?"

"It's just... we've been here three times this week." He said slowly, as though mulling each word over as they spilled from his mouth. "Is something bothering you?"

Deakon smiled at the younger centaur. He was green and didn't know how to speak to him quite yet. Deakon always relished the early days with a new guard, when they were still anxious around him but didn't know what was considered appropriate to ask of a royal. It made him feel normal.

He is observant though, if a new guard is recognizing this... Perhaps I am letting my abilities slip.

Deakon was known for his control of his emotions. The smiling prince. Never unhappy, always a star of charisma. Yet at the festival... he scarcely remembered what happened when he left the hall. All he knew was that his guards suddenly were acting odd around him. They only said he seemed out of it, but that they got him to his room before anyone else saw.

"I find it relaxing to look at this art," He lied. "It is important to appreciate such things, as this is the result of an empire that is thriving. Not just surviving."

This answer impressed the young centaur, his eyes were practically glowing as he watched Deakon prance down the hall and weave between various pieces. The pieces were quite beautiful, but he did not come here for the calm they were supposed to bring. Rather the image it gave. The prince taking time to appreciate the historical art of the empire? It made him appear as an intellectual and a creative.

The next event in the festival is coming soon.

Will that happen again?

Those strange thoughts?

That anger towards the emperor?

Why shouldn't you be angry? A small voice whispered in his mind. *Look at how he will be leaving things. A court far stronger than the emperor, a people who view the royals as a joke... The challenge is coming soon.*

Should I make it happen sooner?

Deakon shook his head again, trying to focus on the statues of the Aspects that stood before him. Yet he couldn't. The beautifully etched marble statues were merely shapes before him as his mind fought with itself. His veins were burning yet cold.

Was mother wrong?

Am I becoming the emperor?

Deakon wanted to crumble there on the spot, but he didn't as three guards watched from nearby.

The challenge will begin soon. A voice much like Deakon's spoke in his head, but these thoughts were not his own.

Will you be the one who starts it?

No, I will control these thoughts... I will be my mother's peaceful starlight.

Won't I?

8

A CHANGE OF HEART

LEANDRE

The heart of man is a complicated thing. It does not exist solely for the purpose of beating blood, and it can drive a man to mad decisions at the drop of a coin. It was the first open day of the festival when commoners and aristocrats alike could mingle. The amphitheatre of the Citadel was packed with all sorts of people. Outside large tables of food stood to the average humans shoulders for any centaurs or skorvians who attended. As a celebration of the harvest season and the festival — grand outdoor feasts were held in the center of the Citadel, with markets lining the streets outside and a play that was about to happen within the amphitheatre.

Leandre couldn't help but feel irked by the many types of inter-actions that played out before him. It was as though he stood before a stage, or watched from the edges of the Colosseum. Which was ironic considering people were still making their way inside to watch the play.

From the men who aimlessly flirted with every woman in desperation, to the women who needlessly insulted one another for their garb at this event, and aristocrats giving disgusted looks to the commoners who made their way into the amphitheatre along with them — it was all so tiring to even witness as a bystander. The only nice thing here was the crisp and comforting autumn air which blew a breeze throughout the Citadel.

Leandre stood a few feet behind Calypso, keeping an eye on every movement and every person who even glanced their way. The other royal scions were out and about as well: Echo was enjoying the pastries by a shorter table, Avalon and Adonys chatting together by the edge of the crowd, and Hectyr watching the dancing with an almost jealous expression. The emperor though was already seated in the amphitheatre waiting for the play to begin.

Outside of the amphitheatre there was also music being played and a small clearing of people dancing carelessly. Moving their feet to the strings of the lyre and singing songs of the Aspects in all their glory. They didn't have a care in the world.

"We should make our way inside soon," Leandre said to Calypso. She watched the dancing with awe.

"Perhaps soon," she agreed. "But right now I am enjoying watching the dancing."

"Did you want to join?" He asked.

Calypso laughed, "I would if I knew the steps. Dancing is much more complicated than combat to me."

Leandre watched the crowds with her, he would join in but only if Calypso wished for it. He spotted one young woman who watched them both.

Why would someone dancing be staring and Cal and I? Should I be worried?

He met her gaze, hoping his cold stare might deter her from considering trying anything to endanger Cal. She looked him over before beginning to dance her way around the circle towards them. Leandre rested his hand on his sheathed blade. The woman slowed her dancing and stopped by them, her gaze fixated upon Leandre. Cheeks bright red, he presumed from the strenuous dances she performed.

"Care to join me?" She asked with a silvery tone.

Leandre's face flushed. He had miscalculated the situation. He quickly cast a glance at Calypso who looked amused by the situation at hand.

"I am sorry, but I am currently on duty," he responded curtly.

The young woman simply smiled and shrugged it off. Eyes still creased with a grin as she galloped back into the dance along with the others.

"Really Leandre, *on duty*?" Cal laughed.

Leandre frowned, "Well, I am — am I not?"

"So would you have accepted if you weren't?"

He rested his fingers against his temple and sighed, "Let's just go inside now."

Calypso snorted at his response but obliged as she began to make her way into the amphitheatre. The building was large and open to the chilly autumn air. The seats curved around the open space left for the play to take place. The seats closest to the stage were for royals and aristocrats — so Ophelya was nearby. Further back was left for commoners and lower lords and ladies. They found their seats were close to the other royal scions with the exception of Deakon, who was close but in a centaur section with seating prepared for them to kneel onto properly — similarly to the skorvian seating. Royal guards however, were an exception.

Leandre stood until Calypso was comfortably seated, and then he seated himself next to her. He almost laughed as he imagined how silly it must have been when guards stood by their royals in the decades prior. It must have made it difficult for those behind to focus on the play.

The play for the festival was a reenactment of the life and death of Cronys. Cronys, who killed his sister Cressyda decades ago. Cressyda, the last royal under the White Tern's star. Cressyda, the one who almost destroyed the empire. Cressyda, who everyone expected Calypso to become simply because she fit the vague omen from who knows how many years ago.

It wasn't Cronys who killed her — at least it may not have been. Some believe it was a soldier and a poet who managed to defeat Cressyda. Yet it is Cronys's name that was remembered. For who would focus on a soldier or poet when a would-be emperor could be crowned the victor? Cronys's name would be remembered with that honor. If you asked anyone how Cressyda died you would never get the same answer twice. Everyone had a different idea or theory on the subject – but the most believed ones usually involved her brother Cronys in some way.

"Why do they have to do this play every year?" Calypso whispered to Leandre. "Isn't it a little... on the nose?"

Leandre nodded in agreement. The play served as a constant reminder of why the royals fought one another. To keep the power in check — to keep the royals from becoming powerful and waging wars for the throne — wars that affected the people. Yet with magick outlawed, the royal scions were never really as powerful as their barbaric ancestors. Not anymore at least.

The people in the play were rather... silly. At least to Leandre. While the actors galloped and shouted on the stage others in the crowd were moved to tears at their acting abilities. Though as Cressyda came onto the stage, Calypso tensed up as many eyes in the crowd turned onto her.

As the 'magick' part of the play begins with Cronys and Cressyda throwing colored sand and ribbons at one another, some arguing can be heard from the centaur section.

Deakon was bickering with his guards and the centaurs that surrounded him. Lord Harkyn watched his nephew through narrowed eyes as he began to act out.

"What a folly this is!" He shouted out making everyone stop and stare. Even the actors slowly began to stop throwing the fake spells to watch.

"Prince Deakon, what is the matter with you?" One of his guards asked as he stood and made his way to the stage. Leandre rested his hand on his blade and braced himself as the centaur prince neared them.

"Why are we spending this important time of the year mulling over the past, when we could be changing our future?!" He shouted. The people begin muttering amongst themselves.

"Look at the emperor now!" Deakon motioned towards his father angrily, hands shaking as he did. "My own father, once the fire of the empire — reduced to a pitiful sight."

"*Boy.*" The emperor said threateningly, "You'd best choose your next words very carefully."

"Why should we even wait to begin the challenge? We should begin the Challenge of Cressyda right now!"

Deakon stepped onto the stage and yanked a spear away from one of the actors. He turned his wild gaze around the crowd until he spotted the nearest royal scion — Calypso. He looked at her for a moment before he charged.

"Stop him now!" The emperor shrieked, but the guards near him didn't react fast enough. Leandre caught his blade against the spear. The loud clang of metal filled the air. He clenched his teeth as he held the centaur back. Leandre looked up at Deakon as his heart began to race. The royal scion's eyes were bloodshot. Leandre recalled when their eyes had met at the opening of the festival, they had looked different back then. Something was missing. Something was wrong. Or perhaps he had finally snapped.

"What in the Aspect's name has gotten into him!" A woman cried out. The crowds around the royals quickly lunged from their seats. Making a safe distance between themselves and the wild prince.

"Something is wrong, Deakon isn't like this... right?"

"I wish he wasn't stopped."

Leandre curled his nose in a snarl at that last comment from a bystander. He shoved Deakon off, directing the spear to hit the ground as he took a defensive stance in front of Calypso. He glanced back over his shoulder.

"Princess Calypso, are you alright?"

"Y... Yes. Nothing hit me," her voice shook. It has been a long time since Leandre ever let an attempt on her life get so close. He looked back at the elder scion. Deakon gripped the spear and glared at Leandre, baring his teeth at him angrily as he grunted. He charged again, and as Leandre deflected the blow this time the spearhead broke flesh — but not that of his intended target.

Leandre and Calypso backed away quickly as Deakon was finally surrounded by other guards. A small figure nearby gripped their arm as blood spilled from a deep gash. Royal blood.

"Echo!" A guard screeched nearby. The young cyclops girl's eye was huge as she shakily backed away from her attacker. He did that much damage with a prop?

The emperor had not stopped shouting orders as he stood by his seat, his cold glare pinpointed on what once might have been his favorite child.

Is he actually defensive of Calypso now? Leandre wondered as he watched the gaze of the emperor glance at his youngest daughter's head.

"You're an embarrassment to the Pallas family name —" He collapsed back into his seat, heaving and clutching at his chest. Servants and guards alike rushed to the emperor's side — with Avalon Pallas at the lead.

"Get everyone out of here now and get us some healers!" She demands. Immediately guards began ushering people out — Deakon's three personal guards struggled to usher him out the side entrance with his skorvian guard doing the most to keep him from charging back into battle.

"Is he dying?" One guard asked her.

"I won't let him," Avalon responds through grit teeth.

Does she actually want him to live? Or is this a front?

Aspects don't let him die... yet.

"We need to get out of here Cal," Leandre quietly said as he looked back at her. Her eyes were wide and she was shaking. She may have seen battle before — but an attempt on her life in the middle of broad daylight? During a public event? That was enough to shake up anyone.

Leandre held out his hand to her and she took it after a moment. As he guided Calypso the safest route out of the amphitheatre he could feel her hand shaking. She held on so tight it made Leandre's hand hurt, but he said nothing. They took the steps to the entrance as quickly as they could as others ahead also made their way out.

"It is alright Cal, I won't allow anything to happen to you." He reassured her calmly. Leandre's lips quivered as he spoke and his eyes constantly scanned their surroundings as they made their way back to the Citadel. As they broke free of the crowds Leandre forced his shoulders to relax

I can't let her see that Deakon even scared me in that situation. Right now she needs to feel safe.

Besides, it's pitiful for a guard to be afraid like this.

What could have driven him to do that? Deakon of all of them? Perhaps Kyril was a fool enough but Deakon?

He was always the most level-headed of them all. Was that just an act? Or did something set him off?

"The emperor... He is going to die soon isn't he?" Calypso asked nobody in particular.

Leandre sighs, "Cal —"

"I don't have much time left do I?" Her voice grew shakier with every word. Leandre almost didn't understand what she was saying as her eyes began to well up and her breathing quickened.

"We won't let anything happen to you Cal, I —"

"What can you even do for me? Nothing!" She shouted. "You or even Ophelya cannot do anything to stop what is coming! If my plan doesn't work then..."

"What plan?" Leandre asked, "If you have something in mind, we can help you."

"No," Cal said bitterly. "There is nothing you can do for me. If I pull you in any further you'll only drown along with me."

She finally pulled her hand away.

"I have to go. Don't follow me."

Leandre watched as Calypso ran away through the great halls of the Citadel. She ran like she had a goal in mind, but Leandre did not know where that goal led her. He began to follow her.

"Leandre!"

As another voice called out his name, Leandre turned around. It was Ophelya. Her hair was a wild mess from running after them.

"Where did Cal go?" She asked as she matched his stride as she followed alongside him. He sighed.

"She just ran off towards her room... She said she has a plan but..."

"But?"

"She won't share it. She thinks we would harm ourselves by helping."

"Of course we will!" Ophelya shouted, "Just as she would do for us! If she has a plan Leandre, we need to know so we can help her."

Leandre shook his head, "At this point, we need to make our own plans, just in case."

Ophelya frowned as they paused, she grabbed his hand and held it out in her palm. "You're shaking too, are you alright?" She asked.

Leandre couldn't help but laugh, "I'm fine, I'm not the one who had someone try to kill me."

"But you were in his path just the same," Ophelya furrowed her brows in concern. "I'm sure that would shake up even the strongest of men."

"Always the older sister, huh?" Leandre pulled his hands away. "It wasn't scary for me." He lied. "I'm not the one who needs this care right now, you should go to her."

Ophelya frowned, "Only fools wouldn't be scared by that situation, and you aren't a fool Leandre."

Leandre clenched a fist behind his back, trying to keep his hands from shaking anymore.

"That wasn't natural, something is wrong with Deakon, and with the emperor. We need to keep a watch on them now." Ophelya dipped her head. "I am going after Calypso now. You go take care of yourself, I can protect us if needed."

Without another word, Ophelya revealed a small hooked blade built like a claw of a griffin. A karambit, a blade from the neighboring country Pilavia. She quickly hid it again beneath her cloak before rushing off after Calypso.

Leandre watched her go. When she vanished from sight he felt lost.

Calypso is right, the emperor might not be saved from what happened to him today.

I need to find something else I can do for her... but what?

"You there! Guard!"

With a sigh, he turned to see who else could want him, he was met with General Arys.

What could a general of the Citadel guards want with me at a time like this?

"Meet me at the barracks, we need to talk."

9
A SAVIOR APPEARS
CALYPSO

Three nights had passed since Cal had first found the hidden staircase leading underneath the garden. Three nights since her first sign of hope in her life. Yet it had also been two nights since her eyes had been opened by Deakon and the emperor. Calypso was relieved at first when she had made her plan, but that relief quickly shifted into desperation as the emperor's death was looming in front of her. There was still no word of whether the emperor survived or not. Since his heart attack in the amphitheatre, nobody had seen him. Calypso had to be sure this plan would work, but she had to hide it — not wanting to get Leandre and Ophelya's hopes up until she could be absolutely sure of this new plan. She didn't even think about what would happen should it fail. She couldn't bring herself to. She didn't have to. She knew her fate should this not work.

It took Calypso a few days longer than she had originally expected to put this plan into motion. From studying the guards shifts to looking into the rumors around the capital — but today was the day. She had found the best passage out from her mother's garden and into the city. Nobody would see her, or the strange heavy armor until she was out on the streets. It had to be night, as she couldn't manage the escape in broad daylight. Not with such noticeably different armor, that couldn't work.

Hopefully, sneaking out at night only isn't off-putting for some. Cal thought to herself.

As Calypso put each piece of heavy armor on, she could only imagine how difficult it would be to sneak around in. Normally, her armor was extremely lightweight and allowed for increased mobility. This armor set, on the other hand, covered every inch of skin or clothing showing and weighed a ton. It must have been crafted for a muscular and large male knight because it fit her better than the average female armor she found which cut too tight around her arms and midriff. This armor felt nothing like her normal training gear. As Calypso began to make her way out of the tunnel, she felt her heart soar with each step as she looked down at the gleam of metal in the dim lighting.

Armor like this hasn't been seen in decades or more — imagine how much of a story this can become! Once I've built up enough of a reputation anonymously, once I reveal myself people will be unable to

*continue to believe the gloomy omen around the star I was born under!
Right?*

Calypso made her way out of the tunnel with a sword sheathed on her hip. It was odd, how familiar she had become with the tunnel to the strange hideaway, and how often she had visited to be sure she wasn't imagining things. Yet every time it was still there.

The Dreamweavers had yet to leave the cave, oddly enough. Calypso had thought that once it had been opened they would leave in search of other's dreams to feast upon. Something must have been wrong with the spiders in the tunnels, but she didn't give it too much thought. Cal had more important matters at hand.

Feeling as though eyes were on her as she snuck from the garden to the walls, she saw nobody. Not even patrolling guards were by that point of the wall yet. Still, she felt a presence just the same. As she made her way to the nearest servants' entry it was not difficult to sneak through to the outside. Cal made a note to alert someone of this later if only someone would take it seriously. Though the end of the Citadel nearer to where she stayed was lacking in terms of defense. Was it a miracle she had made it this long without any assassination attempts? Or something else? Either way, it was a concerning breach — but for what Calypso needed it was as though the Aspect's had cleared the path for her. Perhaps this would be how she changed her fate?

Things were not so difficult once Cal made it past the wall surrounding the Citadel. The air was humid from rain earlier in the day, yet it was still fairly nice with the chills of night. While getting out of the Citadel might have been easy, the next difficult part would be once she was in the city.

The lamppost's flames flickered aimlessly, illuminating stone pathways and closed markets. A few markets were still open as hired hands were closing up and cleaning up the storefronts for the next day. The air was especially bitter tonight with the smell of booze heavy as she made her way past small taverns. With the surplus of people visiting for the festival within the capital city, it was no surprise that every bar or tavern in the city would be bustling during the opening of this festival. Though not everyone came for the opening, the city would be busier during the mid to end point of the long celebration.

The plan was simple — Cal would listen to chatter within the bars and ask around until she found something worthy of chasing. It could be as simple as bandits or as harsh as beasts nearing the city again — whatever it took to get attention on herself as a strange knight doing more than the city's knights. She had considered going to the taverns in regular garb to pick up quests — but then that would defeat the purpose of being seen taking on requests in the first place. The problem was — she had never done that before. At least, not within the upper districts of the city. She would visit the lower district later, but first needed to start somewhere that would spread word of it like wildfire.

Calypso reached the square, the fountain spell was only held during the day by water magick users. The statue in the center depicted the main three Aspects of the sky, lands, and seas. They seemed to watch her as she passed. The silence without the flowing water made them seem quite ominous. Very few people were outside at the capital center, but those who were stared at Cal as though trying to figure out who was inside the armor. Or perhaps that was in her head. That was the biggest advantage of heavy armor. It hid her identity by hiding more of her from sight. Though it was a little louder than light armor.

Here I go, Calypso thought to herself as she pushed her way into the busiest tavern on the road. This place was far busier than the lower district one, especially this late into the night. She received a lot of odd looks as she entered, especially from those dressed in working-class clothes — but the knights within the tavern hardly gave her a second look as they were far too into their game of Byzack to care. That and the wine held their attention enough already. Calypso rolled her eyes before sitting at the last empty seat at the bar. The bartender warily approached, glancing around the tavern as he stood before her.

"Welcome, we have wine if you're thirsty, and food if you're hungry." the small human barkeep said.

Calypso shook her head, "I'm not looking for either."

"A mercenary then?" they asked, looking her up and down. "If you're looking for a job, a few travelers have posted some requests on the board." They nodded to a large wooden board on the wall next to the bar. Many knives are stabbed into it, names carved, and a few torn pieces of paper littered it along with one new page upon it.

She dipped her head, "Thank you."

Calypso sat for a few more moments before making her way to the board. Glancing over the sheet left behind. It was a request for the knights of course, for someone to look into reports of a strange group ambushing travelers coming to the capital for the festival. Cal frowned, she had fought humans before yes — but mostly she stuck to defeating beasts and creatures that were too dangerous at the city's edge or the shores of the capital. Killing people? That wasn't something she had much practice in.

Just think of them as beasts — if you can't solve this peacefully and they attack it's not like I'm in the wrong. After all... they've killed several travelers already.

Ripping the page off of the board, Calypso shoves it into her satchel attached to her belt before leaving the bar.

As Calypso reached the outskirts of the city and neared the forests, the moon was high in the sky. *I can only stay out for so long, so let's hope this can be dealt with swiftly...*

The dirt roads out this far had many markings in them from being so well traveled, but Calypso was following one set in particular — she could tell which carriage had been in a rush as the variation in hoof prints showed the speed was much more rushed than others. It could easily be chalked up to someone eager to reach the city, but this was the only thing Calypso could go on. As she continued to follow it, she had to hold up her lantern as the path led away from the main one and deeper into the woods. She realized that a few travelers had taken a side route — it was less safe to do but must have guaranteed a faster travel time overall if they were willing to take that risk.

Calypso watched the small camp from a distance, none of them were aware of her appearance yet — though one of the oddly dressed bandits stopped talking and listened for sounds from the woods. There were four of them, they also seemed to be on their way to the capital yet they stopped there. Cal watched the way they interacted — they seemed to be making a plan of sorts as three sat at a makeshift table and one kept watch. The flames dancing around the fire began to die off, Cal grinned, perhaps this would be her chance for an ambush?

One of the strange bandits stepped towards the fire and held a hand towards it, small sparks fizzled and danced away from their hand until a small flame fell upon the logs and gave the fire new life.

They use magick?

All magicks had been outlawed except for water magick and only that was used by priests of the empire. So where were they able to learn this, and why were they using it so casually?

As the flame grew brighter, Calypso was able to see the strange group better — and why their armor was different. Their armor was adorned with feathers — and not mock feathers as most fashion styles followed due to the sacred nature of birds within the empire. No, these were real feathers. They weren't stringy like those made of rope or shiny like fake silken feathers. These people not only were committed to going against the law of magick — but they were willing to destroy the seen messengers of God in all their Aspects for their own appearances. It was no small number of feathers embellishing their armor either.

What faction can use magick and adorns themselves with feathers?

...Could this possibly be? No... it's just bandits Cal.

Don't make a mountain out of a hillside.

The one guard stood suddenly, staring off into the woods.

"Did you hear that?" they asked gruffly, the others shook their heads and paid him little attention. He sighed and began making their way out of the little clearing.

"I'll be right back," he muttered.

Calypso clenched her jaw as she slowly unsheathed her sword. She would have to be quick while she still had the element of surprise on her side. She was far enough away from the camp that if she managed to take down the guard she could still keep the others unaware of her presence. As the guard passed by the tree she hid behind, his eyes quickly caught the glint of moonlight against the metal of her armor — he opened his mouth just as Cal slammed his head into the tree. The guard fell to the ground immediately, unconscious but not dead. As Calypso held her sword towards his throat she frowned at his face.

There's no reason to kill him...

Yet still, she felt a small urge inside her to end this man's life with the smallest swing of her blade. Where that urge came from she did not know.

No! She shook her head. *I need to turn them in — after all, they are using magick. They are dangerous to travelers coming in for the festival.*

Calypso stepped over the unconscious man towards the others, they turned to her as she stepped into the light with her sword drawn.

As they realized their guard was gone they drew their weapons. Two carry spears, but one held out their hand to reveal sparks of flames erupting from their palm. She charged at them, blocking one attack, and catching the end of a spear as she used their force to pull them down. As the magick user faced her they shot a blast of charged flames at her. Cal rushed at them through the flames, the armor absorbing it all without harming her. She felt warm, but none of the heat burned her.

This time as Calypso felt her own magick surging through her veins, she did not stop it as she lifted her blade and struck the bandit.

Vasyla needed a savior, and Calypso needed to be saved.

Thus, a savior was born.

10
THE PHILOSOPHERS' LIES
OPHELYA

Nothing ends as the philosophers would think: horribly, wretchedly, and tragically. An era may end, but it takes the strongest of souls to build the world back up again. Yet as Ophelya looked around to see the empire's current court members, she couldn't help but wonder if they were doomed to shrivel up in a cycle of stupidity and ill-begotten traditions. As court members meet outside the official discussion, they would talk about which of the emperor's children would live or die like they were speaking of an epic — a tale of great dramatics with an exciting ending. Since the accident at the amphitheatre, there hasn't been word of the emperor's condition since. He could be dead but nobody could know until the priests who healed him in his chambers revealed that information. Such a pivotal event that could change the outcome of the empire's fate — and here his court sat making a mockery of itself. Talking about who could become the next ruler as if it were a game.

Like it's anything but an archaic and primal tradition, sibling murdering sibling for a crown. Each member of the board had a different royal they were placing their bets on. Which sibling they thought matched their own morals and opinions the best. Ophelya's own parents were foolish enough to say aloud who they wanted like it wouldn't come back to bite them if a different royal was to get the crown. They bet on Deakon, the eldest, yet Lord Harkyn had yet to show who he wanted to win. His silence was almost as scary as knowing his thoughts.

I know it won't be Calypso who he is betting on... but who will it be? Would he show support for them behind the scenes? Give them the upper hand somehow?

The North was known for its magicks — while most were outlawed in the empire it was no secret that petty low magicks were still in use in Lord Harkyn's territory. So, would he use that to assist the royal of his choice?

Most others bet on one of the twins. Ophelya found that situation to be the most awful. Princess Avalon and Prince Adonys. The two looked so much like each other that it was hard to tell which was which at times. The royal scions were all raised apart from one another, to prevent attachments to their other siblings, but the twins? They were raised together from birth. They had spent hardly a day without seeing each other. Yet with this tradition... One would have to kill the other. This was the cruelest of traditions in Vasyla.

Why hasn't it been changed in so many years? Surely by now, we're better than our more brutal magick-using ancestors... right? It is easy to say we are in a modern era... but how much is actually different from the rule of the emperor before Calypso's father? And the empress before him? Nothing seems different. We were caught in a cycle, but how could this be broken?

"Lady Ophelya? You seem deep in thought, what is it you are so enthralled by in that head of yours?"

Ophelya was pulled away from her thoughts by Lord Harkyn's voice, she quickly found herself pinned by his icy blue gaze as his words directed the attention of the court to rest upon her. Each ruler of each territory had their eyes fixated upon her like predators to prey — even the archbishop who had a seat on the court seemed hungry in his eerie, hazed eyes. She glanced at the empty seat at the head of the table. If only Emperor Oryon was healed quickly and able to attend — if he was even still alive at all. Then perhaps this conversation wouldn't be happening.

As she began to open her mouth to respond, Lord Nephus was quick to interrupt.

"She is just thinking about her study period after this meeting. Her mother and I have urgent business to attend to, so she will have free time to prepare for her private studies once the festival is over. We will have to rush after this meeting to even arrive on time," he said with a nervous laugh. Lady Nephus struggled to not scowl at his cowardly nature as the others smiled or laughed slightly — not with him, of course, but at him. Ophelya sighed. Apparently, her father had been a stronger and more prominent figure until the death of his first wife — Maeve's mother. Did that strong man disappear along with his wife? Or did the new Lady Nephus destroy any remaining willpower with her ceaseless nagging? It certainly wasn't a father she had ever known.

"If it will be such a rush," Lord Harkyn said with a grin,

"Don't let us hold you up with our bets on the royals, hurry off!"

"Are you... Are you sure?" Her father asked anxiously, glancing at her mother for assurance, but she just narrowed her eyes at him. The moment they were out of earshot, Ophelya knew he would not have a moment's peace as her mother would unleash hell upon him.

"Of course! We shouldn't hold them up when the meeting is pretty much over," Lord Harkyn said as he looked to the others. As his gaze befell the other members they nodded and flashed their fangs in yellow smiles of agreement.

As Lord Nephus stood to leave her mother followed, casting annoyed glances back at her daughter as a thousand things to say to her passed through her mind, yet she was unable to say them. It wouldn't be terribly hard to guess what some of them were.

"So," Lord Harkyn began as soon as the door closed from her parents' departure. "We haven't heard what your position is regarding the next emperor, who are you placing your faith in?"

She didn't react as the other lords and ladies of the court exchanged glances and watched her expression for even the slightest movement. Even though they seemed confused by Harkyn's interest in her, they also seemed intrigued enough to want to know her answer. The slightest muscle spasm by Ophelya's mouth, twitch of her eye, or even wrong infliction of her voice could give the wrong idea. She was surrounded by enemies, but she couldn't run. Couldn't hide. Couldn't avoid it behind her sister as she once might have done.

Did Maeve want to run? How did she handle these situations? If only I had been intelligent enough to ask her such questions when she was still with us.

"I can't say I've been able to give it much thought with my studies, but you have all given very compelling arguments for all sides." She gives an awkward smile, half furrowing a brow and shrugging slightly as she did. It was the same way she had seen sheepish students act when teachers would scold them for forgetting an assignment. Best to play aloof. *While Lord Harkyn can afford to puff his feathers to show his strengths, it is far too early for me to show mine. Perhaps by doing this, I will be boring to Lord Harkyn.*

"Is it not Princess Calypso?" Lord Harkyn asked. One other member of the court laughed, and others almost joined in until Lord Harkyn glanced in their direction.

I must be against her, but not obviously so.

"No, why would she win?" Ophelya laughed. "Even Hectyr has better chances to win than her, and I hear he hardly even wants to compete."

After she finished speaking she glanced around the table, awaiting a response. *I should be able to leave soon, claiming to want to hurry to study before returning to my private tutor back in our territory.*

A few chuckled but stopped as they waited for Harkyn's reaction, he smirked at her answer and relaxed his shoulders slightly.

Seemingly satisfied.

"Yes, Hectyr does fare better than the last royal scion. I wonder how well he will do against the others. After all, he wasn't raised in the capital as long as any of the others."

Laughter like that of a scheming crocotta filled the room yet again. Ophelya smiled and let out a laugh as she held a hand over her mouth, watching Lord Harkyn. *How did he get the room so wrapped around his finger? Was it because his sister was married to the emperor?* Then again, Ophelya had not heard of any case like Harkyn in history.

The marriage of a family member to a royal didn't guarantee excellent treatment amongst the upper class, and, usually, they didn't keep their positions as lord or lady of the court.

He wasn't wrong about Hectyr though, he had grown up hidden away for a long time before it was discovered that his mother — one of the concubines of the emperor — had hidden him away at an orphanage. Needless to say, she was banished for trying to hide a child of royal blood away, and died shortly after that. Though Ophelya often wondered what it was like for him, growing up there for eighteen years of his life. That was almost a decade ago.

"Do you believe the challenge will be coming any time soon?" she asked Lord Harkyn boldly. The room went silent at this. It was a stupid question to ask, so stupid it almost made Ophelya grin. Playing dumb was easy.

"What makes you ask this?" another court member asked.

She tilted her head and frowned. "I only wondered since the conversation seems to keep turning back to the speculation of the next ruler." She tried to not keep her gaze fixated upon one person too long — while she may be interrogating Harkyn, they didn't all need to know that.

"I pray to the All-Aspects that it doesn't, but there is no harm in talking theoretical and speculating," he answered without skipping a beat.

Ophelya almost sighed, *as if* they were talking theoretically. Harkyn was playing everyone for a fool, and everyone was willing to play his game for reasons unknown.

The rest of the meeting wasn't anything important, Harkyn became an observer and everyone floundered for a new subject. The unofficial meeting ended once Lord Harkyn stood. Ophelya had almost forgotten that the archbishop had even attended until he finally stood after everyone else and seemingly disappeared as he hurried out of the room without a word. He had been silent the whole meeting. Then again, how much fun would an archbishop have at a meeting that became rabble and guesswork on the state of the royals?

Ophelya didn't wait either as she hurried to leave the temple of the court. Instead of making her way back to their temporary place in the Citadel, she took the long route around to where Princess Calypso's room was. As she passed pillars leading to outside she looked up at the sky. *It is still fairly early... surely I can still catch her before she leaves the Citadel or goes to her own lessons?*

"Cal?"

Ophelya frowned as she spotted a large figure dressed in a silk cloak nearby through the pillars leading to a garden. With long off-white hair and a spear at her side, Ophelya immediately recognized it was Cal. She was trembling, still bothered by what had happened the other day. *The emperor might have lived but... There isn't much time left now.*

"Cal?" She raised her head from her hands as she spotted her friend.

"Ophelya!"

As she stood and put her arms out, Ophelya noticed her eyes were red and puffy. Stepping over she pulled her friend into a warm embrace.

"What are you doing here?" Ophelya asked, glancing around. They were in her mother's garden. She frowned at the death that surrounded them through unkempt plants and what should have been greenery. The only plant that was alive was the Clematis blooms that grew up the sides of pillars unchecked.

"I just... needed to go somewhere to be alone."

"Is this really a good place to be though?" Ophelya asked as she glanced around. There was an odd feeling in the air — yet Calypso didn't seem to notice it.

"It's fine enough... Nobody comes here anyways, even my mother hardly did."

Ophelya frowned as she thought of Cal's mother. While Calypso didn't remember much about her mother, Ophelya did. She was older than Cal, and so she remembered more of before her mother passed — and while Calypso seemingly forgot or suppressed the memories of her mother, Ophelya never did.

She could still recall the cries of her best friend as her mother scrubbed and tore at her hair with potassium and rubbed a pomade of light florals through each strand. She remembered at the time wondering what had made her mother angry, but now looking back she could recall the desperation in her eyes as she struggled to make her child worthy. To make Calypso like the others so she would have fewer reasons to be othered.

To make her more of a Pallas, and less of a curse.

As Ophelya put her arm around Cal and held her close, she cried. Ophelya recalled how Cal did the same for her when her sister passed away. Yet as Cal wept, Ophelya could sense a rage beneath it all. Like she was hatching a plan as she gazed upon the statue beneath the gazebo nearby.

Is this really the life laid out for us? To suffer in positions laid out for us and smile to the public?

Ophelya desperately wanted to ask Cal what they should plan, and how they could get her out of this. Yet she could never find the words. For once, Ophelya felt frozen next to her closest friend.

The Nephus family's temporary place at the Citadel was one of many guest buildings located close to the capital building. The polished ivory pillars were in fine shape despite how old they were, the garden surrounding the building clearly well-groomed, and as she stepped through the front entrance she saw servants scurry out of sight.

Have mother and father not gotten back yet? Ophelya felt the ache from her shoulders disappear as though a weight had been lifted. Then she recalled how hostile her mother had gotten when she went near her room. She had a room separate from her father here, from what Ophelya had heard from the servant's gossip at least. None were allowed inside.

Now she had the chance to see what she had been up to. She walked down the open common area to the hall leading to their chambers without glancing to see if anyone was watching because she knew she was alone there. Or at least, might as well be alone with the attitude of those serving at the guest house. She began to go to her room, needing to work on more of her higher-class studies. Before her sister had passed away, Ophelya had been following a different curriculum for a different path, one that looked far more foolish in hindsight — The path of the poet. It seemed too silly in hindsight. Ophelya had once regarded the idea with such reverence. To have a poet in an important family showed that Vasyla was thriving and not just surviving. Yet she was quickly pushed back to understand survival was all that would remain. Once Maeve died she had a lot of catching up to do as the heiress of their position on the court.

Instead of continuing to her room, Ophelya stopped at a doorway earlier than her own. She looked through the doorway.

She had seen her mother go into this room. Normally Ophelya would just walk past but... Something told her she should go inside. She wasn't sure if it was because of how much more hostile she had been on the trip or her own desire to not study, but either way, she entered.

As she entered her mother's room, she frowned. It was far cleaner and plainer than expected. Far cleaner and nicer than her mother can usually keep a place. Back at home, servants had to plan extra time to clean anywhere she had visited. Ophelya only knew that much because Maeve told her everything the servants would share. She wanted to be sure her younger sister had a handle on everything going on around them. It was a shame she was only ever around when Ophelya was still but a foolish child who would smile and nod in the hopes that the lesson would be over quickly so she could do whatever she wanted.

As she stepped into the room she slowly shut the door behind her, praying to the Aspects that she might be spared from her mother returning home early for once. She never was the kind to be early, or even on time in most cases, but by this point, Ophelya knew better than to rely on luck — and to always leave a little extra time in case this time was the oddity of the usual behavior of Lady Nephus.

Gliding across the room Ophelya went to where she knew most of her mother's belongings would be — under the mattress, hidden in the nearest potted plants, and various other odd places to hide jewelry, books, and other such things. Her mother was once a servant, so it came as no surprise that she still sought to hide the things she considered her own. Ophelya wouldn't think much of it if she hadn't suddenly kept servants from entering, and if she hadn't suddenly kept a separate room from her father. She noticed a painting on the wall. *It is... crooked?* A small scratch could be seen on the wall. Ophelya could easily chalk it up to her mother's cleaning abilities being poor, despite being a servant once she wasn't actually very good at cleaning, but the scratch? She still felt the need to inspect it closer.

Stepping towards the painting she began to lift it up, and as she did a book fell from behind it. Ophelya felt a pit open in her stomach as she immediately recognized the leather-bound book. That was Maeve's journal. She had written almost everything down all the time, she had multiple journals, but the last one... They could never find it.

Lifting it up she slowly opened it. *I don't recognize it at all. The dates written, the names mentioned... It is all in her handwriting, but this is not one of the journals of hers that were given to me.*

This is the last copy.

The missing piece.

The one we couldn't find when she passed on.

Why would my mother have it? I needed to read it but... If she were keeping it behind this painting on a trip to the capital, surely she would be checking it constantly?

Ophelya hurried out of the room and down the hall to her own chambers, rummaging through her things until she found another identical journal. It was another one of Maeve's journals, one that she had been given at her passing. She stared at it for a moment before hurrying back to her mother's room with it. Carefully lifting the painting from the wall, she fit the different journal into the wooden border the canvas was wrapped around. Carefully laying it back against the wall, she stepped away and watched with her hands raised ready to catch it if it fell — but it never did. Ophelya let out a relieved sigh, making her way back to her room once she decided everything looked to be in order.

Ophelya stopped in the doorway and stared at the journal left on her bed warily.

Do I want to know? What would she hide about Maeve from me? Maeve may have been more outgoing than she had wanted — but why hide her writing from me?

She felt an ache deep in her bones as she approached the journal.

I hope this isn't against your wishes, sister. Ophelya muttered a prayer as she slowly opened the journal. A letter fell out.

What the...?

The Struggles of Change

Oktobus-Novum, 1057 AH (Anno Harmonia)
It is the month of Oktobus, bringing with it the eerie season of myths and tales of doom. Frost begins to cover the lands, and all of Vasyla's wildlife begins to settle in for a long winter ahead.
The Zodiac of Oktobus is the White Tern. The symbol is most recognized for the cursed royals born under it. One born recently and another born over a century ago. A fitting Zodiac for such a haunting season.
The Festival of Halved Souls is underway.

11
AN OFFER ONE CANNOT REFUSE
LEANDRE

A bird may pluck its feathers and change its song, but it will never be a man. Just as General Arys will never be a true knight — he will always just be an aristocrat in a comfortable position. Leandre tried not to judge him too harshly for his background, but when the general looked at him with such disdain as he entered the barracks he couldn't help but judge the sour man. Slipping back into old ways of judgment and hatred, Leandre clenched his teeth as he smiled at the general. General Arys merely narrowed his eyes, lips twitching in disgust. He was acting as though Leandre had done something wrong.

"Yes, General Arys?"

"Took you long enough to get here." He looked Leandre up and down. "So, you're Calypso's favorite guard?"

"Yes, I am *Princess* Calypso's only royal guard," he replied curtly.

"I'm not sorry to say this, but you're being reassigned." Leandre froze. "What?"

"Calypso let it slip that you were the one training her to become a knight," the general said.

He frowned. *Calypso! How would telling them this give you any advantage in joining the knights?*

The general continued, "Any training outside of her regular combat training gives her an unfair advantage in the Royal Challenge of Cressyda."

Leandre curled his lip in a snarl. "Like the others aren't doing the same. Admit it, you're only doing this because it is Calypso."

"*Princess* Calypso," he replied snidely.

Leandre didn't say a word, staring at the general. Waiting for him to say anything else. He simply turned away. "You will be expected to join the knights in patrolling the perimeter of the Citadel. You can pick what time group to join with the others." The general began to step away, but he grabbed his arm.

"And what if I keep watch over Cal- Princess Calypso?"

The general stopped and didn't even look back at him. "Then we will have you moved outside of the Citadel, no, out of the capital. Perhaps you'd enjoy going back north?"

Go back? *What is he talking about? Does he know something about my past?*

The general pulled his arm away. "Did you really think teaching her to use her magick wouldn't have any consequences?"

Wait... Magick?

Before Leandre could even try to formulate an answer, the general left the barracks, leaving him to stand there like a fool.

What do I even do now? Leandre clenched a fist and began to walk. He needed to move as he thought about Calypso. *Why did she have to be so... so... foolish?!* He hated to think even the slightest ill thought of her, but he could think of nothing else to describe the situation before him. *She destroyed all of my work as her knight and now I would be a petty patrolman. How am I to protect her now?*

Do you even want to protect her?

He shook his head quickly. *Of course, I do! Right?*

Then again... She was the one who chose me as her royal guard. If she didn't... Would I have more of a say in what happened in my life? Would I have been able to forge my own path back then?

No! Don't think like that, she saved you.

But did she? You don't really know what awaited you before, after all... your memory is hazy.

Suddenly a large hand grasped his shoulder, and Leandre spun around — eyes wide.

"Sir Leandre!"

Grabbing the hand and shoving it off, Leandre glared at the centaur in front of him. He backed up as he recognized the eerily symmetrical face of Lord Harkyn.

Leandre bowed his head. "I am sorry, my lord, I did not recognize it was you for a moment."

it began with s asmile for some reason

He laughed heartily. "No, I suppose not. I saw you standing there blankly and I called out to you but you didn't respond." Harkyn stared at Leandre. "Must have been deep in thought, though I wonder what of."

Leandre glanced around. *When did I get to the archives?*

"You seem out of it, care to share what is wrong?"

"I wouldn't want to take up any more of your Highness's time," Leandre said quickly and began to back away.

"Ah, but you see, I was looking to speak with you either way," he said, taking a step towards him. "I heard you very recently found yourself with a great deal of time on your hands."

Leandre grit his teeth. "Yes, I will be working patrolling the Citadel, more protection was needed with the festival beginning."

"Funny, I would think that Calypso would require more protection than anyone else."

It's Princess Calypso, Leandre thought to himself. He didn't bother correcting him though. It was getting tiring correcting everyone all the time.

"It has been a while since I've needed to request your assistance in a project of mine, but it seems I need to call on you once more," Lord Harkyn said, relaxing his shoulders.

"What are you talking about, once more?"

"I am sure you're quite done watching over Calypso, no?" he continued, ignoring his question. "After all, it is because of her that you are here."

Chills ran up his spine as Leandre struggled to rack his brain for a single memory of this. *How would Lord Harkyn know even if it was Calypso? Was I wrong in thinking she helped me?*

Was I right to blame her for my being here?

No!

You cannot think like this! Cal is your friend.

...Right?

"What is it you are getting at?" Leandre asked impatiently, making Lord Harkyn laugh.

"And here I thought all royal guards had manners, good to see you don't put up the typical act and dance for me." He leaned in towards him. "Then I suppose I should drop the act as well."

He leaned back up and suddenly the doors to the library closed. Leandre jolted at the sudden sound and Lord Harkyn began to meander around the room as he spoke — hooves clacking and breaking the silence left.

"I am here to request your services, as a royal guard of your age — it is impressive how long you have kept Calypso safe despite all the odds stacked against her." He looked over at Leandre. "How many assassination attempts have you stopped? Or have you stopped counting?"

"Who is to say she has needed that much protection?" Leandre replied as nonchalantly as he could. After all, how could he know about that? *I've done everything I can to keep those who have tried to attack her hidden — even from Cal. Nobody needs to believe that there have been attempts on her life. That would only push the rumors further.*

"And here I thought we had agreed to drop the act." He narrowed his eyes at books left out on the higher tables as though skimming over the subject matter. "Believe me, there is nothing you can hide from me. I am on the court, after all, I have eyes and ears everywhere."

He picked up a book and flipped through it as Leandre stood at a loss for words. Moments later the silence was broken as he tossed the book aside.

"Let me make it clear to you, the emperor is reaching his end, and I find myself in need of a few loyal and powerful guards for my plans for the empire."

"As a lord, right?"

"Of course, I must be a strong and powerful lord to be able to support the next emperor," Harkyn said with a grin. "In order for these plans to succeed — I first need to make a venture with a small group outside of the capital for... something important. You will help me with this, Knight Leandre."

"And why should I? Give me one reason I shouldn't walk out of here right now and inform the emperor."

He laughed. "I think you'll find it hard to convince Oryon that his brother-in-law consulted a lowly patrol officer to assist him in anything. Besides..." He began walking about the library yet again. "I do believe you'll desire what I can give you in return."

"So, he is alive?"

"Barely," Lord Harkyn huffed. "But yes, he is alive." Leandre let out a relieved breath.

That means there is still time.

"What could I gain from helping you?" Leandre asked. "A position of power, and the freedom to do as you please."

What?

Leandre rolled his eyes at his offer. *He is asking me to assist him on a mission in return for that? How can I trust him? What if he is just using me?*

But what is the alternative? Calypso seems to have her own plans now — ones that don't include me. What am I to do amidst all of this chaos?

Is this the one path that can lead to being able to plan a future? A path forged by my own hand, and not by those around me?

"What position and title would I be given?" Leandre asked angrily, trying to hide the fear in his voice.

"You would be given that of my heir, next Lord in the Northern Territory of Cor Telos."

"Don't you plan on having your own children play that role?"

He dipped his head. "I am unable to have children."

Leandre raised a brow, surprised that he would reveal such a thing. To be impotent was a sign of weakness in Vasyla, yet he admitted this freely.

"Besides-" Harkyn continued. "After what I have planned, the adoption of a child in a lord's house will be the least shocking thing to face the empire."

If something goes wrong... I could always spin it back to hurt him and not myself... Hopefully.

"Just one expedition outside of the capital?" Leandre asked, "That is all you request of me?"

"Yes."

Cal... I hope whatever you have planned works...

Because it's time I started thinking for myself as well.

Backed into a corner with nowhere to go, Leandre only saw one way out.

"I accept your offer, Lord Harkyn."

12
WHAT REMAINS IN THE DARK
CALYPSO

It was hard to find the light when one was already shrouded in darkness. Harder still to convince one that something of the dark is truly good. This was the task that would be the most difficult for Calypso when it came time to reveal herself. It had only been a few nights since her first venture in the mysterious armor, and just as she expected word of her deeds spread like fire. From her dealing with bandits attacking travelers to completing requests of those in the lower district — this mystery hero was seen as a blessing from above. A sign that the Aspects were grateful for the thanks of the people given during the Festival of Halved Souls.

Calypso was making her way to the port, she needed to get out and see the ocean one last time in case... In case any plans went wrong. Another festival event would be happening the next day, and the emperor wasn't getting any better. Calypso had to use her time wisely.

The capital was a port city, so to other countries, this was seen as a weakness — but the reality was that the country's ships and defenses at sea were the strongest. Especially the magicks.

All magicks had been outlawed except for water magicks, and this was because the sheer strength of Vasylian sea mages was what kept other empires from striking. *Though, it seems a bit wrong to me. To outlaw all other magicks, calling them primal and evil, and then allow the one kind that is most beneficial to the empire to be the not evil one.*

Cal didn't even bother finding Leandre to tell him she was leaving, afraid that he would try to stop her. *It has been a while since we last spoke... I should speak with him soon. But not until I am sure of my plan.* This time, Cal was a little smarter about going out with her light off-white hair. Mixing henna powders into her hair to stain the color darker. It ended up looking messy, but the servants didn't bother her as she left the Citadel.

Perhaps this time I won't be interrupted before my meeting. Calypso scoffed at the thought as she reached the streets of the city outside the Citadel. *With my luck, everything that can go wrong, will.* Though she didn't really believe in the omen of being born in the same month as one other royal centuries ago. Just because now was the assumed time period in which the omen would happen didn't mean it would be through her Calypso did believe this is why she had the worst luck possible. *I can't wait weeks before we can arrange another meeting — who knows how long it will be before they are back on Vasylian shores.*

Passing through the streets, Calypso was tempted to stop by the warm smell of cranberry loaf and various spices coming from the market. The warm smells make the bitter cold slightly more bearable during her travels, but still, she continued past it and the crowds towards the docks.

As she got closer to the sounds and smells of the ocean, the more she saw churches and priests along the busy roads that bound the city together. Many of the churches left praised the Water Aspect. In the Empire of Vasyla, most people believed in The One, a single god who was praised in his many forms called the Aspects. Yet the most worshiped Aspects were the main three: Earth, Land, and Sea. The Sea Aspect, also called the Water Aspect, was the most worshiped among them, as Vasyla's powers came from its ships for trade and defense.

Even better, those who give thanks to the Water Aspect hated Calypso the most. Since the last royal born under the White Tern supposedly destroyed the ocean-side churches and almost outlawed water magicks.

Yet another thing I am now blamed for.

Calypso tugged her hood a little further down over her head. Even with hiding her hair color, it was better to not take any chances. One of the servants of the capital could be gathering supplies or visiting family and recognize her. Or one of the other royal children could be out and about. *I don't know why we called each other the royal children, considering that I am the youngest and I'm over twenty. It was that or royal scions. Yet still, it is what we would be referred to as until... Well, until there would only be one left.*

As Calypso reached the pier the smell of salt and sea overtook any other smell. Well, almost all others. The smell of fish certainly wasn't covered up, that was for sure. It would have been almost relaxing if it weren't for the bitter cold and the splash of icy waters up onto the docks.

The sky was rather gloomy looking over the vibrant seaside. The water glimmered slightly as the sun was high in the sky. It was midday already. Which meant many tradesmen and dock workers were busy beyond belief. Luckily the person Cal was here for could always make time. It was an easy thing to do when those beneath you held the highest respect for you. Most captains didn't work the down-and-dirty jobs with their crew, but this captain did.

Calypso glanced up to see a large Skorvis woman stride across the docks towards her, carrying quite a load of boxes. Skorvians made the best crew for a ship, as the sweet call of sirens had no effect on them. She wasn't very large for a Skorvis woman, but she was far more muscular than most. With eight legs, rough tan-colored chitin, rough and muscular arms, a segmented tail with a large stinger on the end, and on the more scorpion half of her she had two smaller claws — she looked nothing like Calypso. Yet to her, this was the closest thing she had to a mother.

"This isn't the best of places for *aristoi* to be getting in the way." *Noblewoman.* She spoke bluntly. Her voice was creaky and had a hint of a silvery tone to it. For some, it could be grating to hear, but to

Cal, it was familiar and calming. She spoke not in a manner that was unfriendly, only a matter-of-fact type one.

"Captain Zagora," Calypso greeted her.

Only now did she actually look at Cal, a surprisingly youthful energy in her sunburnt eyes. She smiled, which was not seen through her pincer mouth but in her eyes.

"Ah! It's my little bird!" she said joyfully.

"You know, you don't have to keep calling me that," Calypso said sheepishly. "It's been years since that incident at the Citadel."

"It is a happy memory from when I was your guard," Zagora said, dipping her head.

If only she could stay as one of my guards. She was the first to protect Calypso as a child as she had known her mother. She chose to be a stand-in as Leandre was in training, mainly because she didn't trust the other two guards assigned to her at that time, but left once he had become her new royal guard.

She must trust Leandre a great deal.

"Hold on a moment, and I'll meet you on the ship," she said with a grin as she continued past her.

Calypso walked down the deck past the jolly workers who followed their captain in unloading the cargo. Workers from other ships nearby glared as their captains barked orders from their shaded spots on the piers. Most of the crew looked like Captain Zagora. With deeper tan chitin shells, more distinct facial features, and deep brown eyes, at least half of the crew were Skorvians. There were also a few centaurs, humans, and cyclops aboard as well.

A few humans passed and dipped their heads respectfully to her and continued with their words. Besides Leandre, these were the only Pilavians she had met. From the country across the sea, Pilavia was a kingdom much smaller than Vasyla, because borders were open between the two it wasn't uncommon to see people from there, but not a lot of them stayed within the capital city because of magick being outlawed. In fact, most went north, into Lord Harkyn's territory. Though Calypso wasn't sure why.

If this plan works... Then I can actually begin planning my future... Perhaps I will want to learn more about the Pilavians in the north and why they go there. Perhaps Leandre would want to learn more about his people as well.

This plan has to work, not just for me, but for Leandre. He deserves to have a better life than as my guard.

Calypso frowned as she climbed aboard the ship along with the crew. *Perhaps then Leandre will tell me more about why he came to be in life service as a royal guard. For me of all people. I chose him when I was young... but he had to have someone put him forward into training.*

Once on the deck, Cal stood off to the side and watched the workers carry more shipment crates up from below deck.

Knowing the royal court, this probably had something to do with the Festival of Halved Souls. Cal frowned as she tried to guess what was within each box. *Overpriced decor? More masks? Hopefully, it has nothing to do with the competition. I know deep in my heart that the emperor is nearing his end, and as much as I didn't want to think about it — I have to. My plan has to work, because if it doesn't...*

What would happen to Leandre and Ophelya? The pair have shown support to me for years... If I can't find a way out of this mess... What will happen to them?

"Cal?"

She was pulled out of her thoughts as Captain Zagora called her name. Cal turned to see the tall woman waiting for her with arms crossed.

"Sorry I wasn't able to make it to our last meeting, something came up," she said as she stopped in front of Calypso. "What was so urgent?"

"It's about the emperor, I think..." Cal glanced around, the other workers weren't paying them any attention. "...I think he isn't going to last much longer."

That is, if he isn't already dead.

Zagora's bright demeanor was suddenly gone as she looked at her. "Then the rumors are true... and the challenge will begin soon." She sighed and pressed her hand to her forehead. "What do you plan to do? Did you come here to see if you can hide away on the ship?"

Calypso shook her head. "If I disappear, all the court leaders and whoever wins will hunt me down — or go after those close to me. Maybe if it weren't for the prophecy that would work, but... I have a different plan."

"You know I would protect you..." she said solemnly.

"I'd rather not have you dragged any further into this, Zagora."

She sighed and smiled. "You're far too much like your mother... and me. Well — whatever it is you have more than one thing to keep an eye on."

"What do you mean?"

"There has been word of a knight wearing ancient armor appearing in the city and helping a great deal of people, serving the church, and... Well, with the 'prophecy' he may target you next." She shook her head. "It's odd, nobody can seem to catch or stop him to see where he got such a relic..."

Perhaps I should tell her a bit... lest she orders her crew to hunt them on my behalf.

"About that... The thing is —" Calypso began.

"He was last seen this morning near the docks, Cal," Zagora said suddenly, making her stop.

This morning?

That's impossible.

I left it in the tunnel during the night.

That would mean...

"Zagora, I need you to stay ashore for a while if possible," Calypso said quickly.

"Of course, little bird," she said, dipping her head. "My crew has been wanting a break for a while now. I suppose they deserved one eventually. Though, might I ask why?"

"I'm going to need you to stick around if my plan is to succeed."

I didn't want it to come to this... but if she cannot help me by getting the docks to show support for me as a knight...

At the very least she may still be able to save Leandre and Ophelya should anyone go after them after I'm gone.

Zagora nodded. "Of course, I'm on your side, you know this."

"Good," Calypso said quickly. "I'm sorry, there is more I wanted to discuss with you but... something has come up."

Zagora frowned but said nothing as Cal pulled her hood tighter around her head and hurried off of the ship and onto the docks.

How could it be?

How can that armor be out and about now?

Who else found it?

I left it in that place and only wore it out at night so...

Who found it?

Calypso didn't stop as she rushed from the docks back to the Citadel, so deep in her thoughts that she didn't even realize she was there until the looming halls and pillars were before her. Since she had been coming through almost every night for the past several days now — it felt like a familiar road well-traveled. The Dreamweavers remained within the tunnels oddly enough. Calypso didn't pay it much mind though. Perhaps they would slowly make their way out to find dreams to feast upon.

As she reached the end of the hall, she felt her heart quicken as she scanned the small room. Calypso let out an exasperated sigh. The armor was still there. Standing in the corner of the room. *Wait... standing?*

Whoever took it was still within the armor.

"Who's there?" she called out. Cal watched the armored figure. None of their features were visible as this style of armor completely hid its wearer. The armor didn't respond — Calypso held her breath, listening for any sign of life — the slightest shift of armor, the heavy breathing of the person inside, anything.

The armor shifted into a bow.

"*Graceless scion,*" it began. "What is your business here? You were the one who awakened me, so why is it you look at me with such disdain?" A silvery laugh came from inside the armor, Calypso could not tell if it was a man or woman's voice. "Ahh... so you've discovered something, have you? Who have you spoken with? The Lady Bryony? Or perhaps it was the great warrior Solairys who spoke to you?"

Who are you, what are you doing here? Bryony? Warrior? What is... All of those questions slipped from her mind as she heard their question.

Calypso frowned at it. "There isn't anyone in the Citadel who goes by those names."

The armored figure leaned back against the wall. "Ah, forgive me, it seems I need to be caught up. What is the year?"

"It is ten fifty-seven."

"I suppose it is no longer Tempus Magicae then?"

"Tempus Magicae..." That was what the last era was once called... but only those who still believe in the goodness of magick still refer to it as such. Why didn't they say Ante Lapsum? Before the Fall? "It is Anno Harmonia. The Years of Harmony."

The warrior Solairys, Silver Era, and perhaps by Lady Bryony they mean Bryonyer the Star of Vasyla... Why is this person talking of only ancient things? Are they trying to throw me off? Do they think they can pretend this armor really belonged to them?

But what if... What if this someone was actually around during the time of Cressyda and Cronys?

"Who is it within the armor?" Calypso asked. "Tell me your name."

"I doubt it is recognizable, but I am Oboryn, Sword of the Vasylian Empire."

"Why did you put my armor on? And how did you even manage to get down here?"

The stranger laughed again, an unsettling laugh that echoed in the room and made her skin crawl. "Your armor? I've been in this armor for much longer than you have been."

"What does that mean?" Cal asked through grit teeth. "I found this armor covered in cobwebs, it hasn't seen the light of day in years!"

"I dreamt for such a long time of what would happen when I was found and of whom would find me. I didn't expect someone so pitiful."

Though she couldn't see their eyes through the helmet, Calypso felt the stranger's gaze as they scanned her body.

"What are you-"

The stranger lifted the winged helmet from their head, Calypso held up the lamplight to see their face. Yet no face was to be seen. The armor was empty.

A deep laugh filled the room and reverberated within the hollow armor.

13
THE DEAD NEVER REST
OPHELYA

Fear is a fickle thing, it can make the wisest of men fools and the smartest of women stupid. Ophelya couldn't even think of a poetic way to put it as she had lived in fear for days. Days had gone by since Ophelya had taken the journal from her mother's room. In those days since, she felt fear strike her heart with every interaction the two shared. No matter how big or small. Even passing her in the halls on her way to study, Ophelya was keenly aware of every movement her mother made. Reading every glance, head shake, or sigh as her about to accuse Ophelya of the theft. Yet no such interaction ever happened. She hadn't even opened the book again since stealing it away once the letter fell from it. This was the last of her sister's journals — perhaps she was too scared, a coward after all. Unable to make even the smallest decision to open a book not handed to her by her teachers or parents. This was why she had survived for so long, but it was also why she was unable to truly thrive. Her title as an heiress weighed heavily on her shoulders — as the people of her territory had high expectations of her.

All she read was that single page — and that was only because it had fallen out. That single letter said a lot — and only Ophelya could understand it. It was because she knew Maeve was looking into the supposed curse of Calypso's Zodiac and the court. Knowing this, she still couldn't read the journal itself.

What would Maeve think of me now? I have changed so much since her passing. Would my sister still recognize me? Or would she see me for what I am, a husk of what I once was? Now being forced down the same path she had been forced into? Though... Perhaps she did fight against it more than I knew.

It was the middle of the day as Ophelya sat in the capital library, preferring the change of scenery to only being in the meeting room or her own room during the duration of her stay in the capital. Another event was coming up soon, which was also why very few others took the time to come to the library. Why stop and read now when that can be done at home? Yet Ophelya had far too important studies to keep up with before having to continue her private lessons once they returned to their territory of Vaales. She had seen Avalon and Adonys in the halls outside of the library — the pair were always together, it wasn't unusual. Yet the sight of them nearby with everything going on made her... unsettled to say the least.

As she sat and stared down at the book in front of her, she couldn't make sense of any of the shapes on the page. It was a book she was fairly familiar with, but all of the letters had become just that — shapes. No meaning behind them whatsoever. The sounds of a few servants walking past or shelving books reverberated in her head. The sound was magnified by her annoyance with the scribbles on the page. Ophelya gripped her hair in her hands and tried to force herself to pay attention when she heard a voice nearby. "Need any help, Lady Ophelya?"

She sighed, looking up half expecting to see a concerned servant who was worried she'd damage the books in her struggle — instead she was met with Prince Hectyr.

Ophelya quickly stood and dipped her head at him. "Prince Hectyr, so sorry — I did not notice you approaching."

Odd, I never heard footsteps come near me? She looked him up and down scarcely, even he didn't recognize he was being scanned by observant eyes. He wore a long robe with a rope tied around his waist, the skirt of it reached the floor — in fact, it went so far that it gathered below him and dragged on the ground — so she could not see the type of shoes he had on. Odd *indeed*, as Ophelya never let her awareness of her surroundings falter.

"Sorry, I did not mean to disturb you — it just looked as though you were struggling a little and I wondered if I might offer some assistance?"

She rested her hand on the table as she continued to stand. "I'm not sure I could bother Your Highness over my private studies," she said anxiously as she felt the eyes of the servants burning into her back.

He frowned as he noticed her hesitation, and mouthed to her, "Are the servants bothering you?"

Ophelya almost laughed at him never even thinking it was him who might be bothering her. Yet still, he wasn't wrong. Would it be wise to make him aware of this? *Hmm, Hectyr is timid and quite weak looking so I doubt anything bad could happen should we be alone.* Still, it was better to not underestimate your enemies.

Is he an enemy though? After all, if I recall correctly — Maeve did work as his mother's lady-in-waiting and she never spoke a word against him.

Ophelya slowly nodded, and Hectyr stepped aside to the servant nearest to them instead of beckoning them over and whispered something. Immediately, the servant motioned to the others, and the room was cleared almost immediately.

"What did you tell them?" she asked as he walked back to stand nearby.

"I told them I needed the library cleared so I could begin my studies, they didn't question it. Would that be enough to help?"

Ophelya nodded. "Yes... Thank you?"

"Glad I could be of assistance."

He smiled before taking a step back to leave, it was bright and genuine and made her uncomfortable as she couldn't understand it. *What was his angle if he was just going to go away?*

"Wait!" she said quickly, making him pause. *This could be my only chance to question him. Perhaps he knew more of my sister than I got to.*

Perhaps that can help Calypso somehow.

"Yes?"

"Could I ask you a few questions?" she asked.

He furrowed his brow but still smiled. "Of course, I'll answer as best I can." He motioned to the chairs at the table and as she began to turn to sit he pulled out the chair for her.

"Thank you," Ophelya said quickly as she sat down and waited for him to do the same.

"Now, can I ask what this is regarding?" He glanced at the books at the table. "If it helps with studying, I have been told I can be a great tutor-" He rubbed his neck awkwardly. "At least before I came to the Citadel."

"It isn't regarding that..." she said hesitantly. As good an opportunity as it was, it felt off speaking to one of Cal's half-siblings without her being aware. What if she found out and made an assumption?

No, this is all for Cal. Whatever Maeve was doing, in the end, will be the lead we need to help her out of the cursed situation... right?

"Is this about my sister, Princess Calypso?"

"Sister?"

He shrugged. "It is what she is, is it not?"

"Half-sister," she corrected him. Calypso would hate to hear him say that...

"Besides, wouldn't you rather not think of them as siblings considering the challenge?"

Hectyr's smile suddenly disappeared, he sighed and hung his head. "I believe I have made my stance on that matter quite clear to the court and to the people." He looked up at her through his brows. "I am sure you of all people know where I came from and why that is."

"Being raised in an orphanage away from it all does not guarantee you would be a good person once introduced to this world within the Citadel."

"That is true," he agreed. "No matter how you are raised does not guarantee a positive individual — though I like to think I am better than wanting to continue a lineage of needless bloodshed."

"So what do you plan on doing once the competition begins?" she challenged him. "The emperor isn't getting any younger, and when the All-Aspects call he will have to take heed just as anyone else."

"What exactly are you trying to get at, Lady Ophelya, if you do not mind my asking?"

"I believe you can take a guess at it."

"If you are trying to figure out if you can trust me with your questions, there aren't enough words in the world that will help you with that. It can only be proven through actions." He let out a halfhearted laugh. "I highly doubt I could do that as easily as this new knight sweeping the capital could."

"I suppose you're right." She sighed. "I am not here to question you about Cal- Princess Calypso," she corrected herself quickly. "I am here to ask you about Maeve."

"Your half-sister?"

"My *sister*," she corrected him. They may not have been full siblings much like the royals, but they certainly were not raised in any similar manner.

He frowned. "I believe she was my mother's lady-in-waiting before she passed away, but what does that have to do with me?"

"Since your mother has passed away — you received all of her belongings... yes?"

He nodded, and Ophelya glanced around before pulling a book out of a secret pouch in her bag. She held it up to him.

"Have you seen a book like this?" She quickly opened it up and pulled the letter out. "Or anything with handwriting like it?"

He froze, blue eyes fixated upon the writing in front of him.

Dear Tyr, If you're reading this, then I've given it to you for an important reason. My name is Maeve Nephus, daughter of Lord Pollus Nephus, lady-in-waiting to the concubine Lyra Appadexys.I began investigating members who suddenly began joining the church and began meddling in court affairs as one day I will have a seat on the court. I have found much concerning information that must be brought to light. I have been investigating rumors regarding the church and their uses of magick and any affiliations it may have to the court and I have discovered an underground network within both.It seems Witch Cultists have found a way within the church and are extending their reach to court

— I am unsure of how deep this reaches, but this may have grim meaning for times ahead. The final born of Emperor Oryon, Princess Calypso Pallas must be watched, for if not the omen regarding her similarities with the last royal scion born under the Zodiac of the White Tern may come true — though I am not yet sure in what way. We must prepare for the worst. I understand this situation does not directly involve you, but I do believe you deserve to know as I fear this is what your mother was trying to protect you from. My sister, Ophelya, is unaware of this now — but once I know more I will be telling her everything soon.

Hectyr paused for a moment before he tilted his head at her. "I've read that letter before but... It went missing years ago not too long after my mother's death."

"I don't know how, but I believe my mother found a way to steal it back."

"What is it you want to ask me for?"

"I need to know — Was Maeve working with your mother? Do you have any other information that could help lead me to find out what she was looking into when she..."

Strange. Ophelya suddenly found herself unable to finish the sentence.

Hectyr gave her a pitying look and sighed.

"I am not aware of any other journal like that one — I only recognize the letter." He frowned. "Though I do remember when she would visit me at the orphanage, she was getting... stressed. More and more before I was brought to the capital she was always looking over her shoulder and afraid. At first, I thought it was because she was hiding me with my mother, but when she died a few months after I was brought to the Citadel... Well, I'm sorry I don't know much to help."

"Is there anything else you could tell me? Anything that might help?"

"I apologize, I don't think there is."

Ophelya looked up at him. "One final thing then."

He sat up. "Of course, anything that will help."

"What do you think they were looking into?"

It was stupid to ask, he could lie and say whatever suited him — yet Ophelya had a feeling that he wouldn't.

Why else would Maeve write to him? He must be useful somehow.

"It isn't much to go on but... My mother was a devout believer in the All-Aspects. Even in exile she attended the church frequently."

"And?"

"In her final days, she stopped attending the church." He glanced at her. "Don't you think it a little odd that someone so religious would suddenly stop going to their place of worship?"

She frowned but dipped her head to him. "Thank you Prince Hectyr. You've given me a great deal to think about."

He smiled sadly. "Of course, let me know if there is anything else I can do for you."

She smiled back, and the muscles on her face didn't twitch as they usually do when she forced a smile.

Hectyr stood to leave, and as he walked away still no footsteps echoed within the library. He paused. "I will remind the servants to steer clear of this room for the next few hours, good luck Lady Ophelya."

As he disappeared around the corner, Ophelya clutched the journal in her hand.

I must read her journal. Now. I cannot let it wait another moment.

If there is even the slightest chance the church is involved in the curse Cal is dealing with I needed to know. Ophelya grit her teeth and pushed the books aside. It wasn't safe enough here. She had to take it elsewhere.

Sorry Hectyr, but your good deed didn't do much in the end.

Still, at least he provided some *action rather than just words.*

I will wait until the next court meeting — after the blessing. I will be safe then — nobody will interrupt me... Right?

14
TO TURN A BLIND EYE
ECHO

One should observe not just with their eyes, but also with their mind. As the empire was reaching a turning point — being observant was crucial for survival. Like a mouse listening for the tiniest crunch of a leaf, Echo felt as though her life were only made for her to watch others. It was almost ironic, how observant she was. With only a single eye, the young cyclops was known for her keen observations and extraordinary tactician capabilities.

She observed, though she was never really observed herself.

Only by one other was she ever observed.

Calypso.

Echo sat, legs crossed in a pile of leaves. In the middle of the forest near the capital city where she often hid. It was ironic really, how often she managed to get away from the capital. This would only become more difficult, Cyclops never really stopped growing. At twenty-one years old, Echo was still only 5'5 — but when she would hit fifty or beyond she would be above 6'2.

Echo bit her lip with her two small tusks as she held out her hands. Rumbling could be heard from the ground beneath her, leaves shivered as the rocks beneath them trembled. Earth magick. One that was feared as the opposite the water magick. Echo learned it for that reason.

Calypso is the only threat.

She had seen it once. At the shores. A young princess, a skorvian knight, and a secret lesson in magick.

The young girl was already older looking than Echo, despite being the younger of the two. With long blonde hair with bleached patches and a chubby build. She was bigger than Echo — who was tiny and scrawny even for a cyclops.

The two never saw her, sneaking around the docks when she saw them upon an empty ship. Practicing. In broad daylight. Yet anyone who saw was loyal to the skorvian, and felt no obligation to say anything. To report anything. To recall what they saw to the authorities.

Echo knew since then, that Calypso had some level of control over magick. Only Calypso and Echo could get away with such things. Calypso was cursed, and people would rather avoid such a thing. Echo was small and covert, and could get away with a lot since her appearance was childlike when compared to humans.

She almost felt excited to fight her. Would she corner her in secret — between the challenges they would face — and fight her with magick out of sight? Or would she be bold enough to try her magick in the arena despite it's outlawed status?

She was so excited to face off with another magick user of her own blood and yet...

Why did I defend her?

When Deakon struck, people assumed that Echo was hit as she had been sitting close to Calypso. The royal scion's were seated in accordance to age besides Deakon who was in the centaur seating. Collateral damage. When the reality was Echo herself moved into the path of the spear, expecting very little pain from the prop.

As Echo continued to make the ground beneath her rumble and shake, she felt the pain in her arm growing.

Perhaps I should learn Controlled Magick rather than Wild Magick... It may be weaker but it would allow me to use it for longer.

Yet Wild Magick has a certain pull to it. I may weaken faster but the strength behind it is unbelievable.

She slowly stopped. *I could make the whole capital shake if I wanted. I can feel it. I can move it. But I cannot reveal it yet...*

Her arm throbbed, and glanced down at the wrappings.

Still. Why defend her? If I let him strike her... She would be easier to defeat. The challenge is coming soon — she is not the only one I will have to face.

Without her though... The challenge will be dull.

Echo could see much, but there was little beyond the challenge she could think about. The Challenge of Cressyda. This would be the peak of her existence, the reason she was born.

So why leave Calypso alive?

It may make the games more thrilling, but what if I cannot defeat her?

Then... is that it?

She hadn't planned for anything past the challenge beyond what teachers and court members spoke of — becoming the next empress. Echo couldn't see herself on the throne even if she won. What would she even do there?

No matter.

Just as Cronys was the one to defeat Cressyda.

I will be the one to defeat Calypso.

The earth around her continued to shake, but it wasn't Echo's doing. She stood to her feet, teeth clenched as the pain in her arm returned. She looked to the wrappings, little beads of red began to bleed through. She had ripped it open again, but that didn't matter.

Echo began making her way towards the source of this magick. Able to sense it like she could sense a fallen leaf on her skin. It became like a second nature, once one learned to use magick it became easier to sense when it was near. This was how she knew Calypso must have still been training since she had felt it recently within the Citadel.

A small band of four could be seen in the woods ahead of her. On the side paths near the main roads leading to the capital city of Lyreas. This was not an unfamiliar sight. Even with the first few events of the festival already passed, people would still be making their way to the capital.

What was strange, was that they were using magick. Three of the people scowl and nudge the last member of the group. The one using magick. They were showing off, using it as commonly as children use toy spears.

Strange... They also use magick.

They wore feathered garb, and Echo was quickly able to tell it wasn't mock feathers. She had seen many mock feathered robes and dresses since she was young. She had seen real feathers that fell off of birds. Once, she almost picked up a fallen feather — until her teacher had seen what she was about to do and screamed bloody murder. To even touch such a sacred object was not tolerated. These strange people though, they didn't have a mere few feathers on their garb. It was enough to cover several birds.

They use magick, and they adorn themselves in true feathers...
Are they from outside of Vasyla?

Echo knew she wouldn't be seen. She was small, lithe, and was already making her way back to the Citadel.

Despite what Echo saw, she did not plan to report it. Or even make a hint at what she saw to another soul. She would keep this information to herself. A dragon with a hoard of words. After all, she was only an observer. She was echo. Echoes only reflected words already spoken — and she would not be the first to utter such words.

15
BLOOD IS THICKER THAN WATER
CALYPSO

"Where is my guard?"

A patrolman standing an awkward distance from Calypso glanced at the two guards tailing her from an equally awkward distance.

"There are two of them right there, Your Highness."

Calypso sighed. "Where is *my* guard, Leandre?"

The patrolman just dipped his head and quickly hurried away, Calypso squinted at them in disbelief as they went from a half-jog into a full run. *Now that's a first.*

She turned to the two guards tailing her to ask them the same question and they quickly averted their gaze.

Perhaps it is better I not include him in this anymore — after all, the closer to the challenge time we get the more in danger he would be. Still, I wonder what he could be working on?

Looking at the female guard she caught her eyes for a second and she quickly looked away. Out of the two other guards, the female cyclops seemed to be the nicer of the pair — yet Calypso still did not know their names as they hardly spoke to her.

"Do either of you have any idea where Leandre is?"

They exchanged a glance but both shrugged their shoulders at Calypso.

She sighed. "Then you can both go now, in fact, you don't need to tail me in the first place."

"I — don't believe we can do that," the girl responded begrudgingly. "If something were to happen, we would be held accountable."

"At least, before the challenge begins that is." The human male coughed.

"Oh come on," Calypso groaned. "Since when did other guards care? If anything were to happen it would have by now — besides we all already know where my path ends."

She frowned, but it was clearly fake as her facial muscles twitched as she struggled to not smile in front of Cal. She dipped her head and the two scurried away, light armor clanking echoed in the halls as they did. *Perfect.* Now Calypso could return to the secret tunnel and deal with the armor.

What will I do with it now though? What does one even do when they find old armor that can speak? Calypso had heard of cases of people using magick to speak through objects, but that was thousands of years ago — and even that didn't sound anything like what she was dealing with...

I'm lucky I was able to shut it down there again — but still, how did it even get out in the first place? Had she left the door open when she left due to exhaustion from being up all night and getting scarcely an hour of sleep before her day began? Did it open the door? But if it knew how, why didn't it leave sooner?

Calypso hurried through the great halls of the Citadel, past the many servants doing final preparations for the next event of the festival. Great floral vines were being delicately wrapped around each pillar and slowly grew to attach to it, banners were being raised, and everything had been polished several times over – yet as she reached her mother's garden, not a single servant was in sight. *Perfect.* A little sad, but Cal wouldn't have it any other way right now.

Hurrying towards the gazebo, she began to make her way up the steps when a voice rang out across the garden.

"Princess Calypso!"

She spun around quickly, pushing her hand beneath her robe to where a blade rested against her belt hidden beneath the thick fabric. The cold metal against her hand made her shiver as she looked at who entered her mother's garden. Cal scrunched her nose in disgust as she recognized the intruder who followed her. With the distinctive white hair and blue eyes of the royal lineage, the unfashionable long cloak which dragged with his every step wherever he went, and the awkward slouch which made him still above average height — that was Prince Hectyr, alright.

Was I right to worry then? Is he looking to take me out early so the challenge is easier for him?

"What do you want?" Cal asked loudly, bitterness spilling from her lips.

He dipped his head and stopped a good few feet away from her. "I saw you rushing in the halls, you looked rather distraught so I wanted to see if you needed assistance with something."

She shook her head and stepped back onto the gazebo. *Curse my face! Why do I have to be so horrible at hiding emotions?*

"I am doing just fine on my own," she retorted.

"I know we're not close, not like normal siblings should be... but I'm here for you if you need a friend," he said awkwardly, fidgeting in place. "And you seem like you need one."

Calypso laughed. "What is it you're getting at? Think you can trick me?"

He frowned. "What?" He watched her stepping back, eyebrows furrowed in confusion. He sounded rather genuine — was he really that foolish?

He began to come forward. "Calypso, you have no reason to be scared of me. I do not care for this challenge between-" He stopped and his eyes went wide as she continued to step back.

"Calypso!"

As Calypso quickly backed up, the floor disappeared from beneath her feet. As she fell back Hectyr leapt forward and grabbed ahold of her hand and was pulled along with her. The two tumbled down the stairs until they hit the bottom. Cal groaned as she struggled to sit up while Hectyr awkwardly pulled himself off of the ground.

Why was it open?! I thought they agreed to stay put! What happened?

"Calypso, what is this place?!" he said as he looked down the hall — just then the lights all blazed and lit up the path. Hectyr almost fell back in surprise.

"You really shouldn't be here," she said. "It's dangerous."

Hectyr looked down at her and frowned, extending a hand to help her up but she ignored it as she slowly struggled to her feet alone.

"If it's dangerous then why are you down here?"

Calypso snorted. "My whole life is dangerous, what's one more thing going to do? Kill me?" She glared at him. "Isn't that what you're here to do anyways? The emperor is dead isn't he? So why not get ahead of the competition?"

He stepped back and put his hands up, eyes wide. "No! The emperor is still alive!"

He isn't dead? Then... If the healers aren't releasing that information...

He might be really close to it.

"I was looking for you because I-"

"*Looking*? I thought you followed me because I looked distressed?"

"Well, that too." Hectyr looked down. "I spoke with Ophelya and she kept asking me questions about you... Questions that made me think she was worried about you and... Questions that led me to believe you're suspicious of me for some reason. Now I realize I was correct." He looked ahead deeper into the tunnel. "But what does this lead to?"

He began to move forward, Calypso reached out to stop him but she missed. She quickly began walking after him.

"Hectyr, wait! You need to leave!"

He shook his head. "Not until I see what is dangerous here."

Calypso followed behind him, with every step she could feel her pulse race. This was an enemy before her, so why didn't she get the rush she got before combat? Why had he not struck at her yet?

Does he suspect me of being up to something? What did Ophelya tell him that made him want to talk to me? I wouldn't mistrust her for a second, if she said something to him it would be to our mutual advantage... but why would she speak with him? The two aren't close. Are they?

As they neared the end of the hall, Calypso took a deep breath. "At least let me take the lead, just for a moment." Hectyr paused and looked back at her meeting her gaze. He dipped his head and allowed her to pass. She continued down the hall and into the small room.

"Don't panic too much, it should be fine —" As she looked around the room she felt her heart drop. It was gone again.

"Why is it gone?!" Calypso cried as she spun around, looking at all corners of the room. "It's not even midday yet!" Hectyr moved into the room and jumped away from something on the floor. He leaned down to look at it.

"Dreamweavers? Here?" He looked up at Cal, horrified. "Calypso, don't tell me you've been *sleeping* in here? With all of these rusted swords and hunks of metal lying around?!"

"Of course not! But... something might have been." Calypso sighed. "Come on, I need to look for something and you can't stay here." As she began to hurry back down the hall, Hectyr followed.

"What is it we're looking for?"

"We?" she asked him. He nodded quickly and she groaned.

He already does know far too much... If I let him go now who knows who he will tell about this secret tunnel?

Perhaps it is better to keep him close while I continue the search. That way I can keep a better eye on him. I need to ask Ophelya why he would come after me though...

"It's something I found. A suit of armor."

"Armor? Did you really join the knights after all?!" He grinned. "Then have you met Aneurin?"

"We've met," she replied quickly. "But no, I have not become a knight after all — wait how do you even know about that?"

"Well, Aneurin told me about your request, but nothing else."

As they exited the tunnels, Calypso pulled a piece of the statue that closed off the tunnel once more before stopping outside the gazebo. "Why would a young knight like that be reporting to you?"

"Because he is my brother, why wouldn't he?"

Calypso gasped. *Does the emperor really have more hidden children? Emperor Oryon really is a who- Oh!* Slowly realization set in for her. "He isn't a royal scion, you were talking about your life before you were brought here, weren't you?"

Hectyr nodded before looking towards the Citadel. "So what is it we're looking for exactly? Just... regular armor?"

"It's anything but regular but... Yes, we're looking for armor."

"Did someone steal it from you?"

Cal frowned "It's difficult to explain... Not necessarily. Do you know that strange hero that has appeared in the capital? Helping others and such at night, and seen roaming in the day?"

Hectyr nodded quickly. "Yes, I have been following that story a lot lately. They're wearing an ancient suit of armor, it's surprising they haven't been questioned yet. Is that your armor?" He gasped. "Did they steal it?"

"That was me — at night at least." Calypso struggled to not laugh at the shocked expression on his face, he must not think Cal could handle that much. "I need to stop the... person taking it out in the day."

"Sooo, we have to leave the Citadel then?"

She raised a brow at him. Why was he not asking more questions? Cal slowly nodded, looking him over. "But first we're going to need you to look less suspicious."

This was going to be difficult, considering how noticeable Hectyr was. Standing at almost seven feet tall if he wasn't slouching — and the posture was already noticeable on its own.

"That should be easy, right?" Hectyr asked.

"I never would have thought making a paste with spices and using it as a hair mask would help hide the color!" Hectyr whispered excitedly as he followed behind Calypso on the streets. "But why the cloaks if our hair color is different?"

"Because hair color alone is not enough."

How often does this man go out? She glared up at him. *It's hard to imagine him having the same blood as me. Even if it's only partial. We're nothing alike.*

"So, why is it you've been going out at night anyway? Doing all of those chivalrous deeds? Trying to gain points with the Aspects?"

Calypso snorted. "More like trying to lengthen my time before meeting them."

Hectyr went silent at that. Yet a look of confusion was on his face.

He probably believe the plan to be foolish. But what else is there?

I've spent years trying to find a way and the only ones end with me leaving like a coward. My name forever tarnished in the eyes of my people.

No matter.

At least I can now have some peace and quiet while we — I *hunt for this... thing.*

It had been hours of searching, and Cal's head was spinning as she tried to imagine where else within the city it could be. If they left the city... there was almost no chance she could track it down in time. She had to hope that it stayed within the capital for now.

Calypso didn't notice the merchant turn into the street carrying bags full of fruit until she crashed right into them. Falling back as fruit flew everywhere, and her hood fell back as well. People began to stare, this time though, it was most likely due to two cloaked figures — one ridiculously tall — having knocked someone over. Even if it was by accident.

Not again.

Before she could slap Hectyr's hand away, Cal spotted one ominous figure in the crowd watching. A knight from the capital. A Skorvis knight to be exact — they were similar to Zagora only they were far bigger and had the hardened chitin of a Skorvian warrior. The way they watched Calypso, they clearly recognized her, yet they didn't notice Hectyr... yet.

Calypso grabbed her hood and this time took Hectyr's hand for help.

"We need to go now," Calypso said quickly as she dipped her head and apologized to the woman she ran into. As the woman looked into her eyes she looked confused for a moment then horrified. If she recognized her though, she said nothing, instead collecting her figs and fruit and scurrying off.

"Why, did you see them?"

Calypso looked back, the knight was getting closer. Hectyr then glanced up and noticed them, tensing up.

"That isn't them but-"

"Excuse me," a raspy voice said next to the pair. They both spun around to face the stranger. "You look like someone reliable — could I ask that you walk with me to the docks, young lady?"

Just before the Skorvian knight reached them the newcomer stepped in the way. Cal stepped back as she gleaned them over. Winged arms, a large beak, and a hunched neck? It was a Voltuan. No less, they were a priest Voltuan.

"Of course, we can!" Hectyr answered before she could respond, Cal glared back at him. "Play along," he mouthed at her. Calypso grimaced but smiled at the Voltuan as they begin to walk along with him to the docks. *At least we're moving, I can still search...* Calypso glanced up at the bird man.

They were a priest of the church, as they wore the robes of an Earth Aspect priest, odd since most Voltuans worshiped the Sky Aspect. Embroidered stones and roots covered the robe with sage greens and deep russet mud colors. The Voltuan stood two feet taller than Cal, looming overhead as they stared at the path ahead. Despite how ominous they appeared, he did not seem to have ill intent toward the royal scions. Based on their dull feathers and glazed eyes they were rather old. Why would such an old bishop not be accompanied by the younger deacons? Calypso silently thanked the Aspects as the Skorvian knight scowled before spinning away. After all, knights were afraid to cause trouble around the feathered race. Birds are sacred in Vasyla, and in turn so were the Voltuans.

Considered to be a holy people.

Yet to find one in holy robes was still odd — they might worship the Aspects like many within Vasyla, but they never did in the same ways of the church.

Either way, it was perhaps clever of Hectyr to go along with it, even if it was unintentional it got the pair out of a rough situation.

Perhaps he is smarter than I give him credit for. That did come with its worries, but Cal would have to wait and worry about that later.

"With all of these rumors about this strange knight, I didn't want to travel alone," the Voltuan began as they walked together. Cal frowned at them. *Was he afraid?*

Well, it isn't just me using it anymore...

"Do you not believe the knight is good?" Hectyr asked.

The Voltuan shook their head. "They may be good or bad, I do not know."

"What reason would a Voltuan have to be nervous in the Vasyla Empire capital?" Calypso asked boldly, making even Hectyr frown at her forwardness.

"No matter who you are or where you come from, it is better to proceed with caution."

Cal looked away from the Voltuan's intense gaze.

As they reached the less busy streets nearer to the docks, the Voltuan looked at her. "You are Princess Calypso, are you not?"

She froze up, and suddenly Hectyr stepped between them.

"Who's asking?"

The Voltuan put their talons up, wings spreading slightly as they raised their head back. They had a rather long neck. "I don't mean any harm to you, in fact — quite the opposite."

They began to continue walking and Hectyr and Cal exchanged a glance before following them.

"Most of my people do not believe in the ill-fated prophecy. There is no such thing as an ill-omen through the stars, young royal."

"Then what has my whole life been? What do you call my ill-fated prophecy?" she asked angrily. "A mockery for nothing?"

The Voltuan shut his eyes and dipped their head for a moment, thinking.

"Just because someone signals change, doesn't always mean they bring bad changes with them. Besides, who is to say the prophecy is about you? Has anyone ever been sure they have heard the whole thing?"

"When Vasyla has over a thousand moons in its skies,
When the star of the white tern brings us a royal scion,
When the night outlasts the day, Vasyla will crumble
once more..."

Calypso no longer met the Voltuan's gaze as he looked upon her. He frowned. "Who can say what the rest of it was? For what prophecy ever fell so short in the history of the empire?"

The old Voltuan stopped as they neared a small church. They turned to the royals and dipped their head. "Thank you again, royal scion, for giving an old man someone to ramble on to for a short walk."

Without another word, they shuffled towards the church, not looking back.

"What in the Aspects' name was that?" Calypso asked, resting her hand against her temple. She sighed. "No matter, we're at the docks now which means we can look for the armor here."

It was late in the evening, and they never found the armor.

"I can't believe we found nothing," Calypso said, "What am I going to do tonight?"

"You mean you were planning on being out all day and crusading all night?" Hectyr let out a tired yawn.

"Whatever it takes to clear my name with the people," Cal grunted in response.

Hectyr sighed. "I'm not sure how well that plan will work but I'm glad we can finally work together like this."

"What do you mean?" Cal asked, glancing down. Her hands were shaking. *Why didn't I notice that? I'm not anxious, am I?*

Why would I be?

Why wouldn't *you be, more like?*

"As brother and sister," he said cheerily. "It has been a while since I have been able to do something like this." She couldn't help but laugh out loud at that, surprising even herself.

"What?" Hectyr asked, dumbfounded, "Ah! Sorry I forget that is odd within the capital, to call one another that. Does that bother you as well?" He looked at her confused, and all she could focus on were his disgustingly blue eyes. The blue eyes of the royal scions — one of the important features that she did not inherit from the emperor. Instead left with the almost amber-hazel eyes of her mother. The last royal concubine, and the most hated even before her passing.

"*Sister?*" Calypso asked. "After all I have been put through because of blood ties, no, I don't like you calling me that. Let me guess, blood is thicker than water to you now?"

He dipped his head. "Sorry since I was raised in a-"

"Yes, you were raised in an orphanage before being brought to the Citadel, everyone knows it! It's how you get away with so much!" Calypso curled her nose in a snarl. "Do you even talk to those you grew up with there anymore? Bother them and call them brother and sister?" she continued snidely. "Or did you just leave them behind as you will me?"

Hectyr's cheery demeanor suddenly disappeared and he stood to his full height, and Calypso immediately regretted making such a rude comment.

"I will never allow anyone to question my loyalty to those I grew up with."

"That's not an answer, *brother*."

He clenched his jaw. "Irys just got engaged to the woman of her dreams and I will be attending her wedding at the end of Dekem, Aneurin finished his training to become a knight and at my recommendation has joined the knight's squadron here in the Citadel, my youngest sister Althyns, has finally been brought into a nice family in the southern territory and sends me letters almost every week — shall I go on?" He laughed. "And that phrase, that is not the whole thing. The blood of the covenant is thicker than the water of the womb — the quote isn't about blood ties being more important, rather chosen family being stronger than what you are born with."

Cal grit her teeth. "If your chosen family is so close to you, why are you helping me and not them? Is it just because you feel it is an obligation? Helping your cursed sister to earn some points with the Aspects?"

He stopped and Calypso continued for a few steps before noticing.

She turned around to look at him. "What?" "It's not that I believe in the curse... but-"

"But?"

"You and I have more in common than I'd like to admit." He sighed. "Follow me."

He slunk away into the nearest alleyway. Calypso glanced around at the passerby, nobody seemed to care. She followed behind him.

"What is it you can't say out there? What could a prince like you be hiding?" Cal asked mockingly.

"Well." He ducked his head. "It's because of this."

He opened the front of his cloak and Cal began to look away until she noticed one face, then another, and another. Hundreds of snakes resided underneath Hectyr's cloak. Where Hectyr's legs should be were instead the bodies of many serpents. Curved so that their bodies slithered on the ground and their heads remained just above it.

That was why I could never hear him approaching!

Of course, it all made sense now. Why he would offer help to her over all of the other half-siblings he could be aiding right now? He was also cursed.

He was an Ophiophor — born of a curse in his lineage. His ancestors killed the last dragons.

"I'm sure you've heard of an Ophiophor before," he said as he dropped his skirt back over the many serpent heads who went silent once covered again. "I may be different, and unable to live out the same life as many others – but that doesn't mean my fate is sealed."

"But you're cursed!" Calypso shouted. "Descended of those who killed dragons! That is the curse is it not? At random, those of your lineage will be cursed with the bodies of incomplete dragons — a sin against their kind. Serpents! Do you really not believe your curse is a bad thing?"

"Who is to say it is a bad thing? After all, it is the last emperor of the dragons who melted a whole city on the island of Prym just for its riches. If you ask me, it is a sign that I am descended from good men and women who would fight up against gods if it meant it would save their country."

"But you said it yourself, you must live differently because of it."

He nodded. "Yes, but different isn't always a bad thing Calypso. I live within the Citadel differently than I did back at the orphanage and it wasn't a bad life with my family there. A curse doesn't decide your future."

She frowned. "Then what of my curse?"

"What of it! It isn't even a curse, it is only speculation. So what, you share the same birth month as one other royal? Just because they chose a selfish and cruel fate doesn't mean they have to. We don't really know if you are cursed to bring the downfall of Vasyla, just as we don't know what will happen even tomorrow."

"Do you... Do you really think fate can be controlled?" she choked out. "How can I control something that has changed everyone's perception of me?!"

"You can't." He spoke slowly after some thought. "But you wouldn't be able to do that even without the curse. Nobody can."

"No, I have to believe I can change their perceptions of me — if I can't do that I can't do anything."

Hectyr gave her a sad look but said nothing as she turned away.

"Let's go back to the capital now," she said quickly.

He sighed. "I hope you aren't planning to go back to the garden again tonight."

She didn't answer him.

As they began to make their way back to the Citadel, Calypso's mind was a mess of falling feathers.

Conflicted after Hectyr revealed that great deal of information about himself to her, and wishing for Ophelya or Leandre to speak with her to help her come to a better decision on the situation. Despite her confusion, Cal couldn't help but feel like Hectyr could be a good ally and someone she could trust. Though she might not ever get used to him treating her as a sister, or her treating him as a brother — they were bound by blood whether they liked it or not.

I don't think I have a lot of options on who to trust anymore if I am to survive — and likely he didn't either.

As they continued making their way back to the capital Cal pulled her hood back over her head as they passed by a group of knights. As she glanced up, she spotted a centaur and recognized Lord Harkyn leading the small squadron. Hardly even glancing over the others Calypso spotted one shorter than the others with a familiar face. Calypso felt her heart drop into a deep, unending pit.

"Isn't that Leandre?" Hectyr whispered. "Why is he with Lord Harkyn?"

Leandre glanced over them, but there was a flash of recognition in his eyes. Calypso turned quickly and hurried to walk away.

"I don't know," she said angrily as she scowled, struggling to hide the tears that welled up in her eyes.

She looked back, the other knights bolstered him onward and he shook his head before following them. Before following Harkyn, and leaving Calypso behind.

Did he choose a different ally than me? Something as serious as working with Harkyn of all people he would share with me, right?

That must be why he hasn't been around lately.

But why? After everything together why would he do that?

Calypso glanced back, watching as her close ally grew further and further away. She couldn't help but feel worried as well as betrayed — but she didn't know what to do as her trust for him snapped.

Trust can be a fickle thing, can't it?

16
THE GUISE OF A BLESSING
OPHELYA

Something was haunting about the churches in Lyreas. Their great looming walls were not as comforting as the ones Ophelya knew back at home. The statue of the Aspect first being split into three, with smaller breakages off of him becoming the lesser Aspects struck fear in her heart as she gazed upon it. All eyes from every figure on the one looming creation seem to stare at her. Their cold marble eyes staring through her to her very core.

Thinking back to the figures in the temples back in Vaales, and their warm comforting expressions, she couldn't help but wonder why the two depictions were so... different.

They really know how to capitalize on religious guilt in the capital, Ophelya thought to herself as she looked up at the unwelcoming depiction of their god in all their parts.

Ophelya watched the priests and priestesses waiting for the emperor or at least his court to enter the temple for the blessing ceremony of the festival. The Festival of Halved Souls was one of many events throughout it — after all, this was the celebration of the harvest season and the years end — yet the most populated events were the ones to include the church. After all, nothing makes one look more appealing to the people than their devotion to a higher power. Most of the events were a way to show off status and piety.

The emperor suddenly appeared at the entrance of the temple, but he was only hanging on by a thread. Deep bags gathered beneath his eyes, darkened like a siren's claws, his face hollowed in like something took a bite out of him, and his body while not quite withered away was clearly weakened which was clear by his labored movement. Ophelya glanced at the priests — their expressions were unchanging as he entered slowly. They watched behind him as eventually the members of the court entered, yet one was missing.

Where is Lord Harkyn?

Ophelya raised a brow as the priests and priestesses exchanged worried glances — not from the sight of the emperor but because of the lack of Lord Harkyn's presence. She narrowed her eyes as one priestess met her gaze and looked away quickly.

Odd.

How much power does he hold over the church? He already has strong power and influence over the court... and he is the emperor's brother-in-law but was never made to step down as a lord... There is more going on there than there should be.

Feeling eyes upon her skin, Ophelya glanced over to where the royal scions stood — As she looked for Calypso she found one other staring at her. *Avalon.*

Ophelya didn't waver or turn away as their eyes met, making Avalon frown and look to the front of the temple after a moment. She sighed.

Royal scions... There is always something with them, isn't there?

As the priests began to speak, Ophelya looked at Calypso. She also had dark circles under her eyes, standing amongst her half-siblings she looked almost as worn down as the emperor as she struggled to keep an eye on the front. Cal glanced over at Ophelya for a moment, who smiled back at her — but she quickly looked away.

Something happened, but what else could *have happened after the event at the amphitheatre?*

A loud sound was heard from the entrance as a priest brought something inside. A sacrificial lamb.

Ophelya looked at the lamb, it was young. Too young. It's eyes still round and carrying the soft innocence of youth. Ophelya wondered when she had last felt innocent — but that was many years ago. Not even a decade prior when she was ten did she feel like that. She watched the lamb be carried to the altar for its blood to be spilled. Ophelya could only imagine the screams of its family as it was taken for this challenge. Would that be Calypso soon if they didn't have a plan to get her out of the challenge?

No, don't think too deeply, don't let yourself fall back into the mourning of the poet. You can no longer afford the luxury of letting emotions run freely. Breathe in.... Hold...... Breathe out.

Ophelya took quiet deep breaths as she watched the priests mutter amongst themselves during the sacrifice, not all of them were even fully paying attention to the ceremony they were holding. Looking at all of them, she noticed that those dressed in higher-class robes seemed less focused on the event and more focused on the empty seat Lord Harkyn was not occupying.

Even when the screams were cut off, Ophelya did not find solace in the silence.

Once they cleaned up the body of the sacrificial lamb, Ophelya found she couldn't quite look at it anymore.

Do the Aspects really find that a worthy way of honoring them? Not with real actions with meaning, but by the waste of one of their creations?

It was almost as empty as the court member's words. Hollow. Void. *Worthless.*

Various upper and lower-class people took their money and riches to place around the blood left in the bowl from the lamp to leave at the statue. A few cast glances around as they left a little more or a little less than one another — watching and wanting. Looking for the judgment and opinions of others.

Ophelya may follow the religion of the empire — but she didn't agree with how the vast majority chose to worship.

It was nothing more than a game — who could look more guilty and grief-stricken in their prayers?

Who can give more while under the guise of not having much?

Who has a guaranteed place in the afterlife?

Were those really good ways to show faith? Of course not.

It should not be a self-service.

Though it was not everyone who looked for the approval of others, some gave to the Aspects without any focus on anyone in the room — focusing their thanks and asking for forgiveness of all of the Aspects, yet it was hard to focus on the few faithful over the many into the theatrics of it all.

As soon as the ceremony ended and people began to gather at the entrance to go to the feast, Ophelya nodded at Calypso and began to make her way to their meeting place outside of the main temple. As she made her way out, she ran directly into someone else.

What is wrong with me today?

Ophelya stepped back quickly, dipping her head to the person in question.

"My sincerest apologies, I was not paying attention to where I was —" She stopped as she looked up to see a tall figure with curly white hair. Hectyr.

Meeting him in private was one thing — this is far too public! Ophelya began to turn to look for Calypso but then Hectyr began to speak.

"You don't need to apologize to me, Ophelya. It is crowded, so I am sure you are not the only one bumping into others."

He suddenly put his hand out next to her shoulder, she began to flinch away until she spotted a rather large Skorvian bumping into his hand.

Did he just block them from crashing into me?

"Thank you," Ophelya muttered quietly.

Hectyr grinned. "Of course." He extended a hand to her. "Would you care to join me as we go to feast in the Citadel?"

She froze. While Ophelya felt slightly calmer around him, and felt a slight pull to continue to stay near him — to question him of course — she also knew what Calypso might think if she saw this. So instead, she dipped her head and hurried past him to the alley beside the temple. She waited five minutes before Calypso appeared around the corner from behind the building.

"Is everything alright?" Ophelya asked, grabbing Cal's hands and holding them as she got near. "You seemed down during the event so I thought we could meet up and go to the shore."

"I... I can't meet up with you at the shore," Calypso said after a moment, pulling her hands away.

"What's wrong?" Ophelya asked. "Did you see me with Hectyr? Because that wasn't anything, I swear." She glanced around.

Wait... Where is Leandre?

"What?" Cal furrowed her brows for a moment. "Oh no... I don't mind that — Hectyr is the least worrying of the bunch and he helped me recently."

"Wait... what?"

Hectyr helped Calypso? So is he trustworthy? Or is this a twisted game?

Before Ophelya could ask any more questions, Calypso continued speaking. "I have a plan, so don't worry but... I can't involve you in it."

"Cal, whatever is it you are working on, you need to include Leandre or me —"

"No!" she interrupted, making Ophelya jump. She quickly rested a hand on her other arm and took a step back. "Just, no. I don't need help and I don't need you two to get any further involved. Especially not Leandre right now."

"*Especially* not Leandre?" Ophelya glanced around quickly, he was still nowhere in sight. He was always near Cal, so where could he be? "Cal... Where is Leandre?"

"He's... I don't know," she said after a moment, as though calculating each word before she said it. Ophelya's eyes widened.

Is he ok?

She opened her mouth to ask, but Calypso was beginning to back away.

"Calypso..." Ophelya reached for her hand again but Cal pulled away.

"You should go," she said quickly. "Before you're spotted with me again. It's not as safe as it was when we were children."

Ophelya watched as Cal met her eyes for a moment. She looked pained as she spoke, whatever was wrong though she would not say. She watched as Cal spun around and walked away until she vanished around the corner out of sight.

If she won't let me in on her plan... Then I have to come up with my own plan.

But first... Why is Hectyr getting involved?

The screams of the lamb, the fake worship of the upper class, and now Cal turning her back on her — Ophelya felt as though her mind were unraveling as the sound of the people in the streets seem to get louder and louder.

Ophelya strode out onto the cobblestone streets and made a bee-line for the tallest royal scion — not caring for who was watching or listening. In that moment, Ophelya allowed her emotions to get the better of her.

As she neared him, she bumped into someone else. She backed away and looked up to see an older man whose eyes were already on her. He smiled, flashing all of his teeth but never taking his eyes off of her.

"Ah, Lady Ophelya. I was looking for you."

She scarcely looked at him, it was one of the lesser lords not on the court. She dipped her head. "Sorry, I'm in quite the hurry, Lord…" She squinted at him for a moment and found she could not recall his family name as her mind spun in circles. She continued past him. *I don't have the time anymore.*

"Hectyr —" As she reached out for Hectyr, Ophelya felt herself get pulled back.

"How dare you speak to me in such a manner!" he said quietly. "I expected better from you, *Ophelya.*"

"Lord Hylio," Hectyr pushed his way in between the pair. "I do not believe that is the proper way to speak to a lady of the court."

Ophelya stepped back and looked up at Hectyr, who gave her a small smile.

What is he doing?

"Sorry, I believe there was some... misunderstanding of some kind, Prince Hectyr," the man said with a flourish. "Lady Ophelya and I were about to go to the feast together, weren't we?"

"No, I don't believe we were," Ophelya snapped back unaware of her surroundings as she glared at the man before her.

The man — or Lord Hylio — glanced between Ophelya and Hectyr, gritting his teeth as he recognized how much attention they had gained. He dipped his head once more before slithering off into the crowd. Out of sight. Out of mind.

"Lady Ophelya," Hectyr said after a moment. Relaxing slightly. "What can I do for you?" He kept his focus on her as he spoke, ignoring the whispers and glances from those that surrounded them.

"What is it you're planning with Cal?"

Hectyr frowned. "I'm not planning anything, I decided to look in on her after you seemed... anxious for her the other day." He whispered the last part. "Since then, I've been helping her with — well, something."

Ophelya furrowed her brows. "She let you in on her plans and not me?"

Calypso, what are you doing?

I understand why you would keep Leandre and I out of this — but to involve another royal scion?

Though it was Hectyr, the least intimidating of the bunch, Ophelya still didn't know how to feel about the whole situation. She froze up, stuck in her thoughts.

Hectyr looked around. "Perhaps you'd like to go sit and discuss this further?"

Ophelya looked around for the first time, feeling a pit grow in her stomach as she saw one set of eyes in the crowd upon her. *Mother.*

"Yes... I think I'd like that." *Don't panic, don't panic.*

You can always tell her it was part of a scheme to snag a royal as she wants so badly.

Even with a plan in mind, Ophelya felt her heart race as she anxiously thought of all of the ways her mother would confront her later.

What is the wort that could happen? She could try to take my old poetry books away —

She could find the journal.

She could keep you from going out and sneaking away to aid Cal and Leandre.

"Ophelya?"

She looked up, snapped away from her thoughts and quickly followed Hectyr through the crowd and deeper into the market area. Ophelya glanced at his expression as she realized they were nearing the lower district.

"Where are we going?" she asked.

"To a safe place."

Suddenly he stopped in front of a small store, well, house. It looked as though someone had built their shop half in and half out of their own home — whatever it was.

Hectyr motioned for Ophelya to enter first, she cast a weary glance at him, but when she saw how innocent his expression was she obliged. *He is much like that sacrificial lamb. Too innocent for his own good.*

As she stepped into the entryway of the house she found herself in a small home converted to a bakery. With many wonderful smells filling each room.

"Irys? It's Hectyr! I'm back!"

Hectyr walked deeper into the house — bakery. Leaving Ophelya at the entrance alone.

Irys?

She glanced around. Bread loaves shaped like pumpkins and breads filled with cranberries and seeds lined the counters — though many spots were empty from massive sales on this festival day. Surely more would follow now that the blessing had ended. Ophelya spotted olive cheese breads, warm and fresh out of the oven which filled the air with their savory and tangy scent.

Calypso would love that, Ophelya thought with a sigh.

Hectyr reappeared with a slightly older woman at his side — she looked to be mid-thirties. She was a centaur — but rather small for the average centaur woman so perhaps... half-centaur? Her long chestnut hair was braided down to her stomach, she had a noticeable distinct nose, and her face was stuck in a frown as she narrowed her eyes at Ophelya. She crossed her arms across her chest.

"Who is this?"

Hectyr grinned as he motioned towards her. "This is Lady Ophelya Nephus. Lady Ophelya, this is my sister, Irys."

Sister? Ophelya looked her up and down. They clearly weren't related and looked nothing like one another. The emperor had no other children nor did Hectyr's mother.

The orphanage perhaps? So, he kept in contact with them...

Ophelya glanced at Hectyr, he was smiling as he looked at her. She though he seemed happy within the Citadel — but here one could see he was truly glowing as he looked more comfortable than ever.

Interesting.

"Why is a daughter of the court here?" she asked, giving Hectyr a wary glance.

Hectyr raised a brow at her attitude. "She is here with me. We needed somewhere away from prying eyes to chat for a moment."

"Good, then you brought a customer. I could use some more of that." She sighed loudly. "Aspects know that Saffya's parents are asking for too high a dowry."

Hectyr snorted. "I thought you told them no price was too high for a woman of such caliber?"

Irys softened up at his laugh. "Yeah well, even she thought their asking price was too high."

Ophelya frowned, it wasn't rare to see same sex marriage in Vasyla — but among court members and lords and ladies it was pushed to marry for offspring to continue the lineage. It was enough to make Ophelya not want to have children.

"You two can rest in the dining room, Saffya won't be here for another hour so that is all you get, alright?" Irys said, ruffling up Hectyr's curls like a child. Hectyr laughed.

"Thank you Irys."

Ophelya dipped her head at the hostess. "Thank you." She passed her and followed Hectyr into another room. It was only now that she realized just how much this place had helped her to calm down.

I wonder if that was intentional or not?

She watched as Hectyr pulled a seat out at a shabby little table for her.

He may not seem like it, but Hectyr reminds me a lot of Maeve — he definitely has her knack of reading people even if he is a lot more… bubbly.

She took her seat and he sat across from her moments later. "You said you've been… helping Calypso?"

He nodded. "She has been… searching for something that she believes will help her prove herself to the people."

"And what might that be?"

Hectyr frowned. "I'm only telling you this because Calypso seems to trust you a great deal… I don't know why she won't tell you herself but I believe you should know. She is looking for armor which was stolen from her."

"So then that strange warrior…"

"It was Calypso."

Ophelya sat straighter in her seat. "So you're saying she thought that by… gallivanting around as a knight and revealing herself later she could win their trust?" Hectyr nodded.

Oh Cal, if only it were so simple.

She must have no other plan… and it is close to when the emperor will pass… All this time I thought we would have come up with a plan… fake her death, smuggle her out of the country, anything, but Cal has always wanted to prove herself to the people. To live and remove the shadow over her name.

"I noticed something... Wherever we were she had many people watching her. Even when we had tried to hide our identities... I believe we were being followed."

"Calypso is believed to fill what is expected of a prophecy. There hasn't been a White Tern scion to survive past birth for decades — that's all that is surely?"

"It's more than that, I-" He glanced around. "We went through the city together and I noticed a lot of people watching her. Strange people. Some wore mock feathers but... I'm not really sure they were fake."

He's definitely observant if he noticed down to the little details. "So why are you helping her?"

Hectyr sighed. "Everyone seems so surprised that siblings should want to help each other." He looked up at her. "I've been trying to befriend even one of the royal scions since my arrival a few years back. If you recall... Well, Calypso was much more skittish around me then so I didn't want to scare her."

Ophelya snorted. "Yes, when she was eighteen she was quite something."

"I can tell by the way you speak of her you think her akin to family as well, don't you?"

"...Yes, and that is why I need to get her out of this pathetic and barbaric challenge." Ophelya suddenly stood. "Thank you, for making things clearer for me. I'm afraid I need to go work on something now." She began to turn to walk away but paused. "Oh, and Hectyr?"

"Yes?"

"Please continue to help Calypso. While I am not sure her plan will work... She shouldn't face it alone."

"You trust me enough for that?"

Ophelya turned to look at him. Just before she arrived at the capital for this season, she would have turned away from him without a second thought. Yet now as she looked up at him she felt at ease... as she hated to admit it she believed she was beginning to trust him.

She nodded, and Hectyr dipped his head. "Of course. Please let me know if there is anything else I can do for you."

As Ophelya made her way out of the bakery she rested her hand on her bag.

Maeve... I know you wrote these journals for a reason... I'm sure you even expected me to speak with Hectyr... What do you want now?

Ophelya opened her bag. Checking the hidden pouch in her bag to ensure the journal was there. There were few places she could find absolute peace — and she knew where she had to go now.

The shore.

It was midnight by the time Ophelya managed to sneak out of the Citadel to the rocky alcove by the shore where Cal, Leandre, and her used to gather in secret. She dropped her bag onto the rough sand and stared out at the looming ocean. She watched the sirens that peer at her from a distance. They were quite a ways away from her, further out in the sea. Yet they watched through dark beady eyes — considering if she was worthy prey or not.

Perhaps listening to the sweet siren call and drifting away in the ocean for life's last moments would have been a peaceful option. Anything felt better than the stress that Ophelya could see in her future. She sighed as she rested her head on her knees and stared out at the glimmering scales of the sirens. *At least they are free.*

If only I could leave with Calypso and Leandre... She sat up. *The only way I will ever see a future worth having will be with my friends at my side. Otherwise, it's the twisted idea my mother expects for me... If I want any future worth having I must read this book... Even if my sister should not wish it.*

Maeve, I hope by following your path this closely I will be able to finish what you started.

She leaned down and pulled the journal out of the bag, kneeling on the sand carefully. The moon and stars above provided enough light that she could read without needing a torch. She looked down at the elegant handwriting that danced across each page. She began to read, feeling her heart quicken. Ophelya began skimming through pages quickly, rereading pages in disbelief. *There is... There is no way this can be true! If that was the case then —*

Suddenly, the journal was torn away from her hands.

"I knew it, I wasn't wrong when I saw you in the library with it. Where did you get this?!" the thief shouted.

Ophelya scurried to her feet and spun to see who had found her. "What —"

"That journal belonged to my friend, so I will as you one last time," they threatened. "Where did you get it?"

She looked at the newcomer with terror. How did they recognize this book?

Their white hair and blue eyes are illuminated by the torch they held. It was a royal scion... And it was not Hectyr.

17

THE SWORD AND THE SHIELD

CALYPSO

It was nearly dawn by the time Calypso slipped into her room, silent as a serpent. The ivory walls made the room feel ominously large — that paired with the sparse furniture made her never really feel comfortable. She had seen the emperor's room filled with riches and gifts, compared to her room it was a different world. With a small bed, a chest for her belongings, and a small table for a water pitcher and cup. The room almost looked as though it was vacant. The fragrant smells from the gardens were null as well. Only the smells of old bed cover and a metallic polish she used to maintain her weapons filled the air.

Calypso felt barren, not because of the room, but because of the lack of a guard at her door. The lack of Leandre made her feel vulnerable.

We haven't had many assassination attempts overall... surprisingly. At least, that is what Leandre said but I can't help but wonder...

How have I been so lucky?

Did Leandre lie?

Without her shield nearby, Calypso found that she scarcely felt like a sword, like a knight. They had trained together so long and traveled the Citadel together so commonly that it almost felt like being naked without him nearby. The feeling of loss at having him around made her reminisce on times he used to travel with her for her odd excursions...

"Are you sure this is a safe place?" Leandre asked as he followed her across the shore. His face far rounder than it was now that he was eighteen. In the four years that followed he matured a great deal, but he still looked the same overall. While he was only fourteen during this excursion, Cal was sixteen. Both of them were equally foolish, which was why Zagora was still around. He followed Calypso across the sand clutching his sword and shield anxiously. Cal laughed at him.

"We need to clear a place to meet safely with Ophelya when she arrives!" she said loudly as they made their way towards the cove. "Who knows what could have made a den in the coves?"

"Exactly my point!" Leandre said with a shiver. "We *don't* know what lives here!"

"What, are you scared?" she asked teasingly.

He shook his head and stood taller. "Of course I'm not!"

She rolled her eyes at him as they neared the rocky outcrop and cavern-like structures that blended into the land from the sea.

As they reached the edge of the cavernous structure they peered inside. Cal held up the torch she carried in her left hand, holding her spear in her right.

"It looks mostly empty…"

Eyes shone in the darkest corner of the cave, and a low growl came from it.

"Cal!" Leandre jumped in front of her with his shield as it pounced. Almost falling back as the beast knocked into the metal. As Leandre was shoved against her, Cal dropped the torch. The creature remained scarcely visible as the torch went out — but not enough to identify it. Cal dodged around the shield and pierced the beasts arm with her spear. It roared in agony and threw it's body against her — throwing her against the rocky wall. Feathers flew everywhere.

Feathers? Is it… some type of bird?

Cal felt her heart drop. *We could get in serious trouble if it's —*

Leandre ran to her side, still taking the defense as he continued to block or deflect the beast. Calypso groaned as she got to her feet.

"You need to shift tactics! Remember what Zagora says!" Leandre shouted as he drove the creature away from her.

"Why can't I be the aggressive one?!" she shouted back as she ran forward to jump back into the battle. She raised her spear, but just before she could land the killing blow a cry was heard from the darkest parts of the cavern. *Babies?*

Cal stopped, leaving herself open to strike as the creature's children ran to it. The beast now visible in full light — was a griffin. A rarity in Vasyla, as the empire was a traveling point for the beasts but not one that they stayed in for long as they migrate.

She stepped towards the beast, dropping her weapon. Leandre's eyes widened.

"What are you doing?!"

"I have to heal it," Cal said slowly as she tried to approach it. The griffin flared its wings and struck, long claws gashing into her own arm. She grit her teeth, but didn't recede from her position near it. The creature narrowed its eyes at her.

"Griffin's are intelligent creatures Leandre, it won't kill me now."

"Cal," Leandre said through grit teeth. "You shouldn't use magick... that's dangerous and you don't have full control over it."

Cal slowly put her hand near the wound she left in its arm. "Water magick isn't outlawed at least..." She pulled out a flask and poured it into her palm. The water gathered into a small sphere and landed on the creature's arm. After a moment, the wound sealed together, leaving a bare yet clean spot on its arm.

The griffin stepped away from her afterwards, casting a glance between her and Leandre uncertainly. "Let's go," Cal said quickly.

"But weren't we clearing —"

She shook her head. "They won't stay here too long, we can come back once they have left."

"Why did you spare it?" Leandre said as the cove grew distant behind them. "We've fought many beasts off from
the capital, what is different with a griffin?"

Cal sighed. "Not every parent protects it's children, why take that away from them and have them struggle in life?" She brightened up after a moment. "Besides, who can say they got that close to a griffin and lived in the empire?!"

The griffins didn't stay in the cove much longer, and with its scent lingering and soon after Cal and Leandre's scent covering that it became less common for any creatures to be seen within the cove. She could still remember Ophelya's excitement in her glittering eyes as the two told that story at the makeshift campfire they built in their first excursion there as a group.

Calypso remembered a free feeling with her youth — a feeling of hope. Believing she could truly change her fate.

Now she wasn't so sure.

Now, was it even possible to change the thoughts of her people regarding her?

To change the so called prophecy and her image within the empire?

Were the two even separate things anymore?

She sighed as she laid on her bed, not bothering to even pull a cover over herself. The cool air of autumn was comforting even as it became colder with the approach of winter. As she shut her eyes, all she could think of was the armor, Oboryn.

It's a common name, but why do I feel like it's important?

And why can I not find them anywhere? They couldn't have just disappeared right?

And what if they do something cruel and then I have that name on all of my hard work? What then?

Cal grit her teeth as she struggled to get comfortable. The wind was far too loud, and her room had a few small windows which allowed the sound to affect her.

I thought this would be... not easy but at least doable on my own.

Should I have included Leandre and Ophelya more before using the armor?

Is it wrong that I want to prove myself to the people instead of finding another way?

Perhaps I should tell them —

Calypso felt movement near her, and it wasn't the wind. She opened her eyes to a figure looming over her. She began to sit up, but they quickly shoved her down. A metallic glint shone in the moonlight, they struck down at her, and Calypso moved out of its path quickly.

"What did you do to her?!" they shouted as they brought the blade down again, Cal barely dodged it as it struck through her pillow.

"Who?!" Calypso asked as she caught his wrists, stopping the intruder from striking again.

"Lady Ophelya! I saw you speaking with her in the alley, and afterwards she snapped!" The man was practically foaming at the lips as he spoke of her.

As Calypso looked at him she frowned. *Isn't that the man who wouldn't stop staring at her during the opening of the festival?*

It wasn't uncommon for Ophelya to be admired — but this was just too far.

Cal struggled as the man forced the blade closer and closer to her throat, pushing the blade aside, she felt searing pain as it tore through her cheek. Cal used the force of him falling and shoved him off of her. He rolled off of her bed and landed with a thud — giving Cal the chance to get to her feet and find a weapon. She reached for the spear kept beside her bed, but as she grabbed she found nothing in the darkness. Moonlight glinted against metal across the room. The man had moved it.

Calypso glanced at the pitcher next to her bed, it was filled to the brim with water as she had done so earlier. She felt magick surging through her veins once more. The man charged at her.

No! You cannot rely on magick!

She narrowly avoided his blow as he struck for her chest. Falling back against the table as the man caught himself from falling onto the bed. Cal rushed across the room for her weapon.

"Oh no you don't!"

The man shoved her away from her weapon and kicked it across the room, leaving her cornered and away from the door.

Don't do it, don't do it!

As the man charged at her, Calypso put her hands up.

The sound of water splashing out of the pitcher filled the room like a wave.

The man gasped, suddenly lurching forward as if hit from behind. A powerful focused current struck through him. Wild magick. The magick common with nature, but uncontrollable like the sea. Like Calypso.

He fell forward onto her, the knife useless as his hand went limp. Calypso shoved him off and watched him fall like a sack onto the ground as water washed out from his back, mixed and swirled with blood.

As Cal sat on the floor, listening as the man's breathing slowed to nothing, she looked down at her shaky hands.

So it wasn't an assassin... but still — I haven't had anyone manage to get that close to killing me since Leandre finished his training.

He told me there weren't many attempts he had to stop either was he lying?

How many had there really been? Trying to kill her day and night? How many had Leandre saved her from?

"I just want to live! Is that so much to ask for?! Tell me Aspects, why can't I just be left alone?!" she cried out to the skies, but the skies didn't answer back.

18
BEYOND THE CITADEL
LEANDRE

Eyes. Eyes. *Eyes.* All over his skin Leandre felt eyes upon him. As he followed along the dirt roads with a small group, the cold autumn winds offered no comfort as he felt like eyes were always watching him. Traveling to an unknown destination only made this feeling all the worse. It had been days since they left the capital city, Lyreas. And Leandre still couldn't shake this sense that he was being watched. They passed many people through the capital city from the upper district to the lower — many people stared as they wanted to know why Harkyn would travel at a time like this. Being seen with the lord of a region so openly had been a bone-chilling experience for Leandre. The cold rain didn't help as they followed the unused trade roads that had been long forgotten since faster shortcuts had been made.

The small band was made up of Lord Harkyn, three knights, and two oddly cloaked figures who hid their faces. One figure had a cloak made of very realistic-looking mock feathers, or at least Leandre hoped they weren't real feathers. The lanterns they held illuminated the paths ahead, but as the moon rose high in the sky everyone's eyelids grew heavy. Lord Harkyn, however, showed no signs of stopping any time soon.

As Leandre looked down at his map as he followed the others on foot, he frowned. They had been heading north, and he had assumed they were going to Mythde, the capital of Cor Telos — Lord Harkyn's territory. Yet now they were headed further west, and there weren't many cities in the direction they were traveling now unless they took a detour.

Leandre struggled to catch up to Harkyn at the lead, once beside him he looked up at the tall centaur. "Where exactly is it we're going?" he asked as he looked at the map he held.

Harkyn raised a brow as he glanced down. "Nowhere that is shown on your map." He pulled a piece of parchment from his satchel and lazily tossed it down to Leandre who barely managed to catch it.

This map is... different? Leandre glared down at the map after he unrolled it. The map was almost exactly the same as his own, but where there was nothing but forest on his was one large ominous claw mark deep within the earth.

"We're headed towards *The Abyss*?" he asked. Lord Harkyn merely grunted in response. "But why?"

"There's something there we need if things are to go... properly."

"Something out of an ancient ruin? Isn't this where the capital city used to be?"

Lord Harkyn gave him a surprised look. "I'm shocked you knew that."

Leandre said nothing in response, not wanting to tell him that Calypso used to include him in her studies.

"We're nearly there," Lord Harkyn said.

Their lanterns illuminated the path, but not well. It had been hours since the sun had set, and Leandre felt his eyelids growing incredibly heavy. *Surely the ruins are close... right?*

With the sudden influx of monsters, Leandre was surprised they didn't get attacked along the roads. Yet... something always felt like there was a monster with them. He cast a glance to the two cloaked figures. Something about one of them was... different. Leandre felt his head throbbing as he looked at one of the two. Was it superstition? Or something else?

"Alright, we're far enough from the capital now, I believe," Harkyn announced suddenly before pulling out his lance. Leandre furrowed his brows at him as he rubbed his tired eyes. *What is he —*

Harkyn lunged forward and pierced an unarmed knight. A surprised shriek could be heard before shifting into a disgusting sound.

"What are you doing?!" Leandre shouted out, jumping away from him and grabbing his own weapon as fast as he could.

Harkyn looked to the cloaked figure. "You know what to do."

The figure laughed before lifting their palms, suddenly a gold mist could be seen through the air, forming into a thick cloud and then into a ball of energy and light.

Magick?!

The mysterious figure didn't even have to utter the incantations for the spells! If it's wild magick at that level... How powerful could they be to do that?

Before Leandre could even react the orb split and a mist spread over the remaining two knights. It was like watching sunlight filter through a cloud — the light covered their whole bodies and as it disappeared, so did they.

Leandre held up his blade as the cloaked figure looked at him, his head aching suddenly. They looked to Harkyn who shook his head.

The cloaked figure merely turned away from Leandre, losing interest. All that remained was the one body, two cloaked figures, and Harkyn.

"But why?!" Leandre shouted at him, "Why leave me alive if you were going to kill the other knights?"

"Do you really think I could leave the capital without a few knights on hand? They're worth a Cryss each, if even that, we can get more later. Besides," He loomed over him. "If I had any plans to harm you, I would have already done so back in the North. No, you're too valuable to me alive."

"*Back in the North*? What are you talking about?!" Leandre shouted angrily, but he didn't respond.

"Kyril, there is no longer the need to hide yourself, there are only... allies here."

Leandre looked to the other cloaked figure. *Kyril? He is part of this too?* Kyril pulled his cloak down and glanced at Leandre, his eyes were wide and he was visibly quivering. Yet he scrunched his nose and forcibly laughed at Leandre.

"What, shocked to see me?" he said with a shaky voice.

He signed up for far more than he bargained for, but then again, so did I.

Most royals didn't see a whole lot of bloodshed, and nothing to such a degree. So surely something within him just snapped.

Something within me probably broke as well, Leandre thought to himself as he gripped his aching head.

Lord Harkyn had continued on and as Leandre looked around, he recognized the other body had disappeared. It was disposed of. "Come on then, we don't have all day," Lord Harkyn called.

Leandre warily continued after Harkyn, he was right. They had stopped close to the entrance. Lord Harkyn stopped ahead before a deep chasm. Like a giant beast had taken it's claw and dug it's mark into the ground. Poorly built wooden pillars and bridges were built going down inside. It was so large, it wasn't hard to imagine how the previous capital once was here. Why hadn't anything been built near it though?

Leandre noticed a sign nearby, and didn't wait for the others to go investigate.

Witless travelers, desperate adventurers, and fools of all kinds — these words are for you alone. The mark unseen exists within this basin. Beyond only holds the toils and pains left behind by its creation. The Aspects cannot protect you here, so here we shall not return.

Leandre stared at the sign for another moment and Kyril shoved him as he passed by.

"What, are you scared by a sign?" Kyril skimmed it over. "Some kind of prankster probably put it here to keep anyone away from relics inside."

Leandre clenched his fist and caught the hooded figure watching in his direction. "It isn't the sign that concerns me."

Kyril huffed as he stopped beside Lord Harkyn, who stared into the abyss.

"What is it we're looking for?" Leandre asked, making Harkyn glare over.

Kyril snorted as he looked warily into the chasm. "It's something of great importance! You couldn't even begin to comprehend –"

"Do not speak for me, boy," Harkyn snapped at him as he gazed into the darkness. He turned and stepped away from it.

"Something of far more importance to me than you could ever imagine."

Leandre watched as Lord Harkyn found a tunnel leading down into the chasm — choosing to enter that instead of the shoddy bridge entrance which was half broken. *He talks as if speaking of a loved one every time he mentions this... artifact.*

What could it be?

"Follow," Lord Harkyn demanded gruffly.

The small band quickly followed him into the tunnel. The tunnel was filled with smells of old rotting wood and dust as water damage had weakened the mine props in the tunnels dug for better access to the oddities of the abyss. Once the tunnel opened up the bridges led the way further down into the ruins. Buildings and temples of all sorts were buried within the abyss with parts of them sticking out from the sides of the cavernous walls. The bridges that led from building to building also followed along many odd statues and stone engravings.

"It is time to spread out. Look inside any room or building still accessible and find anything that speaks of a mark." *A mark?*

The others quickly split off, leaving Leandre to look ahead on his own. *Why are we searching for a mark?*

As he continued ahead, Leandre couldn't shake the feeling. Eyes. Eyes. *Eyes.* There was nothing else in sight but... there was something else in the ravine with them. As the sun set overhead forcing Leandre to pull out his lantern the abyss felt even more ominous. Ruins of buildings scattered throughout the claw mark in the earth. If this was the original capital, and it is believed that Cressyda almost destroyed the empire — then how did she do this? How did a whole capital city become part of the earth, only now seen through the slow passage of time wearing away at the earth here and revealing more of what was left behind? And when did this excavation attempt happen?

As Leandre looked down into the bleak darkness below, he couldn't help but wonder if anything was left to stare back at him. He shook his head at the mere thought.

That isn't important right now. First we need to find something... And I need to figure out why Harkyn seems to know me from before my life at the Citadel.

After many more hours of searching, Leandre stopped and sat against the doorway of a strange temple which was stuck in the cave walls. He glanced inside. *How are we even supposed to look when we don't know what we are looking for?* Thousands of skeletons and rusted swords and spears could be found — but nothing with a strange mark. Leandre sighed before he stood up and dusted himself off. Casting a glance back into the abyss he decided to step into the temple to escape the feeling of being watched. Looking around inside Leandre sighed as he held up his lantern to see even more walls covered in words carved into the stone. Was this from before the ruin of this place? Or from the excavation attempt? As Leandre began to make his way forward, steps could be heard from outside. He spun around to see Lord Harkyn, Kyril, and the mage.

"Was this where he said it would be?" Kyril asked in an obnoxiously loud tone.

Lord Harkyn glared down at him. "Quiet! Who knows what lies deep within this abyss, wouldn't want to wake anything would we?" He motioned inside to the mage who dipped his head before leading the way. They passed by Leandre as they began reading the texts upon the walls.

In protection of the empire, let us forever remember, A combatant and a creator, Both gave up their powers for the crown. With their sacrifice, the mark is forever held, And its magick is no more.

The stone tablet containing those words was broken, carved out from the wall. Behind its rightful place sat a pile of rusted pieces of metal. A mask facing a helmet. A sense of peace and love between the two filled the air, and Leandre felt his headache ease as he stood near them. Another hole way in the wall, cracked and broken but still large enough for a man to stand inside. Did armor once stand there?

Harkyn grabbed one of the shards, a metal mask as black as the night split in two pieces. The mask of a poet, back when masks were more common for those of the profession. Leandre reached in a pulled out the other piece, a knight's helm colored in what presumably was once white and gold. The helm was still in one piece, but just barely. Underneath the mask and the helmet were pieces of armor and golden wristbands both of which were shattered into a thousand shards. It almost looked like a mirror had shattered, the way they were broken — but what would break armor like that? And how did the mask and helmet hold on?

Wait... A Soldier and a Poet? Weren't there theories on such a pair being involved in Cressyda's death?

Then... Why do so many believe Cronys did something?
Was he involved?

Leandre glanced over at Harkyn, his eyes moved quickly across the ruined objects in front of them. His hooves stamped the ground as he clenched his jaw. Leandre had never seen him so... not in control of himself.

Most importantly, why does Lord Harkyn have such an interest in this now of all times?

Harkyn shouted angrily at them and tossed the pieces on the floor, stepping on them and making them crumble and shatter into nothing. A chill filled the air like something just broke in the very essence of the world.

"What does this mean?"Leandre asked Lord Harkyn.

"Harkyn, what does the tablet mean?!"

Angrily, Harkyn turned his gaze upon him. "It means that we did it, but not everything was here." He looked at Leandre with wild eyes. "It means that the royal challenge of Cressyda has always had a second survivor, hiding in the shadows as the other takes the crown! I was correct! But first, we must find her... and restore the magick."

Kyril grabbed the helm from Leandre's hand, it breaking in his palms. "You told me that was nothing but a myth, old man! What are you saying?!" He dropped it to the ground. "We searched the Citadel and found nothing!"

As the two argued, Leandre noticed Lord Harkyn had laid down his bag and was no longer paying attention to it. There was a... sword? It was a xiphos. A blade with a leaf shape which had a diamond-shaped cross-section. This blade was not typically crafted anymore — though it did look excellent for powerful strikes. The strangest thing, however, was that it was almost new in appearance in comparison to the mask and helmet that once sat in front of it and had more similar designs than that of modern weapons. Leandre glanced back, they weren't watching him. He traded his blade out with this one, placing it on his belt within its sheathe.

Leandre snuck out of the room to look around the walls of the tomb. Words were written all over, but many were still legible. Across all the words he could find, Leandre walked away from the small room where Harkyn and Kyril fought and continued back out to the excavation bridges that loomed over the eerily deep pits below. It was clear that this once had been a temple of sorts, but how did it end up down here? Did something pull it down? It was known that this capital was lost centuries ago... but to what? It couldn't have possibly been Cressyda... Right? Is this what the people feared Calypso could do? Leandre couldn't help but shiver at the thought of what horrors could lurk deep inside the earth in this abyss, or how these structures were still standing to this day — but that wasn't important. Leandre had to focus. What could he gleam from the walls before the others noticed him? Since important objects were inside the writing outside the temple must have some importance as well. He ran his slender fingers along the etched stone, reading the words and struggling to figure out what the cracks in the stone had destroyed.

"What are you doing out here?" Kyril asked.

Leandre glared at him. "I could ask you the same."

"Lord Harkyn and that stupid mage are talking, and they wanted to speak in private."

He laughed. "What are you a child? You a royal scion, and you got sent out of the room?"

Kyril scrunched his nose in disgust at him. "Well, you aren't so bright and clever yourself losing your job guarding the least important royal!"

Leandre grit his teeth, no need to engage in a petty argument now. Taking a deep breath he looked back at the walls. "What is it we were supposed to find anyways?"

"A stupid set of armor! Apparently, we needed it if the mage was to continue to show support for Harkyn, and in turn me."

Leandre shook his head and continued reading words on the walls.

Cursed... through... fell...rise... armor... wait — armor? "What was so special about this armor in particular?" Leandre asked plainly as he continued reading the walls. "Wouldn't you like to know!" Kyril replied snarkily. Leandre sighed. "So you don't know, just say that."

Through cursed armor we fell, and through cursed armor we rise.

"Of course I know! You think a royal scion of my degree wouldn't be kept with insider information?"

"Yes, *especially* a royal scion of your degree." *Is it the armor written here that they are looking for?*

But why?

"It's not the armor really, it's something *inside* the armor."

"What about the strange knight in the capital?"

"Lord Harkyn looked into it, that armor is not the armor of – well... It's not what we're looking for!"

Leandre kept reading the walls, looking for one more familiar word when he finally spotted it.

Under the stars of the White Tern, the Vasyla we know will fall.

Is this the omen associated with Cressyda? And now Calypso? The walls after that point were too damaged to read. Leandre grit his teeth.

Suddenly, shouting could be heard within the room, Leandre and Kyril went quiet and shifted closer to the doorway.

"What are you doing?"

Leandre put a finger to his lip. "Shush!"

"What of the curse?" Lord Harkyn asked quietly. "Are you sure only she can break it?"

The mage responded, but it was so quiet that neither of them could hear it.

"Good, the emperor is almost dead. We can expect the other royals will have all killed one another under its influence before we return."

"What?!" Kyril gasped as Leandre turned towards him. "What in the Aspects is this?!"

Before Leandre could respond, someone grabbed his shoulder and pulled him around. Leandre struggled to pull away as nails dug through his cloak. Turning, he recognized the cloaked magick user.

"I see the hound has gotten tired of his leash," they speak for the first time since Leandre had met them — their voice neither feminine nor masculine. It was hollow. "You're far too curious for your own good, aren't you?"

"What does that mean? What is it you want with Cal?" Leandre asked as he ripped their hand off of his shoulder, cloak tearing.

They took a step back and grin. "The body shall accept the spirit, just as you believe in the Aspects, we believe in the stars of magick — and your... Cal, as you so call it might be required for this." The mage removed their cloak revealing their face. It was covered by many markings of many spells being cast upon themselves. Their eyes bloodshot from all of the energy needed to consistently hold numerous spells, and their face devoid of expression as they stare through him. Kyril stepped back and almost lost his balance in fear. "You're a — You're one of them! You worship Cressyda! A Witch Cultist!"

The Cressydian Cult?! They had been destroyed decades ago! When transfiguration magicks were outlawed!

Lord Harkyn stepped out of the room and onto the bridge behind the mage. Leandre glared at him.

"How dare you — You knew all along that Calypso would die if I helped you didn't you?"

Harkyn frowned. "I expected you of all people to understand. Self-preservation must come first. If you aren't willing to accept that one simple factor in life you are unfit to become my heir."

"Heir?!" Kyril laughed. "You were never going to make him your heir!"

Harkyn stamped his hoof on the ground and pulled out his lance. "Just as I was never going to make you the emperor. That position will be mine once I find my empress."

"Wait... What?" Leandre's voice quivered as he spoke. "Your empress? What are you talking about?"

Harkyn grinned. "It no longer matters, I see you two have lost your value to me. Getting rid of you here means a simpler job back at home."

Harkyn held out his lance and the magick user grinned as they prepared a spell.

As the mage began to cast a spell, Leandre recalled the other knights as he felt panic rise in his chest. Leandre charged at him, knocking them to the ground before the spell reached its completion. He fell onto the mage as well and their eyes widened as they struggled to shove Leandre off. Lord Harkyn reared back onto his hind legs, stomping at Leandre who narrowly avoided his hooves. Rolling off, Leandre was quick to his feet. As the mage stood he slipped on the edge of the bridge, catching himself at the edge barely. He quickly looked to Harkyn for help. Leandre felt a splitting pain through his head as a voice that was not his own made itself known.

Help me! Help me up now!

Leandre began to raise his foot to stamp on the mage's hands but felt uneasiness wash over him as he did.

Don't you dare! You foolish little puppet!

As Leandre felt another pain in his head and pulled back from striking the mage. *Why?!* his own voice wailed in his mind. Before he could move, Harkyn swept the area with his lance, using it like a halberd to knock him back against the rock wall and away from the mage and the edge. This gave the mage a chance to get to his feet and prepare a spell. He aimed for Kyril as Harkyn focused on Leandre. He glanced over as Leandre dodged another strike.

"Kyril, run!"

But he didn't. He was frozen in fear as his face was illuminated by the growing spell that absorbed magick from the surroundings.

If he casts that here... It could destroy the bridges!

While the mage was distracted Leandre knocked their feet out from under them. Not hesitating this time as he shoved them over the side. They grabbed the edge of the bridge just in time.

Turning back to Harkyn, Leandre barely dodged as he reared up and tried to strike with his front hooves.

The mage was starting to clamber back up onto the bridge, but before Leandre could stop them, Kyril anxiously kicked them off the side.

"NO!" Harkyn screamed as he rushed to look over the edge.

The cultist's hollow screams echoed until cutting off abruptly as they reached the bottom with a sickening crack, and the screaming didn't end there.

Leandre felt as though eyes were on him once more, and the screaming continued in his mind.

That's when a splitting pain became unbearable in his head.

The world didn't go black, it turned golden as his surroundings melted into the precious metal.

Even in the end I'm surrounded by fools and gold.

19
BENEATH THE TRADITION
OPHELYA

Layers. There were always layers to everything Ophelya found herself wrapped up in. Her mother, Calypso, the court, Leandre... and now *Maeve*. As Avalon Pallas stood before her, angrily panting as she struggled to catch her breath, Ophelya simply observed her.

Why would Maeve have ever included *her* in anything?

"Give me the journal back, royal scion," Ophelya stated simply as she regained her composure.

Avalon bit her lip and clutched the book tighter as she looked down upon her, making Ophelya roll her eyes. She was the twin known for connections to the church. Praised for her devotion and devout belief in the Aspects — though many believed it was a front to get more support on her side. She certainly acted holier-than-thou.

"Why should I give this back to you? You're a daughter of one of the lords on the court, you'll only try to hide it away again."

She squinted at her. "I am Lady Ophelya, and that journal belonged to my sister, the late Lady Maeve."

"Your sister? So, you're telling me your sister was working with them?"

Ophelya's eyes widened. "Working with who? How much do you know about all of this —"

That's it! The church! Avalon had always been one of the few scions who was a devout believer and known for aiding the church of the All-Aspects, the head of all the divisions of the religious order.

"Whatever it was my sister was investigating... the priest in the meetings — the church was involved in her death somehow, weren't they?!"

Avalon backed up. "What?! No, the church hasn't done anything wrong!" she shouted at her. "It's the court that is corrupt!"

As she began to flip through the book, Avalon frowned. Ophelya snatched the journal back from her. "Perhaps it can be both, *Your Highness.*"

"This journal... it's not the same one," Avalon said as she stared down at her empty hands with a blank expression.

"What do you mean?"

Avalon held her hands together in front of herself and sighed. "This is not at all what I had planned for tonight."

"Nor I," she snarked back. "Now tell me, how were you able to identify this journal?"

"I found a journal like that years ago... but most of its pages were torn out."

"What do you mean — what was inside?!"

She frowned, crossing her arms tight against her chest. "Information about identifying the Cultists of Cressyda."

"What?" Ophelya's eyes went wide. "I thought they were wiped out decades ago!"

"Apparently not, but whatever is in that journal might help me find out where they are so I can snuff them out."

Ophelya opened up the journal, skimming to where she last was. "From where I was before... I think I might know somewhere to look but —" She glared up at Avalon. "What would you do with that information if it was within a church?"

"There is no way a holy place can be corrupted like that... What was it? Ophor?"

"*Ophelya,*" She replied slowly.

"Ophelya!"

It took everything in her to not roll her eyes at the foolish princess before her. Ophelya glanced out at the sea. "We need to go now."

"What, why?"

"We brought attention to ourselves by yelling and it seems the sirens are getting intrigued by our little show." Ophelya began marching away making her way back inland toward the city. Avalon rushed after her.

"Where are you going?"

"To investigate something."

Based on Maeve's writings, most of the churches on the outskirts of the lower district had been abandoned. So perhaps something was going on out there... But wouldn't something have been reported to the local knights?

"You're going to mess with a church aren't you?" Avalon asked as she caught up to her.

As they reached the docks, Ophelya sighed. "Yes, I am."

"Then I'm going with you."

"What for? What do you stand to gain?"

Avalon frowned. "To prove to you it isn't the church."

"Again, what will that gain you?"

"You'll be able to help me look into the court afterward — after all, you have an in."

Ophelya clenched her teeth. "Don't you also have '*an in*' as you put it as a royal scion?" She glared at the blue-eyed woman.

She speaks too casually for a royal scion. How much time does she spend outside of the Citadel at religious events?

Once into the city streets, Ophelya raised her hood to cover her face. Avalon, however, did not.

"Are you not going to hide yourself?"

"Why should I?" she asked. "*I* am a royal scion."

I forget how cushy life must be for the other royals.

Avalon jumped, making Ophelya's whole body tense. "What? What happened?!"

The royal scion shook her head, "It was just a stupid cat. In the alley just there."

Ophelya glanced past her, she saw a shape in the alley, but it wasn't small.

"Why are you still staring? I already said it was only a cat." Avalon said snidely.

"I saw... a strange knight in the alley," Ophelya answered slowly and quietly.

Could it be the knight of the rumors?

Ophelya frowned as she tried to look for a distinguished shape in the darkness of the alley. Even the slightest glint of the candlelight on metal, but there was nothing. "Did you want to go look?"

"Why would I want to go into the alley where someone might be watching us?!"

A shape bolted from the alley, making Ophelya duck in surprise. Avalon laughed.

"It was a cat, look." She calmly pointed out the small dark stray running down the road. "It's eyes were amber. You probably saw that and took it for metallic shine at a glance."

Ophelya looked back at the alley one last time before shaking her head. *I know I saw something... But what knight would be hanging around alleys during a festival? Everyone is busy watching the Citadel right now. Even this rumored knight hasn't been acting in such a manner.*

"The edge of the lower district is not much further," Ophelya said quickly. "Let us keep going."

"What church are we going to?" Avalon asked. "I didn't even know there were any this far out."

"There are, just... not used much anymore from what I saw on my way into the capital," Ophelya said after a moment.

Ahead there were fewer buildings, and streets made way to dirt roads as they neared farmlands. A church could be seen in the distance on a hillside — but it was crumbling partially on itself as the roof had half collapsed. The fields around them were just harvested for the season, and new growth would be planted soon.

"That's it?" Avalon looked appalled as they grew closer to it.

"Hush!" Ophelya said as they stopped by the edge of the collapsed roof. Voices could be heard from inside. She looked ahead, spotting a hole in the wall up on the roof. Climbing up the fallen roof, she made her way to the higher end with Avalon warily following. The two peered through carefully. One person was inside.

"See! Just one odd fellow in worship."

Ophelya frowned, looking down into the church she could see the place was a disaster. Broken chairs and tables were everywhere, and the altar was cracked as well. The one man who sat inside kneeled at the broken altar, whispering to himself.

"Wait... more are coming. From the forest!" Ophelya whispered quickly, ducking down so as not to be seen.

A group of ten or so people made their way into the church, bringing with them lanterns that illuminated the dark building.

Are those... feathers?

All of them were covered in feathered cloaks, and even the floors of the church were covered in feathers which were clearly not the false feathers made by skilled craftsmen — they were real. Markings of spells covered every corner of the building. *The practice of lesser mages?* Yet some of them looked rather complicated. So they were not using the wild magick of the body — they were using controlled spells that needed signs and words to carry them. Every person here had their face hidden beneath a cloak.

"I've been looking into this for years, I thought I could prove Maeve wrong... but I've never..." Avalon paused to take in a deep breath. "I never thought it had gotten this far."

"So what were you doing if you were aware of the Cultists of Cressyda even being within the capital?!" Ophelya growled at her. "Did you never stop to think there could be more?!"

Avalon glared at her. "I couldn't do anything! If I tried to look into it, I could risk people assuming I was with them and be put to death! Or worse, I could have put Adonys into danger."

"Your brother can take care of himself, besides, he is your age."

She shook her head, "We may be twins but he always has been my little brother."

Ophelya frowned at her as she looked back through the broken window where all the cultists had gathered. "Well, we're going to have to do something about it now," Ophelya whispered.

"Like what?! What can we do? This has gotten far worse than I thought — not to mention it goes far deeper!" Avalon looked at the journal in her hands. "You're saying your sister was looking into the court when she found out about this?"

Ophelya nodded. "I'm guessing this is what got her killed." She glared down at them.

"They'll pay for this."

She glanced at Avalon, expecting her to be a sputtering mess at this sight, but instead found a young woman with a focused rage as she watched the cultists. Anyone could see it in her eyes. She was planning their demise. *Perhaps she will be helpful after all.*

Ophelya looked back inside at the feathers strewn about the dilapidated church. Real feathers. The cultists must have injured or killed hundreds of birds to make their cloaks and had some to spare. *What cruel people. They must lack empathy for even the simplest of creatures.*

One of those things down there could be the one that killed my sister.

And one of those things was now going to target my friends.

I have to kill them first, no matter what it takes.

I have to keep Calypso and Leandre safe.

I have to get my revenge.

"Shouldn't he be dead by now?"

The two went silent as they struggled to listen in on the cultists below.

"The fool on the throne only has days left at this point," a Skorvian said gleefully. "I was there, at the amphitheatre when it happened. I hear he lived, but just barely."

Others looked at them in awe. "You were there?! Tell us every detail of it! Was he in agony?"

"I was there too," a woman added from the group. She was gnawing on her fingernails until then. "It wasn't all that entertaining considering he didn't die."

A centaur, whose face was hidden like a few others in the crowd, sighed. "He lived, yet you say the eldest threw a fit about beginning the challenge early?" another asked.

"Don't act like you're in charge just because the lord isn't here!" another one complained. "All you horses from the North think you can trot in here and command the sun to set in the morning and the moon to rise in its place."

"Pipe down, I was simply asking a question, that's all..." They held their chin and squinted at nothing as they struggled to think. Others looked uncomfortable at this response, shifting away from the centaur and Skorvian in fear.

"That would be odd though..." the centaur continued, "It isn't supposed to happen until he is dead."

What could that mean? What would his death have to do with Deakon's rage?

Ophelya and Avalon exchanged a glance.

"Those damn healers must be keeping him alive by the smallest shard."

"We need to be ready when he dies... all hell will break loose among the royal scions."

"But what if the curse is broken?"

All the others cackled at the human's anxieties.

"The curse wouldn't be broken by accident, besides — we have our best going to the Abyss to search for the other link. As long as it is kept safe — the curse will continue just as it has for generations."

A small human giggled. "I can imagine it now! That violent urge slowly creeping into the minds of those royal insects! It will be all the more exciting to take them down."

The centaur shook his head. "Why should we? The curse will make them all kill each other anyways — we just have to kill whoever remains."

"Curse?!" Avalon whispered urgently. "We're cursed?!"

"*Shhh!*"

The cultists inside froze up.

"Did you hear that?" one asked quickly.

"We need to get out of here!" Ophelya mouthed to Avalon.

Ophelya rushed down the roof tiles and grabbed Avalon's hand, helping her down as well.

"Where do we go?!" Avalon whispered as the cultists began to investigate.

Ophelya looked around, the closest thing was the forest... *But wasn't that where they just came from?*

The rest was clearing around them, they had to take that chance.

Grabbing Avalon's hand, Ophelya rushed around the corrupted church and hurried towards the coverage of the foliage and trees ahead. Glancing back, she could see the cultists were only just starting to investigate with a few holding flame magick spells within their palms to light the path as they looked for the intruders.

As they made their way into the woods, Ophelya looked back.

"Who is that?" Avalon asked.

A suit of armor approached the cultists, they braced themselves and called out to the armor — confused and afraid.

"I — I don't know," Ophelya answered.

They didn't wait around to find out.

As they continued deeper into the woods to hide, they quickly climbed up into a tree and hid within the foliage.

"Ophelya?" Avalon whispered her name. "There are... more in the woods."

As Ophelya looked ahead other feathered cloaks could be seen scarcely from their hiding point. They would have to hide until dawn — perhaps even later if the forest was crawling with so many of them.

"Let's just... wait for an opening."

As the pair rested surrounded by the thick leaves of the tree, Ophelya couldn't drive a horrible thought from her head. *That voice... was familiar, but there's no way.*

Please.

Let it not be true.

After all... why would she be there?

"Ophelya?" Avalon whispered. "You heard all that back there, right?"

She nodded slowly. "The challenge... this curse... There is more to the tradition in your bloodline than I originally thought."

"But what does this mean? What can we do?!"

She shook her head at the royal. "I — I do not know."

If it's a curse... By the Aspects.

The royal challenge was never about keeping the royals in check to prevent pitiful wars among themselves and spare the people. It was to keep the head of the empire weak so another power could grow, and now the forests outside the capital were crawling with a cult in Cressyda's name. *But why now?*

   Calypso, Leandre — please stay safe until I can return.

20
DEEP WOUNDS
CALYPSO

It was sudden, like when a predator lunges at its prey. Calypso was woken by a cascade of servants ushering her to get ready quickly — since she didn't have a lady in waiting, it was a mess. It wasn't until she was up and ready to start the day that it was revealed to her why there was such urgency.

The emperor was dying.

He had been slowly withering away from years now, but the events of the amphitheatre were enough to break him.

There was no going back.

The emperor had requested to speak with the royal scions, one at a time. Leaving Calypso for last. The final child he had to speak with.

It was in the halls outside the emperor's chambers — Every scion was there but Avalon and Kyril. Perhaps one was already inside speaking with him? Calypso glanced at Adonys. He was quite the feminine man, and it was hard to differentiate him from his sister. It was odd to see one twin without the other, especially at a time like this. Even stranger still was the absence of Lord Harkyn, when all the other lords and ladies of the court were present, and the consorts of the emperor were all there, too. Cal leaned against a pillar outside of the emperor's chambers as she awaited her call.

Should I even go if I am summoned? Or will he perhaps not include me?

After all, he hates me... right?

"Calypso!" Hectyr urgently whispered to her as he stood on the opposite side of the pillar in the shadows. "Have you seen —"

"The armor? No... and it's been days." Calypso sighed as she watched the other royal scions as they stood around. The hall was packed with guards, all keeping an eye on Deakon. Cal noted that there were more Skorvians and centaur guards watching him — probably because he would be more difficult to control should something happen. As Echo stepped out of the chambers she cast wary glances his way, clutching the bandages on her shoulder as she left. Not even bothering to stand around and wait to hear of when he would pass. "No... well yes, but that isn't what I was asking."

"Oh, well then what do you want?" Calypso asked harshly.

"It's Ophelya, I haven't seen her."

Calypso raised a brow and scanned the crowds around her. He was right, her parents were nearby as all court members were close for this but Ophelya herself was nowhere to be seen. But why was he looking for her?

Perhaps she's hanging around outside the Citadel — getting a breath of air away from the crowd. Why else would she not be here?

Surely nothing had happened to her? Right?

She looked back at the chamber entrance. If Echo just came out, then perhaps she would be called in soon.

"I'll go look for her," Calypso said quickly, beginning to take a step away.

Hectyr stepped out from behind the pillar. "Wait! Don't you think you should wait and speak with him?"

Calypso frowned. "Why?" she muttered under her breath. "It's not like he will say anything that could fix what comes after."

"Not for him, for you. For closure before he is gone." Hectyr glanced around. "Besides, I don't think anyone plans on jumping into combat until the competition is announced other than Deakon."

"Not even you?" Calypso joked. Hectyr glared at her.

"Don't even jest about that."

Cal put her hands up. "Alright sorry…" She glanced around. "Fine, I'll stay."

Just then, a servant rushed out of the emperor's room, he glanced around until his eye landed on her.

"Princess Calypso," the cyclops said with a shaky voice.

"The emperor has summoned you."

Hectyr placed a hand on her shoulder, it was shaking. She glanced back up at him.

"Don't worry, nothing bad will happen," he said through labored breath.

"Hectyr, are you alright?" Calypso asked.

He slowly nodded. "I just... I need to get rest after this," he said with a halfhearted smile. "Now go."

Calypso frowned at him, but said nothing else as she turned and stepped into the emperor's chambers. It was quite the lavish room, riches filled every corner and gifts of flowers and expensive objects littered any clear space. Shades of greens, golds, and ivory filled the room from various silks, metals, and polished stone. In the center was a large bed, which made the emperor look even smaller than he should even in his frail state. The once great man now reduced to this. A pitiful sight of what comes near the end. Something everyone feared as they aged.

The stench of a dying man filled the air, it smelled of decay. It was a sweet pungent smell. Half covered by expensive perfumes and mists sprayed by servants to try and cover it up. Yet the smell was far stronger. Cal felt like she could throw up as she curled her nose at it.

"Calypso," he greeted her gruffly, his breathing ragged, much like Hectyr's breathing a moment ago. "I am surprised to see you heeded my call."

"I do not believe I had much a choice," Cal replied curtly.

"There are... many things I should say to you." He said slowly.

She almost scoffed at him. "I'm sure many of these words could have been said before now."

"There it is... you remind me so much of your mother. She was the only one who was willing to contest me." At this point, Oryon was no longer looking at Calypso, he looked past her at nothing. "Perhaps your mother was right. Maybe it was time, I should have put an end to the games."

"What?" Calypso curled her lips into a snarl.

"I remember killing my own brother — at the time it felt right. It was what we were meant to do but now..." He sighed. "I wish he could be here for my final moments."

Calypso narrowed her eyes at the old man before her. "You could have ended it? And you didn't? Despite having seven children, you never once thought to end it beyond my mother suggesting it?!"

"Perhaps I could have once... I could never be fully sure on whether or not it was something the court would have accepted."

The emperor began to cough, he brought his hand to his mouth to cover it. When he moved it back down, red spots could be seen on his palm.

Calypso's whole body began to tremble as she looked down at Oryon. Her father. He was going to die now. Her world would crumble along with his.

"No," she sighed. "I will not let your death bring me to ruin. You did nothing in life to protect me, only leaving me with one guard as the others had two or more — you allowed favorites. You allowed imbalance. You allowed this primal tradition to continue." Oryon trembled as he focused on her once again, hand shaking as he reached out for her. Not wanting to die with the guilt of knowing she wouldn't forgive him. But that wasn't her job — to make him feel comforted when she was hurt. It may be better to be kind, but not if it was to comfort someone who wasn't genuinely apologetic.

Calypso turned her back to him. "I will find a way to end this." She spotted Hectyr outside the room. "And not just for myself."

The emperor didn't say anything, he just continued to cough — breathing struggling now.

"I hope you find peace with your brother when you see him, and you'd best pray my mother and him accept you in the afterlife," Calypso said as she made her way out of the room. Servants hurried in as his coughing grew louder. She made her way towards Hectyr who seemed to be staring at nothing as he waited.

Deakon laughed as all the royal scions cast anxious glances between one another. Since his last outburst it was impossible to tell who would make another rash decision.

"So, you spoke with him?" Hectyr asked as Calypso stopped next to him.

She glanced around, wary of those who saw them speaking together. "Yes... Yes I did." She glanced up at Hectyr. "What's wrong with your eyes?"

Hectyr looked down at her, his eyes were the same color but... duller. Almost as though the soul behind them had vanished.

"Hectyr... are you sick? What's wrong?"

"What are you talking about —"

"Get the healers quickly!" a servant yelled from his chambers, rushing their direction. "We need to make his passing calmer than this!"

Calypso looked to the ground and shut her eyes. *Was I too harsh with him?*

No. He made his choices in life just as I've made mine. I will change my fate.

The loud coughing and ragged breathing from the chambers stopped. It was only moments until his last breath left his body now. Hectyr shook his head and gripped his hair with tense hands. Cal cast a concerned look at him.

He was fine earlier... how could the emperor's death affect him like this? It's almost like a —

"We don't have much time — if they don't hurry he could already be- "

Before the servant even finished speaking, Deakon and

Adonys both pulled out their weapons and clashed in the center of everything. The servants and other lords and ladies shrieked as they began to fight right then and there. Calypso grabbed Hectyr's hand and pulled him away as she began to edge off to the side of the crowd.

"What are they —"

"We need to get out of here!" Calypso whispered to him quickly.

He looked down at her, frowning. "We?"

Cal dropped his hand and shivered as she recognized what she did. She shook her head as she glanced at the combat one more time before turning down the hall. "You can come with me, or you can fight too." *I need to find the armor,* now!

As Calypso rushed down the hall towards the garden. She sent up a silent prayer to the Aspects that Oboryn has returned to the tunnel and that she wouldn't have to search long. Hectyr followed behind her, but slower. Slagging behind as though he were suddenly stricken ill. As Cal looked back at him, brow furrowed, she noticed he kept his eyes on the ground.

"Are you alright?" she asked as she stopped by the archives entrance.

"I'm fine," he snapped. Calypso flinched at his response.

As they neared the garden, the loud and hollow clang of the armor could be heard ahead. It was a haunting sight, the cream colored armor with deep ebony and gold engravings upon it slowly wandered about. Aimlessly. Just in the halls by the garden.

"Is that.... Is that it? The armor? Who is in it?" Hectyr whispered uncertainly.

"Well... It said it's name was Oboryn."

The armor, Oboryn, turned in their direction and cackled.

"Do you really think I don't know you're here?" It began to walk in their direction.

As they stop a few feet away, Oboryn spotted Hectyr. "Ah, it seems you are not alone. You surprise me, I didn't think you'd be so foolish as to keep another of the blood near during this time."

Calypso looked up at Hectyr, he was shivering now, his eyes kept glancing between herself and the armor ahead.

What is wrong with him?

"Why do you keep running?" Calypso asked. The armor merely let out a shrill laugh.

"Running? Do you really expect me to sit still until you want to parade around again?"

"I cannot allow you to keep going off on your own, and now I need to make use of you once more." Calypso said slowly. It was odd, to speak to armor in such a way. Words felt foreign suddenly as she looked upon it. The armor pulled out a weapon.

"No, I believe now is not the time."

Calypso's eyes widened, it was about to strike as it gripped the hilt of the blade tighter. She pulled out her blade and struck at the armor, knocking off its helmet and revealing the nothingness inside. There wasn't even a scratch left by her knife. *How do I even fight this thing?*

Hectyr let out a delayed gasp as he processed what was before him.

"I would say it best to get away from him," Oboryn said as they picked up their head. "But perhaps it doesn't matter now what happens to you," Oboryn said casually as they glided past the two of them. "After all, the curse should take effect soon. He does seem to be the elder one."

Cal spun around as she watched them stride past. "What do you —"

Before she even finished speaking Hectyr grabbed a blade off Calypso's hip, he gripped it in shaky hands. Striking quickly, but not at Oboryn.

As Calypso felt the blade dig into her skin she didn't even notice the pain, not at first. Hectyr dug the blade deep into the left arm before pulling it out viciously.

Looking up at Hectyr she felt tears as they began to fill her eyes, but Hectyr was already in tears. Suddenly his eyes were back to normal. The same blue of the royals that she had always cursed at.

He let go and stepped away, whole body trembling as he looked at Calypso.

"I — I wasn't... I didn't mean to —" He looked around, as though suddenly taking in his surroundings.

"The emperor is dead!" the cry echoed throughout the great hall.

Calypso didn't wait to hear his excuses. As she began to run away she could hear more fighting break out down the halls as Adonys snapped next and began to fight. Guards and servants alike were quick to rush in and break up the struggle — this was not how the challenge was meant to take place. Yet still, they couldn't harm the royals. They only could try to stop them.

As Calypso rushed down the great halls she gripped around her arm, trying to stop the bleeding.

"Calypso! I'm so sorry!" he yelled after her. Cal couldn't even tell if he was chasing after her as his movement made no sound.

If he'd left the blade in I'd have more time. I should have seen this coming. I shouldn't have trusted him!

But something is off —

Why did he snap just as the emperor died?

Was this her curse Oboryn spoke of? Or was something else at hand?

Calypso slowed as her head grew dizzy from the loss of blood. Looking ahead she saw as knights of the Citadel gathered to stop her from fleeing further. The challenge would begin, and they would not allow her to escape. Not when they wanted her to perish in it.

Calypso felt her body aching from exhaustion and blood loss and couldn't hold on any longer. The embrace of sleep took her quickly as the world around her turned black.

247

21
MEMORIES ONCE LOST
LEANDRE

When one forgets something — it doesn't always have dire consequences. A forgotten task, a harmless recollection, or a hazy scene once familiar. Yet as Leandre lay in darkness, he suddenly felt an ominous feeling that comes with remembrance.

"Leandre!"

Opening his eyes, Leandre stood up as he heard his name being called by a familiar tone.

What happened? "Leandre!" Cal?

As he looked around, he found himself no longer within the tunnels. Instead, he was surrounded by snow. The air left a burning cold sensation on his skin, and it was far colder than anything he remembered from the Citadel.

As someone tugged at his wrist, Leandre almost fell forward onto his face. He looked down at his hands in confusion. Why were they so... small? Why were they held together with rope?

"Leandre!"

Looking back, he spotted who was calling him. A little girl, tears spilled down her face as she cried out his name. She was just a little bigger than him, but still looked very young. Five other children surrounded her, all older — but they had little emotion on their faces as they watched him. A woman, who he assumed was their mother, tugged the little girl away, in her other hand was a heavy-looking pouch.

"Wait! Don't go!" Leandre called out at them without even thinking to say the words.

The woman just gave him a sorrowful look.

"This is for the best, Leandre," she called out. "Go with him, you will have a far better life with them than me."

Leandre frowned, she looked familiar. She shook her head as she struggled to herd the rest of the children away, the youngest still crying out his name.

"Don't take my little brother away!" she cried.

Little brother? But she is so much younger than I am.

Leandre looked ahead at where the rope went. A small squadron of knights stood there, wearing armor with white and blue coloration rather than the gold and red of the capital city Lyreas. One cloaked figure was among them. They glanced back and shared a strange look with the woman before looking down at Leandre. He froze under the figure's gaze.

But we killed you! How is the cultist still alive?

Is this an illusion? Then why is it so familiar?

Suddenly the world around him faded, and standing before Leandre again was Lord Harkyn.

"Are you sure this will work?" he asked as he stalked around the smaller boy, glaring down. "He is your... Well, if anything were to happen to the boy — could you live with that?"

"Trust me, the spells will work. Though I expect you to uphold your end, holding the number of spells you have requested is beginning to take its toll," the mage responded, there was a strained sense of emotion to their voice — like they had limited use left and the bottle was almost empty.

The world around him slipped away into misty gold that grew darker and darker until Leandre was left alone again in darkness.

That was... my father?

Leandre opened his eyes at the sound of Kyril shouting his name. Looking up he saw Lord Harkyn looming over, an intense look in his eyes.

"The spell, the mage... I assume you understand it all now — don't you?" he asked, slowly stepping forward. "I needed someone on the inside, an ally, but you never completed your task. I thought I could still make use of you but again you've proven useless."

"What do you mean?"

"Your resentment towards Calypso? Your bitterness? It should have progressed much faster but it didn't!" Lord Harkyn spit into the abyss. "That pathetic mage couldn't even uphold his end of the bargain!"

Resentment? Spell? Was that why I began to feel bitter towards her? A spell?

I was never a guard chosen by her — I was an assassin planted to fester and grow until the hate outgrew my care for her.

So why did that never happen?

Harkyn pointed his lance at him. "Don't worry, when I get to the capital and find Cressyda I will kill Calypso myself." Kyril kicked a loose plank on the bridge causing the structure to break between Harkyn and him — he reared back and avoided falling but Leandre began to fall along with it. Grabbing onto the edge of the bridge, Leandre looked up at Kyril. He bent down and pulled him up before they made a bolt for the entrance. Leandre cast a glance back at Harkyn, he was already heading around the bridges to the other point where their paths would meet.

"You could have killed me!" Leandre shouted at Kyril. "What were you thinking kicking that support beam?"

Kyril snorted. "Yeah well, I didn't, did I?"

As they ran, Leandre noticed Kyril quickly running short on breath. His breathing was ragged within minutes, and the entrance was still further away. They had just passed the point where the path that wrapped around to Harkyn met, yet he wasn't there yet. Clacking of hooves could be heard close by.

"Keep going!" Leandre shouted at Kyril as he noticed the support beams. One was hardly holding — the wood had begun to rot as a trickle of water through the cracks of the cavern walls hit it. As he stopped Kyril glanced back.

"What are you doing?!" Kyril shouted.

Leandre slammed his body against the wood. "Stopping Harkyn!"

Harkyn's hooves echoed throughout the cavern as he caught up.

"There might be other exits! Why risk it?!"

He continued to slam his weight against it again and heard the wood begin splintering. "We need to slow him down!"

God, Calypso would already have this broken — I need to be stronger than this!

But this is dangerous, Leandre thought as he reared back to slam into it one more time. *If I don't move away quick enough I could be caught in the caverns with Harkyn, who knows where the exit is! I could even be crushed beneath the rocks.*

But what if I don't? If Harkyn escapes? He could outrun us to the capital easily — but first he would kill us.

"Leandre!"

Harkyn stopped a few feet from him, eyes widening as he saw what he was about to do.

"Don't do it!" he screamed. "That is the only exit we know!"

"Give me one reason why I shouldn't."

Leandre didn't wait for him to answer with another lie.

Slamming into the beam one last time a loud crack could be heard. Leandre rushed towards the cavern entrance as the support beam split and rocks began crumbling all around him. Screams echoed from both Harkyn and Kyril which filled his skull, but he kept going. As he neared the entrance a rock slammed into his shoulder and another hit his leg as the ceiling gave way. Leandre leapt forward and landed just outside the cave. Singing pain spread throughout his leg making him grimace as Kyril crouched beside him.

"We made it!" he shouted gleefully as he raised his hands to the sky in joy. He looked back and saw Leandre still on the ground.

"Knight? Are you alright?"

"Did you suddenly forget my name?" Leandre asked as he grit his teeth and struggled to his feet. "It's Leandre." As he stood, a pain filled his leg as weight rested upon it.

"You're hurt? Great." He sighed. "Now it will take us forever to get back to the Citadel!"

"Us?"

"Yes." Kyril grinned. "After all, you must be one hell of a guard to have kept the cursed princess alive this long."

Leandre rolled his eyes at the older boy's lack of seriousness as he looked back at the crumbled entrance.

"Do you really think there is another entrance?"

Kyril shrugged. "If there is, we'd better get started on the journey back."

As Leandre picked up the pace and began hurrying along the path, Kyril rushed to keep up with him.

"Don't you think if you keep that up you'll hurt your leg even more?"

"I don't care, we need to get back — fast." He looked over to Kyril. "You heard him, right? I thought he seemed... emotional this whole time once we got near the artifacts and saw mentions of her. *Cressyda*. Somehow, he seemed to believe she is back."

"But that's impossible, surely?" Kyril frowned. "I feel like I've heard that name recently..."

Leandre shook his head. "Harkyn might be twisted, but he isn't an idiot — he knew damn well what he was talking about. I need to stop him from killing Cal."

"But if he wanted to kill... her," Kyril said bitterly. "Why would he have stopped me from doing that?"

Leandre stopped and turned on him. "What?!"

Kyril put his hands up. "When planning for the challenge! He said I couldn't kill her! He believed the prophecy around her could be useful."

He furrowed his brows at the royal scion. "Was he planning on using her as a scapegoat for his plans?"

"That... actually sounds like the type of plan he would make." Kyril scowled. "Damn it all! I really thought he was going to keep his end of the deal! And what about the curse?"

"Curse?"

"What Harkyn was shouting at that mage... He spoke as though something cursed the royals back in the Citadel. Something to make us all kill one another. That is why I came along, I needed to be away from the capital."

Leandre paused for a moment before realization struck him. "You're right! I remember that but — Didn't he say something about the emperor's death?"

Kyril's skin went pale. "Is that... the trigger for this curse?"

Leandre turned and began to run down the path, Kyril hurrying along with him.

Cressyda... this armor... a curse —

I never should have left Calypso and Ophelya on their own!

The Pain of Rebirth

Dekem, 1057 AH (Anno Harmonia)

The once beautiful starry skies of winter are bleak as a darkness fills the sky. Frost falls across the land and the sun has turned black. As we reach the final month in Dekem, many Vasylians call for the head of the cursed scion, Princess Calypso Pallas.

The Festival of Halved Souls has prematurely ended.

22
THE CHALLENGE BEGINS
CALYPSO

A warm feeling of embrace covered Calypso from head to toe, it was as though she had been wrapped in sunlight. The world around her blurred as she struggled to get the sleep out of her eyes, voices could be heard nearby. As she rubbed her eyes and looked around she quickly recognized the dimly lit room with many beds about. She was in a healer's room? But why? Calypso couldn't get over how much the sense of healing felt like magick- yet it wasn't considered a form of magick.

This doesn't look like the healers' room in the Citadel though... Where am I?

As Calypso heard the sounds of people approaching she quickly shut her eyes and lay back onto the bed.

"Why did we even bother healing her? Aren't we not supposed to heal them once the challenge begins?" a healer asked as the pair stopped next to her.

"It was requested, they did say it was an accident — and it was outside the challenge still." *Accident?* Calypso then remembered Hectyr's attack. Just as the emperor died he snapped. She clenched her jaw shut as she continued to listen to the healers.

"But why would Prince Hectyr request us to heal her? Doesn't that undo his work?"

It was Hectyr who had me brought here? But why would he do that after attacking me?

Was he being genuine? But how could one accidentally attack some-one?

"He said it was an accident!" the healer repeated irritably. "And we had to oblige as this was a very odd situation... Usually, royal scions wouldn't make such requests for one another."

"Perhaps he wanted to face her in the arena himself?"

"Well, either way, she'd better wake up soon. They're expecting her above."

As Calypso felt one of the healers place an arm on her and shake her, she opened her eyes.

"Finally awake," one said with a groan. "Now we can finally get on with it."

She sat up warily as she glanced between the two of them.

"The challenge?" They exchanged a glance before one nodded at her question.

"Follow us."

Calypso stood and followed the two healers out of the healing room, they went through many dark eerie stone hallways lit by the dim light of lanterns on the walls. The stone path through the tunnels beneath the Colosseum almost felt like the tunnel that led to the armor. Except there weren't even Dreamweavers here. No form of life stayed within the Colosseum except the captured beasts held here for combat.

The smell of wet stone and cold autumn chills filled the air that blew through the tunnels. It must have rained... or it could still be raining. Everything spelled doom for this challenge.

And nothing would make this easy.

The two healers motioned to a room ahead of her.

"Go through here to get ready, the others are already prepared. Wait until they call your name, and you will be allowed into the arena."

Two guards stood outside of the door, clearly there to keep her from running.

Without another word the two turned away from her, rushing to alert to speaker that everyone was now ready to begin the challenge.

As Calypso entered the small room leading to the Colosseum, she glanced around. Light armor was set up beside a slab bench, upon it was a spear. Ornamental and useless — it was the very spear left for her by the emperor. While she had once loved the spear, she began to hate it as she recognized what it symbolized. What it meant. *Something meant to be pretty and look useful but something that cannot fight in real battle.* The emperor may have loved her as a daughter, but he never saw her for her value.

Calypso sighed at the sight of it. Something about it always made her uncomfortable.

She looked out into the clearing ahead as she put the armor on. It was light infantry armor, nothing heavy. And the only type that would fit her was for larger men. She shook her head as she looked out towards the Colosseum. Who was to be her opponent? The first challenge was the most brutal as it would include fighting multiple beasts on top of battling one other royal. The quickest way to strike out any weak links.

Calypso may be familiar with fighting monsters of all kinds but *multiple*? All the while fighting for her life against another royal scion?

Will I even make it through the first round?

Once the armor was fully on, Calypso picked up her spear, and the gate down the hall opened up. As dim light filtered into the long room, she took a deep breath and began to make her way towards the combat arena.

As she stepped out into the light and heard her name announced roaring cheers filled the crowd. The people of Vasyla. Her people. Praying for her downfall. The Colosseum was packed to the brim with many people awaiting the outcome of the first rounds — thrilled by the festival and the challenge happening at once.

As Cal looked around the crowd, she felt herself freeze up as she spotted a familiar-looking Voltuan among the masses.

"Wait... That's Cal!" a Voltuan screeched above the rest. "You can't let this happen! We need her out of there!" he shouted as loud as he could. Calypso spotted the Voltuan out of the crowds and felt her heart soar as she recognized Iago. *There are some who believe in me out there... Then that is all I need.*

Calypso continued to scan the crowd but felt her heart drop as she couldn't find Ophelya or Leandre.

What happened to them? Are they unable to face this... or are they going to try something dangerous?

She continued to scan the crowd for the two familiar faces but found them nowhere — even Lord Harkyn was nowhere to be seen.

Did... Leandre and Harkyn never return?

Aspects protect them wherever they are.

Cal continued to look around the crowd and realized multiple court members were not present. Lady Nephus and Lord Teresi were not present either.

The announcer for the challenge even went silent for a moment, a look of disgust on his face as they looked her over. The announcer was a large cyclops, over seven feet tall, he must have been quite old to become such a great size. He may have even been the announcer for the last two generations of this challenge. Echo was also a Cyclops, but being just over twenty she was still small and looked like a child.

Another gate opened on the other side of the Colosseum — there were eight gates in all and the one opposite of Calypso was slowly lifted by guards.

As Calypso watched who left the other entrance she frowned.

"For the first round of the Challenge of Cressyda, we have the silent Echo Pallas against the final born, Calypso!"

The crowd roared as Echo stepped into sight. Not because of her, but because they wanted to her to defeat the one she opposed. Rain began to lightly trickle down into the arena, but nobody showed any signs of wanting to leave, eyes glued to the two contestants before them.

Echo glared at Calypso, a grim look in her eye. She glanced at their surroundings and looked over Cal. As though assessing the situation. As though coming to a decision.

"But that isn't everyone now, is it?" the announcer shouted out gleefully. "No, these two royal scions will not just face one another but also —"

Two gates opened at the eastern and western sides of the arena and great beasts slowly began to rush out of both.

"A lesser dragon and a manticore! Who will defeat both beasts and their rival for the throne?"

Calypso looked between the two beasts and Echo. The manticore had its gaze set upon Adonys. It held its barbed tail up and ready as it stalked him, muscles rippling beneath strong hide — but Adonys's gaze never left Calypso. Something was wrong with him. The lesser dragon, or drake, was already breathing smoke as it turned on Calypso. Cal gripped her spear in her hands.

I won't fight Adonys... but the beasts. She looked back and forth between the manticore and the drake. Focusing on those two might be easier, but she still would have to avoid being struck by the opposing royal scion while distracted by the others.

Cal grit her teeth as the drake began its charge. She ducked just as it leapt at her crashing onto the ground.

Use your wild magick, she heard a voice, yet she couldn't tell where it came from. *I can sense it within you. Overflowing amounts of energy, untapped. Unused.* The armor let out a guttural laugh as Calypso continued to dodge the lesser dragon's slashes and strikes.

I can only play defensive for so long, Calypso thought to herself.

And this is not the only enemy on the field.

Cal looked up to see Echo narrowly avoid the manticore's barbed tail. Wait... how did she avoid it? She didn't seem to move much, only the manticore did. Echo turned and glared at Calypso. Avoiding the beasts, she instead charged for her.

Using wild magick? I know I can do it but... should I? Is there really no other way out of this?

Water Magick was still legal. *I can use that water magick then.*

The rain above was light, but only growing heavier by the minute. Calypso felt an ache in her body as she struggled to focus her emotions and energy into willing the rain to bend to her will. Wild magick does affect its user more than controlled magick — and Calypso felt as though her lungs were crushing in as she gathered the rain to one point.

As Calypso felt the energy surge through her she grinned. *Perhaps I should let this happen. Even if the crowd sees me doing magick, they won't care once they realize all I've been doing for them... right?*

As Echo and the lesser drake lunged at her, Calypso didn't move away as she held her hands forward to them.

The rain that had gathered in the sky above her suddenly became like a wave spilling from a single point in the sky forcing all three of her foes back to the other side of the arena and keeping them pinned to the wall. The water was covering them, within moments all three would drown. Roars of fear, anger, and even excitement could be heard all around her as numerous as the raindrops that fell from the sky.

Cal released the spell, and the remaining water flowed to their end until it dissipated back into the air. She let out a ragged breath as the spell ebbed away.

That was the first time I've willingly used wild magick.

The lesser drake and the manticore watched her in fear as they struggled to their feet.

Echo stood after a moment, her eyes cleared until she looked at Cal. Confusion seemed to wash over her. She began to step forward, and the ground began to shake. Echo's hands shook as she focused on the earth below them. Was this her doing?

Before Calypso could prepare another spell the rain began to fall harder. Calypso could feel a shift in the air. She suddenly felt that odd presence again, like the armor was nearby.

"Oboryn... is this your doing?" she whispered to herself.

The feeling of its presence disappeared, the sun suddenly began shifting to dark and a red glow bloomed around it. Like paint, a blood-orange bloom began to spill forth from the black hole in the sky.

Echo looked up to the skies and glared at Calypso. "How are you doing this?" She screamed across the arena. Her words were not laced with fear, but awe.

"It's her! She's changing the sky!"

The crowd began to shriek in terror at the sky's changing. Torrential rain poured forth and the salty scent of the ocean filled the air as even the seas were brought to a rage.

The people were screeching for her head. Cheering in one voice for her death as they looked up at the dark sun. People began jumping into the Colosseum, but not regular citizens... throwing off robes as they jumped these people revealed bright feathered gowns and twisted grins as they rushed at her. Echo's eye went wide and she began to back into a corner as she struggled to assess the situation. Calypso stepped back. One two... Twelve... Twenty... *How can I face that many of them?!* Calypso raised her spear, ready to strike, but as she did something lunged over the edge away from the crowd and landed in front of her.

Calypso held her arms up to block herself, but as she lowered them she was met with a large Skorvian woman. *Zagora!*

"Zagora, what are you doing?" Calypso asked as she watched a multitude of her crew clamoring over to defend their captain. She snarled as she faced the oncoming crowd.

"They're witch cultists, little bird!" she shouted as she deflected the blade of one of the cultists. "We need to get you out of here!"

"Witch cultists?!"

That has to do with Cressyda but... Why are they striking now?!

"Calypso, go!"

"No! I won't leave you!" Calypso looked up at the sky.

"Oboryn! Did you do this?"

The armor did not say another word, though Calypso still felt their presence within. Calypso raised her spear to strike the nearest witch cultist, but before she could strike Zagora shoved her away.

"Get out of here Calypso! Find your friends and get somewhere safe! This is not the challenge you're expected to face!"

Calypso looked up at Zagora one last time, frowning but she abided by her request as she watched her crew fight alongside her.

This... why do I feel Oboryn's presence? How could they possibly be involved?

I can't keep doing this alone.

I need to find Ophelya... and Leandre if I can. I need to make sure they are safe... and then... Oboryn.

23
THE CULT OF CRESSYDA
LEANDRE

As rain began to trickle overhead Leandre could not shake an ominous feeling that loomed over him like the storm above threatening to unleash at any given moment. *If there is a curse... I need to get to Calypso's side immediately.*

Even Ophelya is in danger now. She has been more obvious in her interactions with Cal as of late... What if someone uses her to get to Cal?

"How much longer until we get back?" Kyril groaned loudly.

"Panagyota is probably getting worried about me by now."

"Panagyota?"

Kyril nodded. "Panagyota of House Teresi." He glanced away, face flushed. Clearly, he didn't want to continue the subject, though he seemed proud of it moments ago.

I never really thought about the lives of the other royal scions before now... What all they planned for themselves if they were to survive... How many people are linked to the other royals? How many would mourn every one of them when they pass?

Calypso only has Ophelya and myself... and of course Captain Zagora.

How many lives were linked to this barbaric tradition?

Leandre raised a brow at him. "We will get there soon enough. I can see the Citadel in the distance already."

"Huh, you're right actually," Kyril said after a moment. He paused and squinted at the road before them. "It looks like more people are going into the capital for the celebrations of the festival."

"Why would more people be coming now? The festival should be halfway over..."

Kyril shrugged. "Perhaps more people are concerned for the emperor's health? He was in pretty poor shape before we left."

"Do you think he died?" Leandre asked as he began to pick up the pace, passing by Kyril. He quickly caught up. "I — I hope not. At least not yet, anyways." Kyril's voice shook as he spoke but he didn't waver his pace as the pair hurried along the path to the capital. It wasn't much farther now, and the rain began to come down a little harder as they neared the gate. By the time they finally reached the capital city of Lyreas the crowd they saw was long ahead of them. Nobody was in sight.

No guards were at the entrance of the capital. Leandre rested his hand on his sheathed sword taken from the abyss as Kyril began to run ahead into the city.

"There must be a festival event going on!" he said cheerily as he ran through the rain. Leandre hurried to catch up to him.

"Kyril wait, something doesn't seem right." He cast glances around as they hurried through the lower district. There wasn't a soul in sight.

What happened to all of those people we saw entering Lyreas?

As Leandre and Kyril neared the city square, loud voices began to echo throughout the streets. The sky roared above as the storm reached its peak and the sun began to change into darkness. Leandre looked up to the sky to see it change, his head began to ache again as he watched it change. The sun turned black, and a red glow bloomed like a fire blazing around it. Red dripped forth from the ring and fell to the seas like a potion being poured slowly. People were rushing out of the Colosseum and screaming in terror. Wide-eyed and scrambling away like prey from predators. Citizens and aristocrats alike were seen fleeing from the Colosseum.

"Kyril, is this something of Harkyn's plan?!" Leandre grabbed the royal scion by the shoulders. "What does this mean?"

Kyril didn't look at him, instead, he looked to the arena.

"The Colosseum isn't in use during the festival of halved souls..." Kyril froze up as he watched people move like a wave of the ocean from the arena.

The pair stopped nearby, watching with furrowed brows as they tried to make sense of what was going on. It was only when cloaked figures began coming out of the Colosseum did it make sense.

"Witch cultists!" Leandre shouted as he shoved Kyril away from an oncoming enemy.

"We need to get to the Citadel!" Kyril shouted.

"No!" Leandre pulled out his sword, "We need to get into the arena to find Calypso and Ophelya!"

As the crowds began to thin, three of the witch cultists turned their gazes upon them. Kyril ducked behind him quickly.

"We can't take on that many!" he cried out, voice cracking.

Leandre shook his head.

"I'll handle it."

Remember what you always have to tell yourself when this happens. You're defending yourself. You're defending your friends.

Leandre waited until one of the witch cultists rushed at him with a dagger alone. With a sidestep he avoided it and cut him down with one swift movement. It was hard to ignore the feeling of a blade breaking through skin and muscle.

You're defending yourself.

The next one clutched their hands in a claw as the rain began to form above into a spell, muttering incantations below their breath. Leandre ducked and avoided a bludgeoning attack from the other cultist and struck the spell caster between the shoulder and the neck. As they fell, Leandre placed a foot upon them and pulled his sword out of the body.

You're defending your friends.

Turning, Leandre barely avoided a strike from a bronze mace, the third cultist was larger than the others. A Skorvis. Leandre frowned. Humans and cyclops were relatively easy for him. Centaurs as well. But Skorvians were a kind he struggled against.

Jumping to avoid the large pinchers of the Skorvian, Leandre landed with a foot on the Skorvian's shoulder, ducking to avoid another swing from the mace he jumped around to their backside and struck between the Skorvian's shoulder blade, but the blade only just cracked the hard chitin shell.

The Skorvian shook Leandre off, and he landed on the brick ground, hitting his back against the edge of the fountain. He looked up, and the world around him shook as the rain above continued to drench him. Leandre watched as Kyril glanced at him and looked at the Skorvian before moving away.

Typical.

Leandre struggled to get to his feet before the Skorvian reached him. Preparing to dodge their next attack. Before he could though, a spear burst through their chest. They gripped the weapon weakly before falling to the ground and shriveling up.

As they fell another Skorvian could be seen behind them.

"Captain Zagora!" Leandre shouted. She leaned down and helped him up with a grim expression. "What happened?"

"Witch cultists happened," she replied simply. "Calypso is making her way to the Citadel now." Their gaze softened after they looked at him for a moment.

"It's been a while, my pupil, you seem... Different somehow." Zagora narrowed her eyes at him. "Was I right about it then? Did you break your own curse?"

Leandre took a step back. "You knew I was cursed?"

"I had my suspicions," Zagora said as she pulled her weapon from her fellow Skorvian's corpse. "But it was not your fate to have me intervene."

"But I was a danger to Calypso! Because of that curse, I could have killed her!"

Zagora shook her head. "I've seen the way you look at her, boy. No matter how deep a curse holds you, killing Calypso is not your fate. It seems emotions do have some semblance of control in the ties of fate after all..."

"What are you talking about?" Leandre frowned. "If you knew, why did you train me as her knight?"

"I could see you were pure of heart, no matter if there was a curse upon you or not."

Leandre frowned, before shaking his head. "The challenge started, didn't it?" Zagora nodded.

"Where is Calypso?"

Captain Zagora nodded towards the Citadel. "I told her to go to the safety of the Citadel. You might be able to catch up to her."

"And Ophelya?"

"I haven't seen her."

He frowned. *Ophelya... wouldn't she have been in the arena? Unless she already escaped...*

Leandre dipped his head. "And what will you do?"

"I will gather my crew and finish off the remaining cultists, they may be spread throughout the city — now go!"

As Zagora followed where the crowds of cultists had vanished Leandre turned and began making his way up towards the Citadel.

I have to get to her and together we can find Ophelya.

As the Citadel came into sight Leandre spotted a figure up ahead. It was Kyril. He caught up to him quickly, as the royal scion was already panting and out of breath.

"You lived?!" Kyril said between ragged breaths.

Leandre pulled him to his feet. "Of course I did." He continued past him. Kyril heaved before struggling to catch up.

"Wait... Wait for me!"

Leandre didn't even bother to respond, instead keeping his eyes on the road ahead of him. He caught glimpses of a strange knight ahead, rushing towards the Citadel.

"Isn't that the strange knight I've been hearing about?"

Are they also going to help? They have been doing many good deeds.... but what could their motive be?

Kyril froze as he saw the armor making its way toward the Citadel, Leandre cast a glance at him. He was shivering, but not because of the rain.

"Kyril, what's wrong with you?" Leandre asked. When he didn't move he grabbed him by the shoulders and shook him. "Kyril?!"

"Cressyda... That's... That's the armor Lord Harkyn was looking for. That's where her last shard remains but why did I hear a voice coming from it?"

Leandre felt a pit grow in his stomach as he looked back at the armor. *Wait... that armor... Calypso's plan and that sudden crusader in the capital - by the Aspects was she using it? Then where it goes, will she be nearby?*

But then... Why are they going towards the Citadel?

24

A SERVANT, A LADY, & A CULTIST

OPHELYA

Hiding away was far more exhausting than Ophelya had thought. Every crack of a twig or shake of a bush had her awake and alert — not to mention the royal scion who sat beside her up in the trees. Nearly a day of hiding wore them out, Ophelya felt exhausted down to her very bones by the time the forest was cleared of cultists. Hours had passed since Ophelya and Avalon had first hidden in the forest — days until they finally could make their way back into the city. The cold of the autumn nights were almost unbearable as it was nearing winter — but within the trees together the two managed to stay warm. As for the cultists, by dawn that day there was no longer a sight or sound from the strangely dressed people. The silence should have been comforting, but it was almost too much to bear. Every whistle of the wind or rustle of a bush brought fear right back to the pair.

It was Ophelya who finally made the call that it was time to leave, Avalon clung to the tree and stared into nothingness as she climbed down — Ophelya waited a moment before offering her a helping hand as she froze up on her way down.

"I have got this," Avalon said through grit teeth as she slowly made her way down. Ophelya rolled her eyes at the elder girl's attitude. As they left the woods and still saw no sight of the cultists, their anxieties slowly began to leave them.

"Isn't it odd?" Avalon asked as the pair made the trek back into the city and through the lower district. She kept rubbing her hands over her arms as she scanned her surroundings. The confident royal from a few days ago striding through the city gone since the encounter with the cultists.

"What about our situation isn't odd?" Ophelya asked, constantly scanning the other woman. *Should I bring her with me? Should I even be around another royal scion? And if there is a curse...*

Avalon wouldn't stop casting anxious glances around herself, making Ophelya furrow her brows. "Avalon, what... What are you doing? We're in the city, it's fine."

She looked at her, but only after a moment did her eyes show recognition of looking at Ophelya. "You're right it's just... I've felt off since yesterday. I can't focus." She shook her head.

Ophelya sighed. "Once we get back to the capital, we can find you a healer but after that, we need to find Calypso." *I also need to find Leandre... I can't keep leaving them in the dark. They need to be aware of what threatens us — even should the emperor die and the challenge begin there is no way we can get Calypso out of the challenge safely with cultists around.*

"Yes, yes, *Princess Calypso.*"

They were nearing the Citadel now, the guards didn't stop them as they recognized Avalon, but they exchanged a glance as the pair passed through. Ophelya narrowed her eyes at them. Usually the guards would at least greet one of the stars of the empire. If not at least dip their head for herself as a lady of a territory. *Ominous indeed.*

"Come on, I know a quick path to the Citadel," Ophelya said as she took the lead, Avalon hardly even nodding in response as she followed.

In the likelihood that there is an event in the city center, it is best we avoid there for now...

Ophelya led the way through the lower district around the western side to the upper district — it was odd how few people they came across. It was so quiet you could hear a pin drop, and the whistling of the autumn wind that blew through the city didn't put either of them at ease.

"A storm is coming soon," Ophelya muttered. "We'd best hurry and get to the Citadel."

Cal, Leandre, please be safely within the citadel.

I'm on my way.

Ophelya rested her hand on her leg where a blade sat against her leg. She wasn't as well trained as Cal or Leandre, but if anything were to happen, her skills were better than nothing. Plus her karambit would tear through anyone who dared get close to her with terrifying ease.

Ophelya glanced back at Avalon, she was shaking and her eyes didn't focus on the path ahead of them.

Could it be the curse is beginning to take effect?

She looked ahead, they were nearing the Citadel now reaching the steep incline leading up to it. Ophelya sighed.

"Avalon... Perhaps it is best if you don't return to the Citadel."

She looked up at Ophelya with wild eyes. "What are you talking about? I have to return!"

"But if there really is a curse and —"

"No! If there is a curse I need to make sure my brother is okay."

"Avalon, listen to yourself," Ophelya said, stopping at the Citadel gate. "If there is a curse... then you could hurt him, too."

Avalon shook her head and passed her by. "I will not stand by and listen to this slander. Adonys is my true brother, I would never harm him. Curse or no curse — we share more blood than the rest of them."

Ophelya watched as she disappeared into the Citadel, glancing around at the gates she frowned. *No guards? At the Citadel?*

Even if there was an event in the town center, no guards at the Citadel was not a good sign. Pulling out her blade, she slowly made her way towards the Citadel. Everything seemed normal and intact. The great pillars of the entrance still held strong, and decorations for the Festival of Halved Souls were still about. Still, there wasn't a guard or a servant in sight. Rain started to pour down as she entered the cover of the Citadel.

The smell of the seas filled the air as the rain spilled forth.

What in the Aspects is going on?

As Ophelya stepped into the great hall, a screech rang out. Avalon fell to her knees in the center of the hall, clematis blooms, and many riches surrounded her as she kneeled next to a chiseled stone slab. Suddenly the grand hall felt small, pillars shrunk Ophelya put a hand up over her mouth as she recognized the figure atop it.

The emperor.

He was dead.

And his body would not be buried without his other children. Not until one of the royal scions won the crown in a twisted tradition. It didn't matter in Vasyla if his body would rot away before the challenge ended, what was important was that his mission be completed, and the next ruler be chosen before he was buried and sent to the Aspects. There was no sweet rotting scent in the air yet, which meant his passing was recent. *Very* recent.

The Challenge of Cressyda has begun... Hasn't it?

She didn't comfort Avalon in her grief, leaving her to mourn her father alone. Turning to go back out to the entrance of the Citadel, she clenched a fist at her side to stop her hands from shaking.

Ophelya looked back out over the capital city, the rain was coming down hard yet over the Colosseum it seemed to be gathering... Like something was pulling all the rain in the vicinity to that one point.

Ophelya's heart dropped.

The challenge has already begun.

"Ophelya!"

A familiar voice pulled her out of her thoughts, spotting a figure coming up the hill through the gate towards her, she frowned.

"Mother?"

"Where have you been?" her mother asked as she hurried up to her. She was dressed up, like she had been at an event. In a dramatic gown following current fashion trends. It looked rather gaudy and was soaked by the rain. Her dark skin was paling though, was she that worried about her? As her mother stopped in front of her and placed a hand on her shoulder, Ophelya felt slightly at ease. Though Ophelya and her mother had a shaky relationship, it was good to know that she cared.

A rare comfort indeed.

"I'm sorry, I was busy looking into something and —"

"No, no, that doesn't matter now!" her mother said quickly, her eyes moving past Ophelya to look into the Citadel. "You missed a lot, but if we hurry then we can —"

She frowned. "Mother, weren't you worried? Don't you want to know where I've been?" Ophelya took a step back, removing her mother's hand from her shoulder, and finally looked down at Lady Nephus's robes.

They were not made of mock feathers.

"Come now Ophelya, that doesn't matter now!" her mother said, grabbing her shoulder again. A wide grin spread across her face, and as she got close Ophelya realized her eyes were bloodshot and dark bags sat beneath them. "Cressyda will be here soon, and we must have a body ready for her. Without Harkyn here there is a chance we can —"

"Cressyda? A body? Mother what are you —"

As Ophelya pulled away her bag fell to the ground, its contents spilling out onto the brick road beneath their feet. The journal fell open onto the ground, its contents immediately soaked by the rain. Ophelya quickly bent down to shove it back into the bag before it was too damaged. As she rose to her feet, Lady Nephus's demeanor instantly shifted.

"I see, still letting that foolish woman get into your head, are you? I thought we could move past this, past her once she was dealt with. I worked my way up from a servant to a lady, and now I can become the mother to the empress that brings back the age of magick! Don't let her continue to get in the way of your fate, my dearest daughter!"

Ophelya took a step away from her mother. Horrified to see her own face looking back at her with wild eyes and lips pursed tight together. As she stepped away and fully looked at her mother, she recognized the markings on her body. *Blood magick.* The most heinous form of wild magicks — instead of using regular energy from the body for spells, it used the energy of the user's life force, or their blood. Her mother's fingers were turning purple and many bruises covered her body.

"That's... That's why you didn't like how outspoken Maeve was. She wasn't just looking into the cult, she was looking into what *you* were doing, wasn't she?"

"I knew I should've burned it!" her mother explained as she reached out for her again. "But she provided so much valuable insight into how we could be found out!" *This isn't my mother — it can't be.*

Why would she do something like this?

Ophelya looked past her mother at the Colosseum. Calypso would be there. She had to get away from her mother and get to her friends.

"Mother," Ophelya began, taking a step towards her mother and constantly glancing past her. "I understand your goal now, but first I must go do something to... perfect my body for Cressyda."

Her mother grinned at her, her teeth red from coughing up blood. "Thank Cressyda, you aren't going to be foolish about this."

Ophelya took a step around her mother, making her way toward the gate when she felt her body freeze.

"I don't think you have any business outside of the Citadel, dearest daughter," her mother said after a moment. Ophelya felt blood in her veins — *felt* it. Her body turned around but she wasn't in control. She looked back at her mother to see her hands twisting and moving in complex patterns as she stared at her daughter.

"Where do you think you got your smarts from? Do you really think I'm that much of a fool?" Her mother stepped towards her and placed her palm against her forehead.

Ophelya felt herself drifting away slowly.

No, no, no! Fight it! Fight it, don't let it get to you!

But it was too late, as Ophelya fell to the ground she faintly heard the last words from her mother's twisted voice.

"You will sleep, and when you wake you will have a whole new purpose."

25
A SERPENT HIDDEN IN PLAIN SIGHT
HECTYR

A serpent was seldom thought of with concern by those in Vasyla. An incomplete dragon. A lesser being. Something to be forgotten in the dark. It wasn't until now that Hectyr felt truly and completely as one with a serpent as he did waiting in the Colosseum. He held his head in his hands as he sat and waited to be sent into the Colosseum for the first round of the challenge.

I always knew this day would come but... I thought that I could disappear before it did.

He could hear outside the crowd cheered as combat began, but he didn't go stand at the gate to watch — no, instead he kept his head low as he gazed upon the floors beneath him.

It was Calypso who had to begin first... Why not me?

Guilt crawled up his skin like a thousand spiders as he kept remembering the sudden violent urge that hit him before he struck down Calypso. He could still see as she turned to him and all the trust in him left her eyes as she fled. *Why didn't she strike back?*

Better yet, why did I strike in the first place? The emperor died and then...

The only question that kept floating through the elder scion's head was *why*.

Cheering roared outside as gates could be heard opening, releasing beasts of the wild into the challenge to remove any weaker scions. The challenges later may be seen as easier, but as each one passed each scion would be further drained thus making it feel more difficult. Hectyr finally stood, slithering over to the gate leading into the arena. He spotted Calypso just as she put a helmet over her head.

He watched the grim expression on Cal's face before she leapt into combat. She was rather impressive, and clearly had a size and weight advantage over the other scion in the area. Hectyr did not doubt that she could survive, she seemed like a tough young woman but still... Killing your own family would have lingering effects on her soul. Rain began to pour down heavier, yet the challenge still ran on.

Why didn't I help her? Why did I attack her? Hectyr still pondered over the sudden urge that he had felt in the halls outside of the emperor's chamber before he died. It was sudden, like a serpent lunging at its prey. Where had that come from? And why did he not feel it as strongly now? *At least it looked like the healers heeded my request, she wasn't favoring her arm when she fought.*

Perhaps I can now.

Should I enter the arena and help her? But then… I would have to fight Echo as well. And what if I get that violent urge again if I am near her?

Hectyr wanted to kick himself if he could, he had finally started to gain the trust of one of his blood relatives and he immediately messed it up. There was Deakon, who gave him cold yet calm smiles as he kept him at arm's length, then there were the more hot-headed royals like Avalon or Kyril who shouted and yelled at his friendly gestures. Why had he snapped at Calypso? *Was it something with my own curse?*

But why would it be acting up now? Why did that happen then?

And why do I still feel this… urge for violence? Do any of the other scions have this?

Deakon. He then recalled the outburst from his elder brother at the amphitheatre.

Deakon went wild the same day the emperor had his heart attack… and Adonys and I both on the day he died…

Is this curse linked to the health of the emperor? Did his dying activate something within us all?

Suddenly screams came from outside and the sky began to change.

Hectyr looked out the gateway, backing up as he saw the people pouring over the edges of their seats and into the Colosseum. *What in the Aspects are they —* Hectyr then saw the weapons in their hands. They were armed. They were running directly for Calypso.

"No! Calypso!" Hectyr shouted out as he gripped the bars of his gate. He could only watch in terror as the enemies neared her, but as they did others fell down in front of her and took up a defensive formation.

I need to get out there, I need to do something!

Hectyr backed up into his room, glancing at the entrance.

Surely the guards will no longer be keeping me here? Not with what is happening outside...

Peering out the door into the tunnels beneath the Colosseum, nobody was to be seen. Not a single guard.

Slithering out into the halls, Hectyr felt chills with the silence inside the Colosseum tunnels compared to the loud rain and people that he could hear moments prior through the gate. The rain bouncing off the Colosseum above was muffled now as he made his way through the complex system beneath it.

He paused at turning points as he stopped to think about the way he came in. It was along with a few guards, and the paths were a lot to try to recollect.

Hectyr frowned as he recalled seeing Aneurin guarding the Citadel as they made their way to the Colosseum.

I was worried with him looking for work in the Citadel... Now I know I was right to be. Hectyr thought about how excited his younger brother was when he told him and felt guilt wash over him as he didn't stop him.

Would he be safe?

Or would the strangely aggressive people make their way towards him?

What if he is already — Hectyr shook his head as he struggled to focus on the winding paths ahead of him. *One step at a time.*

Find Calypso. Then find Aneurin.

He continued through the winding system until finally he found the side entrance and he was out in the city square outside of the Colosseum.

It was beginning to clear as people rushed away through the streets, fleeing for their lives as the strangely dressed figures who had filled the Colosseum now gave chase through the streets. Hectyr stayed within the entrance peering out, he spotted Calypso making her way out of the combat zone and running up towards the Citadel. A few strangely dressed people were chasing after her.

I need to help her! I need to find a weapon...

As Hectyr scanned the fallen for a weapon he noticed a commonality between those who fell and those still being chased. He noticed that those being chased through the streets were dressed quite lavishly, while commonly dressed folk seemed to get away free for the most part — *were they targeting lords and ladies of the empire?*

What was their goal? Why was there an organized attack during the challenge? Did one of the other royal scions make this plan?

Deakon would be the most obvious option, seeing his sudden violent turn in the recent weeks — but Hectyr also had this turn. In fact even Echo didn't seem right during the challenge. Adonys lost it when the emperor died as well...

Is there something more to this?

Hectyr spotted a familiar looking face going towards the Citadel. Waiting until the rest of the combat dispersed Hectyr slithered out after them.

Where have I seen them before?

No matter, I need to get to the Citadel and find Aneurin then help Calypso. I need to make it up to her. And I need to stop the royal scions from fighting one another... If I can find them all.

Hectyr slowly made his way through the streets, jumping at every sound as he looked up at the skies.

The sun was black and as Hectyr watched the red ring drip down to the earth from the skies, he couldn't help but wonder what facet of magic could even create such a thing. Would wild magick do such a thing? Or would it come from a more controlled form of magick?

Is this what brought down the last capital? He had heard the stories of Cressyda, the royal who motivated the empire to create restrictions on magick after having destroyed the original capital, but those were nothing more than stories — and was never recorded in history books. Was there more truth to it than he once thought?

But then, where is this original capital? Surely there would be some remnants of it somewhere, right?

Hectyr felt a pit grow within his gut as he looked to the skies, not even caring that the torrential rains had soaked him he continued carefully to the Citadel.

As he neared the Citadel and the gates came into view, he looked for Aneurin but saw nobody at the gates. Not even a sign of anyone having been there watching the gates.

Hectyr hurried to the gates and as he passed through he saw the familiar stranger yet again. He slowly approached them as he saw them frozen in the entrance of the Citadel but they began to head inside.

"Wait!" Hectyr called out, the man spun around. He had long wavy brown hair, warmer-toned skin, and was far shorter than himself. As Hectyr looked down at him he immediately recalled seeing this person near Ophelya and Calypso. As soon as they saw Hectyr they pulled out an ornate and strange sword. Holding it protectively in front of himself.

"What do *you* want?"

Hectyr slithered over to him with his hands up, stopping a few feet away. "You... You're Calypso's guard... Leandre, right?"

The guard, Leandre, slightly relaxed but still frowned at the royal scion. "Why do you ask? Are you hunting her down?"

"No!" Hectyr denied quickly. "I'm looking for her, I saw her running from... some oddly dressed people towards the Citadel and I lost sight of her."

"Do you really think I'll believe that? There is a curse that has come to fruition, even if you say you don't want to kill her — I can't believe that."

"I won't leave Calypso, not again," Hectyr said as he slowly lowered his hands. "Challenge or not, she is my little sister, I'm supposed to *protect* her."

Leandre raised a brow at him. "Where has this attitude been in the years prior? Hm?"

Hectyr tilted his head. "I... haven't been at the capital as long as the rest of you. Nobody was receptive to a brotherly relationship within the Citadel."

"Well, I believe that should be obvious given the conditions of this family." Leandre snorted. "You seem... fine." He looked him over as he spoke. "Have you been... fighting with any other royal scions?"

Hectyr frowned. *Should I reveal what happened? It will come out sooner or later if we find Calypso... But he may attack if he finds out.*

"When the emperor died... yes I did." Hectyr dipped his head. "I don't know what came over me, but I must make it up to Calypso before anything else happens."

"Make it up to her?" Leandre tensed up, holding the blade back up at Hectyr. "What did you do to her?"

Before either of them could say a word a scream echoed throughout the Citadel. They both turned to look inside. They exchanged glances before they both recognized the voice.

"*Ophelya!*"

26

A RITUAL MOST CRUEL

CALYPSO

As Calypso reached the Citadel her whole body screamed at her. The effects of wild magick surged through her veins making her feel like she was one step away from death. She stopped before the great entrance, putting an arm up on a looming pillar as she leaned over struggling to catch her breath.

No amount of planning could have ever prepared me for this... Is this what I get for simply wanting to live?

She looked up to the skies, the red glow reflecting in her wide eyes. *What even is this?*

Suddenly the loud clanking of armor could be heard coming from behind her, Cal spun around to see three of the *cultists* as Zagora called them running towards her. She held her weapon aggressively and instead of standing firm, she charged.

Two of the cultists stepped back, surprised by her boldness. The third one, however, ducked beneath her strike and sliced at her ankle with their dagger.

As the blade cut through fabric and sliced across skin, Cal winced, but still struck one of the startled cultists down.

As one fell the other two exchanged a glance before attacking at once. Cal dodged beneath one attack and jumped barely over the spear of the other. Landing with a huff, she immediately caught the knife of the bolder enemy with the pole of her spear. The knife slid off it as the enemy jumped away to avoid her attack. Calypso was panting and felt sweat dripping down her brow.

You've already run across the whole city and faced off with a few enemies before.

You don't have too much left in you.

The cultist with the spear struck, knocking Cal to her knees. As the man with the knife jumped forward, Calypso ducked beneath the blow. Resting a palm on the ground as she struggled to maintain a defensive position. They began to strike down upon her, but Cal struck first. Forcing her fist upward and using their force against them as she hit upward into his jaw. He fell to the ground, knocked unconscious.

Only one left. Calypso changed tactics, no longer so aggressive as she dodged beneath the enemy's curved blade and hit them across the face with the butt end of her spear. As they flinched and stumbled back she swept their feet out from under them. They fell onto the ground, and Calypso couldn't help but recall her recent training with Leandre.

Will we ever return to those days?

Cal held her spear to their throat as she stepped on their wrist. With a cry out, they dropped their weapon. Wide eyes fixated upon her.

"Tell me, what is your faction trying to do in Lyreas?"

The cultist laughed anxiously as they looked between the spear tip and Cal. "Why should I tell you? Even if you kill me, I will have died for a just cause." They began laughing hysterically. Calypso looked into their eyes and recognized how bloodshot they were.

Is this... Magick Hysteria? Calypso had learned about the effects of magick on the mind and body if not used properly, but never before did she think she would witness it firsthand.

"When the empress returns, there won't be any more struggle!" they said as they slowly stood, pushing themselves into the spear. "There won't be any lords or ladies, only the empress and magick for all to use freely. We will finally reach to other lands just like she had planned —" Their voice gurgled with their blood until they could no longer speak clear words. They fell back onto the ground but their eyes didn't stop moving to and fro. Calypso stepped back and felt bile rise in her throat.

"Stretch to other lands? Even before Cressyda, the empire was not a conquering —"

Before Calypso could say anything else a scream reverberated within the halls of the Citadel.

Was that —

Calypso didn't face the cultist for another moment, wiping their blood off onto her cloak before running to where she heard the yell come from. It was from the great hall. *I never saw her at the games... Did she find the armor? Did Oboryn do something to her?!*

She cast one last look back at the bodies before running into the Citadel.

I need to get to her before it's too late —

She entered the great hall and the sight before her was almost too much to bear.

Clematis flowers withered around a slab in the center of the room. Riches of all kinds kicked aside and scattered haphazardly as though a drake had stormed through and crashed into it all. A body laid aside the stone slab. Pushed off of its resting place. Already forgotten as the warmth had scarcely left it. *It.* The emperor.

In his place was Ophelya, she was not visibly held down yet as her wide eyes rested upon Calypso and she screeched again it is apparent she was unable to move — left immobile from some other force.

Calypso rushed over to her friend's side. "Ophelya!" She touched her friend's arm as she saw blood smeared across her skin in disgusting yet ornate patterns. It looked like controlled nonverbal magick was being used here.

"What is going on here?! What happened?" Calypso tried to rub the markings away but they didn't budge. *Is there a spell keeping them there?*

"*Get back!*"

Calypso spun around to see a woman standing nearby, a collection of old books in her arms as she entered the great hall. Cal squinted at her for a moment. "Lady Nephus?"

As she came closer, it became visible that she was shaking, her eyes bloodshot and deep bags beneath her eyes. Something about her was twisted as even she couldn't walk straight towards her. She looked weak, she looked mad — yet Calypso had a feeling that the Lady Nephus should not be messed with even in her madness.

Magick Hysteria.

"Stay back!" she hissed as she approached the pair. "The ritual is almost complete and I will not let you further hinder the chances of my daughter!"

Calypso kept her hand on her friend's arm as she stared across at Lady Nephus.

"What do you mean chances? We need to get her out of here!"

Lady Nephus tilted her head. "Oh no! Don't play dumb with me! I know Lord Harkyn wanted to use you, but he isn't here! And I won't allow the next empress to be brought back through a cursed scion!" She dropped her books to the ground and knelt beside them as she flipped through them. "My little girl will have the chance to go down in history! She will bring back the age of magick by giving herself to the true empress of Vasyla!"

Lady Nephus dipped her fingers in a scar on her palm as she began drawing on a marble statue. It was not a statue that was there before, nor was it of a figure Calypso could recognize.

"Her body will be ready for a new soul, and what greater honor is there than to be the host of Cressyda?! The greatest magick user of the millennia!"

As Calypso saw the markings left on the statue for the ritual, she felt a cold chill creep down her spine. Those markings were not new to her.

Those markings... I've seen them inside the armor but weren't there two?

If the armor laid host to a soul... or perhaps more... and now Lady Nephus wished for Ophelya's body to be ready for a new soul...

Does she mean to remove Ophelya's soul from her own body?!

Ophelya's own mother was trying to force her soul out of her body and into an object. A magick forbidden even during the ages of magick being widespread and well-accepted.

As Lady Nephus finished her markings on the statue she turned her gaze to Ophelya.

"Step aside, scion," she said without even glancing at Cal. "You have taken enough of my daughter's time. It is her turn to stand in the light, and yours to step into the darkness."

Calypso held her spear towards Ophelya's mother as she neared. Blood was still caked on the tip of it.

"I will not let you any closer to her. I have only one thing left to me in this world and I will not let you take *any* of my allies away from me."

"Calypso!" A shout came from the entrance of the great hall. They all turn to see two figures, one tall and one short. It was Hectyr and Leandre.

"Calypso I —" Leandre stopped short as he saw Ophelya on the table behind Calypso. "Ophelya!"

Before Leandre even reached the table Hectyr beat him to it. He looked down at Ophelya with a conflicted expression. He turned up to Calypso.

"Who did this?" He asked, his voice had a darker tone to it. Contrary to his usual awkward or cheery voice. He looked to Lady Nephus, who stood a few feet away from them. He stared at her in disbelief.

"There's no way... No true mother could do such a thing." Hectyr's eyes darkened as he looked at her.

Lady Nephus laughed out loud at the sight of the three of them over her daughter stuck on the funeral slab. Her laugh grew weak quickly though and she began hacking.

"My, my, so she really did manage to catch a royal or two after all. Not the best choices from the bunch but still — I am impressed." She took a step forward. "But that plan was only a backup. One which is no longer necessary now that she will be the host of Cressyda."

"NO!" Cal shouted. "Ophelya's soul belongs in her body — and nobody else can take that place."

"And who are you to tell me what her body is and isn't worth?" Lady Nephus challenged.

Calypso didn't wait another moment, she removed her hand from Ophelya's arm to wield her spear and held it out towards her mother. She gripped the weapon so tight you could see the veins in her arms. Hectyr and Leandre pulled out weapons as well.

"Take another step forward and I will not hesitate to attack."

Lady Nephus laughed at this, before muttering under her breath and holding her bleeding palm out to the air.

"I've heard much about what you are capable of through training, youngest scion," she said slowly. "But have you faced wild magicks? Or controlled magicks besides water magicks, for that matter?"

The blood began rising from her palm, being pulled out by a force unseen and turning into an array of tiny splintering blades that surrounded her.

"Blood magick," Leandre whispered fearfully as he watched.

Calypso's stance slightly faltered as she saw the blades pointed at her.

If she sends those flying — they'll hit everyone — Ophelya included!

Calypso quickly spotted the vases nearby. *They must be filled with water from washing the emperor's body!*

That should be enough!

Calypso felt exhaustion already sweeping over her like a wave, but she had no other choice. Focusing her energy, she moved her arms in a flowing motion. Picturing the flow of the water. She forced the water from the pots as Lady Nephus sent the bloody blades flying. The wave met from all sides of the room in the center, barely catching the weapons and slowing them. A few still flew through and caught Calypso on the shoulder and torso — but nothing hit anyone else. The cuts burned at the tiny blood daggers that remained embedded in her skin, like tiny flames dancing on her. She grimaced in pain.

"Cal!" Leandre gasped at the magick before him. "You can still —"

"Yes, I can *still* use magick!" she replied quickly. Now wasn't the time to explain she had been practicing — nor was she sure she could even discuss it with him after seeing him leave with Lord Harkyn.

As Calypso stepped forward to attack, Leandre quickly joined her. She froze for a second — ready to tell him to let her deal with it, but she stopped herself.

No.

I can't keep doing this alone.

I may not want him to get hurt but... If I fall alone then I can't protect any of them.

She didn't stop him as the two faced off against the crazed Lady Nephus.

It felt like training as the two of them charged at Ophelya's mother. Leandre's strikes aimed low to move her back while Calypso struck high. Lady Nephus was more than ready though, using her blood to create horrifyingly sturdy shields that blocked each blow. The terrain was difficult to fight on as well, with riches sprawled across the great hall haphazardly. Cal almost tripped, and Lady Nephus took this chance to move forward and get between them and Ophelya. Moving quick and precisely, she stepped back with each attack she blocked. Lady Nephus loudly groaned in pain as she pulled a large blade out of her hand — made with her blood and magick. Leandre avoided a strike to the head as she swung her blade at him, and began to strike him again. This time knocking him down with horrifying strength even in her weakened state.

So this *is why magick was outlawed...*

As Calypso stepped forward ready to block the full brunt of the attack, Leandre dodged around her and deflected the attack with his blade — startling Lady Nephus. He stepped aside and struck her from the side as Cal tag-teamed and swept the spear at her feet. Lady Nephus lost balance and fell onto the ground. She loudly screeched enchantments and spells and with a forced wave Calypso and Leandre were forced back. Thrown away from where Ophelya laid. All that remained between Lady Nephus and her daughter was Hectyr.

She should be slowing down! The human body only has so much blood that can be spared... So how is she still fighting?!

Hectyr rushed between the two of them, holding nothing more than a heavy ornate statue. He ducked beneath the shards of blood sent flying at him and struck at Lady Nephus — hitting her leg as he did. Calypso's eyes widened as he struck, surprised by his ability to fight — not the best but not the worst either. His strike left a large purple mark on her leg. Her body was bruising very easily now.

Hectyr began to strike again, but Lady Nephus was quicker, snarling like an animal she struck out with her blade and her bare hands. Cutting his face with her knife and with her nails catching his ear. Hectyr fell back onto the ground, revealing the many serpents that made up his legs. They all rear back and hissed at her. Lady Nephus reeled back, horrified.

"An Ophiophor?!" she shouted after a moment, she backed away from him — getting closer to Ophelya. Even Leandre's eyes were wide at the sight, jaw dropped open as he watched Hectyr slither back to his feet and back out of her range. All three of them were bruised, cut, and worn down. Lady Nephus looked the worst of all, yet she still stood firm.

Lady Nephus stopped close to Ophelya, her back to her as she faced the three of them. Cal looked at her friend stuck on the table. Was she moving...?

27

THE CURSES OF BLOOD

OPHELYA

It was a tingling sensation, having your body controlled to stay still. Tingling from head to toe. It had felt like hours and hours had passed in mere seconds of waiting — and Ophelya was no stranger to waiting patiently. Unmoving. Quiet. Not quite dead, but hardly alive either as she stayed in the shadows. The perfect daughter. Better than the first. The first who deserved a much better fate. She had much time to think about the matter, with the dead eyes of the emperor seemingly staring through her from the floor he was pushed to. Pale, unmoving, and dead. *Maeve deserved better.*

All this time I thought it was an accident... How did I never know?

Why didn't she include me in more? Then again... How much have I included others in my own business?

Even Calypso and Leandre?

Slowly Ophelya could feel her fingertips and muscles in her wrists as she watched the others fighting her mother. Only able to see them out of the corner of her eyes, she flexed her hands as she struggled to move. She couldn't even cry as she thought about her sister dying to the woman who fought her allies.

Maeve.

Maeve.

Maeve.

Ophelya felt her feet and then her legs slowly came to life like they had fallen asleep. It felt like static electricity left her skin tingling as she felt her muscles again. She began to shift to grab her blade on her hip.

She tilted her head as she finally felt in control of her body again. Her mother stopped next to the stone slab — she was panting and out of breath — most likely her magick wore off as she was worn down by Calypso and Leandre. It wasn't just her hands that shook, her whole body was trembling. She had a mad look in her dulling eyes. Ophelya took a deep breath as she watched her mother back up, she was cornered and snarled like an animal at them as they approached her. Ophelya looked up at her mother, feeling a deep unfulfilling grief hit her soul.

Maeve.

You never had to care for me — we weren't even fully related. I'm sure my birth turned your world upside down, yet you never let that get in the way. You never showed a grain of resentment towards me. Even when you stepped up and raised me more than my mother did.

Ophelya lunged up and grabbed Lady Nephus — holding the cold metal of the curved blade up against her throat before she could cast another spell. Leandre and Hectyr watched with wide eyes, but Calypso's expression was resigned — as if she knew it might come to this.

"Ophelya — What are you doing?!" her mother shouted. "I've almost done it! I've almost made everything perfect! You will go down in history, so why do you disobey me?"

"I will no longer play a puppet, or shadow as you want," Ophelya hissed into her mother's ear.

Lady Nephus flinched as the blade pressed against her skin, the claw-like blade pricked her skin with its pointed tip.

"You're *my* daughter. You cannot even think of doing this." Her voice cracked at the end, as though even she wasn't sure of what she was saying.

Maeve.

I'm sorry.

"We may share blood, but you were never my mother. You killed her long ago for your gain."

Without another thought, Ophelya clenched her teeth as she pulled the blade away from her mother's throat. Lady Nephus spun around, raising her blade. As she spun around to face her, Ophelya slashed the karambit directly across the lady's chest. The hook caught skin and cut deep. Ophelya let go and stepped back, leaving the blade embedded in her chest.

She didn't deserve to be stabbed through the back — At least not to Ophelya.

Yet either way with such a blade she had no chance of survival.

"Goodbye, Lady Nephus," her voice cracked as she pulled out the blade.

It didn't take much for her to fall as her body was already weakened, but Ophelya didn't look at her face. Nothing could be more haunting than to see your face older, twisted — and dying.

A moment after she fell, when the room fell silent and her breathing stopped — the markings began to fade from Ophelya's arms.

"Ophelya!"

She slowly looked up from where the markings once were. Calypso, Leandre, and Hectyr hurried to her side. All three of them were bruised, cut, and overall worn down from fighting.

Calypso pulled her into a hug and held on tight, "By the Aspects, I was so worried!" she sobbed.

Ophelya laughed. She felt hollow as she hugged her back. "I believe we all are right now." She pulled away after a moment and looked at Leandre and Hectyr. "Wait... How are you here?" she asked Hectyr.

"What do you mean?" he asked. Ophelya glanced at Cal.

"How are you not...?"

"Attacking Calypso?"

Ophelya frowned. "Then you already know of it? The curse, it is true then?"

Leandre was the one who nodded. "It is. Lord Harkyn revealed that while I was..."

"While you were traveling with him?" Cal said accusingly. Ophelya frowned at her. *What had happened?* Calypso crossed her arms and angled away from Leandre. Ophelya looked at him, he was nowhere near as closed off as she was. In fact, he looked at her with... guilt? He continued to cast glances her way before looking at their surroundings.

"I'll admit, I went with him at first for the wrong reasons," Leandre said after a moment. "But I managed to stop him by going with him."

"Stop him from what exactly?"

"If he were here, he was going to..." Leandre glanced at Cal. "Well, he was going to use Calypso to bring back Cressyda."

"Like how my mother wanted to use me... But why?" She noticed Hectyr struggling to keep his eyes fixated on anything as they all spoke. "Hectyr, you are struggling with the curse, aren't you?"

After a moment his eyes met hers, though it took a few more seconds for him to process the question. "Yes... But I am able to control it better now... I think."

Ophelya frowned and looked at Calypso. "What about you? Are you experiencing any... want for violence?"

"Beyond the one I just went through? Not really," Calypso said, not quite meeting her eyes. "But that's beside the point right now, what did Harkyn want? What was his goal?"

Ophelya frowned at Cal, but said nothing more as Leandre began to speak.

"I think he wants to become the emperor to Cressyda as the empress," he said carefully after a moment. "Harkyn was looking for something, a suit of armor containing her somehow."

Ophelya glanced at Calypso, her gaze was suddenly on the floor. "Cal?" she asked, stepping closer to her friend. "You know something don't you?"

"It's the armor... isn't it?" Hectyr said to Cal. She nodded slowly after a moment.

"They said their name was Oboryn... but I believe it is Cressyda."

"Armor? How do you know it —"

"I was the knight going out into the capital, seen in strange ancient armor. I was almost stopped by knights believing I stole it from a museum." She laughed.

Leandre furrowed his brows. "*They*?"

"Yes, they. I... I think there are multiple souls within the armor — though I don't know how many..." She looked down at Lady Nephus's corpse on the ground. "And if my guess is right, seeing how her magick stopped once she died, then perhaps... Perhaps the blood curse is tied to Cressyda's life as well."

Ophelya felt her stomach turn as she thought about her mot — the body lying on the ground. Hectyr glanced at her and frowned.

"We need to get Ophelya somewhere safe to rest — I can only imagine the toll that magick took on her."

Calypso and Leandre nodded, and just as they did, a loud crash echoed throughout the halls.

"What was that?"

Leandre pulled out his sword. "I can investigate."

"Alone?!" Calypso grabbed his shoulder as he started to walk away. "Surely you are aware of what we're facing by now right?"

"Look at you and Ophelya! You both look like you have one foot in the grave."

The pair continued to bicker back and forth while Ophelya leaned against Hectyr for support as she felt herself weakening with every moment.

What is there even for us to do?

Ophelya felt a pit of despair open up before her, and she was teetering at the edge.

Cultists, curses, and death.

Oh, death.

Of all the poems I used to write about death, none of them ever came close to this.

The smell of the blood and bodies in the room made her want to retch. Even the blood on her own body made her sick.

"Why split up at all?" Ophelya said after a moment, looking away from the body on the ground. "The capital is overrun with cultists, there is an ancient spirit haunting the Citadel, and we were almost all killed by my mother." Ophelya let out a choked sob. "First Maeve, now mother — Aspects know if father is even alive. I can't lose anyone else today — no matter the circumstances."

Cal slowly stepped forward and took Ophelya's hand with her own.

"I have to see this through, I let them out Ophelya, I need to stop them."

"Is this to prove yourself to the people? Why does that even matter Cal? Is our good opinion of you not enough?"

Cal lowered her gaze. "It's not about that anymore — no matter what I do... the people of Vasyla will still find a way to blame me." She met Ophelya's gaze. "This is about doing what is right, and protecting you and Leandre." She glanced up at Hectyr. "Even you, *brother*, though I never thought there would come a day when I could call anyone that." Hectyr smiled solemnly.

Leandre stepped forward. "I'm going with Cal, because I owe it to her."

She turned and furrowed her brows at him. "How do you owe me anything? I owe you my life from the number of times you've stopped those who'd want to kill me."

Leandre looked down for a moment, flexing his hands.

"Either way, I am here to keep you and Ophelya safe."

"And I may not be as strong as either of you," Hectyr said, motioning to Cal and Leandre. "But I am here to do my part as well. As I should have done for Calypso as her brother." He trailed off like he was going to say more but stopped.

Ophelya glanced up at him. *What would things have been like if he had joined our little company earlier?*

Could we have all been allies? Friends?

Would Calypso have felt better knowing someone else didn't want to compete?

Would we still be where we are today?

Is there even a future in which we can all survive together?

Ophelya pulled Cal into a hug, motioning at Leandre for him to join. Hectyr also joined the hug, and for a moment, Ophelya felt safe.

"I'll get Ophelya somewhere safe, it's... probably for the best that I stay away from Cal right now," Hectyr said after a moment as they pulled away.

His hands are shaking.

"And you two can go investigate if you really must." Calypso and Leandre exchanged a glance and nodded.

"Please don't try anything too rash," Ophelya said as the pair turned to go out into the halls of the Citadel. She watched as they went off until they disappeared around the corner.

"Are you going to be alright, Ophelya?" Hectyr asked as they began to walk towards the servant door.

"How can I be," she said, struggling to keep upright. "That could have been the last time I see them alive."

28
OF TWO SOULS

When times change those around you change as well – there would be nothing more disconcerting than suddenly returning to old habits. Old events. What once was normal now turned upside down. This was why it felt odd, to be free of the curse and walking next to Calypso again. For Leandre, he felt more... free. More energetic. Like he did when he was young and first came to the Citadel. Yet there was still an underlying exhaustion. As the two walked down the halls he felt a throbbing ache throughout his body after the fight with Lady Nephus. He looked over at Calypso. Dark bags were under her eyes, sweat glistened on her fair skin, and her movement was slightly sluggish. Yet she still had a look of hope in her eyes. Leandre smiled at this and took in a deep breath.

"Calypso, there is something I need to tell you and something I need to apologize for."

As the pair walked through the large ominous halls, the smell of death filled the air. Though no people alive nor dead were anywhere to be seen — the smell of blood and rotting sweetly filled the air with its sickening scent.

"Is now the time?" she asked, her voice quivering. She was quite obviously still mad at him.

Leandre sighed. "I'm assuming you know I went with Lord Harkyn."

She didn't respond, barely glancing at him out of the corner of her eye. Leandre frowned.

"Calypso, I will admit — at first I went with him... for selfish reasons. I saw it as a way to make my own choice and forge my path — in the recent weeks, I've felt... differently towards you. Ill intent toward someone I — care for. I learned why that was by going with him."

Leandre felt his face flush at his inability to say what he wanted.

Calypso stopped, she looked up at him for the first time.

"And why is that?"

"A curse."

Cal narrowed her eyes at him.

Now is better than never. He took in a deep breath.

"Do you remember... how I came to the Citadel?"

She paused for a moment, before shaking her head.

"It was Lord Harkyn's doing. I did not come here by choice, I may have been chosen by you once I was brought before you — but

I was brought to the capital by Harkyn to either kill you or keep you alive for Cressyda ... I don't know which was his plan, but I know a curse was placed upon me to nurture ill-intent towards you." Leandre pulled out his sword. "I also found this."

Calypso's eyes went wide at the sight of the blade. "Where did you —"

"Lord Harkyn took us... Well, Kyril and my... the magick user who cursed me, to the location of the last capital. It was rubble all within a ravine with an excavation built into it and —"

"Leandre, that blade matches the armor containing the souls... Containing Cressyda."

He stopped and looked down at the blade. "Could this contain a soul as well?"

Cal extended a hand towards him and he handed her the blade without hesitation. Calypso started to look at it but stopped.

"Leandre... I need to apologize as well." She looked up at him.

"All this time I focused on clearing my name to the people *and* keeping you two safe... when I should have been focusing on those who believed in me and not the prophecy. I'm sorry I made you feel like you had no choices, and I'm sorry you had to deal with defending me over the years."

He shook his head quickly. "No, never apologize for me defending you. I never would regret that. Even if I could change my life, I wouldn't. Because it wouldn't be the same without you in it." He sighed. "I can't keep wondering what might have been and what was wrong with my past... even as I remember it now. I can only look to the future, and no matter what goes down today... You should do the same. If I can though, I want to remain at your side."

Cal continued to look at him for a moment, eyes tearing up but instead, she turned to the blade and searched for the markings.

She froze as she looked along the blade.

"Did you read the blade? The engravings?"

Leandre looked at the blade and then shook his head. "I didn't notice it until now."

Cal looked up at him with an astonished look. "Leandre this is —" Calypso stopped speaking as she gagged from the smell. She quickly handed him the blade as a screech was cut off nearby and the air grew thick with the fresh scent of blood.

As they neared the archives, the scent of death grew far more pungent than anywhere else.

"What in the Aspects was that?" Leandre said quietly as he stepped forward towards the library entrance where the sound came from.

As Calypso peered inside behind him, he heard a voice echo within the room.

"Yes indeed. The magicks have been pushed back before. They always come back. And in Vesyla, magick has long since been suppressed and hidden away, waiting until someone brought them back to the light..."

They stared at the armor, horrified. How long had they been in here? Out in the open where everyone could see them. Holding a history book in their hands, the armor's bone-chilling voice filled the room as they read aloud. Books were scattered all over the room, and blood splatters covered many of them — yet no bodies were to be seen.

"*With the strength of the Aspects, **we** were undefeatable. The royal scions of old times. Using almost every kind of magick available the empire almost crumbled when the royal lineage was almost wiped out. Because of this, each type of magick eventually became forbidden, and a new tradition was born, one to curb the violent tendencies of the royals and one to keep those keen on the crown from destroying the empire over it. Thus began the Royal Challenge of Cressyda. A natural order, so that only one could hold the power needed to rule this ancient empire, and keep its flame from ever dying. The royal scions would be forced to battle one another until only one remained. But it has been generations since this tradition was born.*" The armored ghost cackled as they tossed the book aside. "Even now, as magick returns, the royal scions continue to struggle unto eternity. Nothing has changed, not in any real way for that matter."

Oboryn turned in their direction and cackled, yet the voice that spoke was not within the armor.

"Do you think I don't know you're here?" They began to walk in their direction. "What is it I should call you now that you know? I believe just Great Niece will have to do, or we would miss the window of opportunity sitting here just saying greats until we've reached the correct amount."

Another stepped out from behind the armor, a person. Human.

Yet... they looked almost dead. Their skin was sickly pale, gray eyes hazy, and skin that looked dry. A fresh marking was carved into their arm. Their blonde hair was half cut short, half left long, and a wide cut spread across their chest ripping into their clothing as a blade had cut across them but left them living. A living corpse. They pulled a blade out of their chest. A fresh mark was visible upon their arm.

"Which one of you is Oboryn?" Calypso asked suddenly.

Leandre furrowed his brows at her.

"What are you —"

"It is still me," the armor responded with its silvery voice. "But I am surprised you are clever enough to ask such a question. What a turn of events for the foolish scion."

The stranger smiled as they stood with one arm tucked into the other and a hand laying daintily against their chin.

Calypso pulled out her spear as she looked at the stranger.

"Then... You're..."

"*Cressyda?*" The stranger spoke — yet their voice wasn't quite something that should suit it. Similar, yet twisted. Like a completed statue suddenly being carved into something else, something new — something *wrong*. The voice was still oddly metallic and was neither feminine nor masculine. A husk of what voice it used to be. "If I've learned one thing since you woke me, it is of the tarnished name of Cressyda."

The way they are speaking... they talk as if it isn't Cressyda. Leandre narrowed his eyes at them. *Is this not who Lord Harkyn was searching for? He was searching for armor. H was searching for Cressyda's armor. But this... This is someone else.*

Cal took a step back.

Leandre stepped beside Calypso, resting his hand on his sword still sheathed. The armor turned towards him.

"Ah, and you're the guard of *this* scion? How ironic this situation is."

"How so?" Leandre challenged as he looked into the eyes of the helmet. Only, there were no eyes where they should have been. He grit his teeth as he felt fear wash over him like a wave.

"Because I too once protected one under the White Tern... and we stopped them from fulfilling the prophecy as well."

"What do you mean? Cressyda wasn't —" Cal looked at Leandre. "Wait... Was the prophecy about... Cressyda? Not me?"

The stranger laughed. "Of course, it was — though it is... fun to know how long my people have gone on believing it true of every *other* royal born under the star. It seems none have even been able to live even a fraction of the time you have."

Calypso's hands began shaking. Struggling to process what they were suggesting. Leandre noticed this as he glanced back at her. He looked at the stranger.

"You speak as though you aren't Cressyda, state your name," he demanded.

The stranger raised a brow at them, dull eyes gaining color back slowly. As though the body had gone through a reversed death. "Now where is the fun in that?"

The armor stepped forward first, wielding a spear it pointed towards them. Calypso and Leandre both pulled out their weapons. Calypso a spear, and Leandre a xiphos sword.

A look is all they shared before the three leapt into combat. The clang of metal rang throughout the room as metal struck metal. Leandre slid down and stuck the shin plates of Oboryn. Calypso blocked a blow from his spear, deflecting it and making it strike the ground. The armor's sabaton, or shoe piece fell away. Yet it stood still, as though balancing on an invisible foot.

"We need to break it apart!" Calypso shouted, she grabbed the sabaton and chucked it across the room before rolling away from its next strike.

Leandre leapt up and blocked its blow with his blade. It knocked him back with ease.

Calypso kept striking, aggressive — but not with strength. Desperation fueled every hit as she continued to knock the armor apart. Piece by piece.

I need to destroy this thing! I let it out, I need to be the one to destroy it! Cal's mind grew fuzzy, only focused on one thing. To destroy Oboryn. What once may have been her hope — which may very well be her doom.

The armor hardly struck or reacted as the pair continued to fight it. Only once its leg was entirely gone and pieces of its gauntlet and shoulder were gone did it finally lose patience. Dropping its weapon, the knight swung at Calypso with its bare gauntlet that remained, striking her in the jaw. She flew across the room, knocking into a shelf. She didn't move for a moment. Leandre turned to her.

"Calypso!"

In his distraction, the armor swung — knocking his sword out of his hand and making Leandre lose balance. He fell onto the ground.

"Stop!" The corpse spoke. Placing a hand on the armor's shoulder as they stepped around them. "That blade..."

Calypso slowly struggled to sit up, unable to get to her feet as she watched the pair stand over Leandre.

"Cressyda —"

"Do not call me by that name again, guard." The corpse spoke sternly yet simply. As though stating a fact. Leandre grabbed his blade and weakly held it up in defense.

"Then who are you?!"

The armor and corpse look down at him in silence. As though both reliving something in their minds.

Leandre pointed the blade at the stranger. "Answer!"

The corpse narrowed their eyes at the blade. "Now isn't this fascinating? Your search for Cressyda, yet you hold the last bit of her being in your very hands."

Leandre and Calypso looked at the blade in shock, making the stranger laugh. The armor stood ominously behind them.

"It seems blood doesn't pool very far from the corpse after all — just as those with shared blood will always be stuck together." They began laughing wildly before shouting out an incantation. Leandre was forced away by a forceful gust. Crashing against the pillar across the hall. Calypso cried out from inside the library as Leandre flew out of her sight. She struggled to her feet, and grabbed her spear.

The knight knocked the sword from Leandre's hand. The blade landed a few feet away from him and a small wail echoed throughout the halls.

The corpse leaned down and began to grab the blade — but the xiphos began glowing. A burst of firelight came from the blade, the corpse screamed and threw the sword as flames erupted up their arm.

The armor quickly took a defensive position beside them as they put out the flame. Singing licks were left in curved patterns on their skin.

They turn to the blade anger deep within their eyes. Eyes which now seemed fully alive. The knight stepped towards the blade, crushing it beneath his foot. The blade shattered from a precise blow — yet the hilt still faintly glowed. Leandre could still hear a faint wailing.

"I will not be overshadowed by another royal ever again! Especially not the final born of a wretch!" The corpse shouted as Calypso stepped through the doorway of the library. "You and all the rest of the world seem to have it all wrong — It wasn't Cressyda that almost destroyed the empire in the past and it isn't Cressyda who stands before you today."

The stranger began to step away from them, but stopped, glancing back at Cal.

"I helped you a great deal when I was in the armor... royal scion. Perhaps now you can return the favor — after all, you fit the bill for the prophecy, and if there is one thing I've learned across time it's that fate can be misconstrued by the masses."

They stepped towards Cal and grabbed her by the hair, forcing her to her feet. She quickly forced her weight against him, pushing him to the ground. They looked up at her with anger in their eyes.

"It seems you need your armor again." They began laughing slowly. She raised her hand to punch him and struck. The armor caught it.

Leandre struggled to his feet and reached for the blade as the armor stopped Calypso from fighting back. Shoving her back to the ground.

"You're weakening already," the stranger said, laughing loudly now. Voice cracking between every word. "I will get you to come with me, whether you like it or not."

They grabbed her arm while she was on the ground and began dragging her. Cal struggled against him but was already weakened from fighting Lady Nephus.

"No! Get back here your monster!" Leandre shouted out as he picked up what remained of the blade and got to his feet. As Leandre began to make his chase after them, the armor stepped in his way.

"Watch your tone, dog." The armor stepped towards him, looming over him. "You are speaking to Cronys — the rightful heir to the throne and Emperor of Vasyla."

Cronys. The brother of Cressyda.

29
BLOOD TIES
AVALON

Avalon never felt unsure of herself or the world through the Aspects. Nothing shook her faith — nothing made her fear. Injustices? These were merely challenges for piety in the royal scion's eyes. There could be no corruption in religion. To Avalon, the world was as it should be. The challenge would come and go. Avalon and Adonys would survive not separately but together. Twin rulers. There was almost no end to her delusions. Yet her world began to shake and spin around her.

It began with Maeve. She questioned those in the religion. Saying that the church was being infiltrated as well as the court. These warnings fell on deaf ears as Avalon did everything to prove her wrong. The world settled for a while with Maeve's death. Then it happened again with Ophelya. The world never stopped spinning. Even when Avalon opened her eyes and slowly made her way to her feet.

Where... Where am I?

She tried to recall her steps. She was with Lady Ophelya... The sister of Lady Maeve... They made their way back to the capital and then.

The emperor is dead.

Our father, Oryon, is no more.

Then the curse... Has it already passed? Or is it underway?

Avalon looked around. She was at the citadel entrance. On the ground with her back against a pillar. She slowly got to her feet and her head began to throb — she put her hand on it and grimaced. When she pulled it away she saw dried bits of red flakes upon her fingertips.

Was I attacked?

The skies above swirled with crimson red as a large black hole loomed from where the sun should have been. Trails of red bled down to the earth like water poured from a vase. It was as though the Aspects themselves were bleeding out into Vasyla. It was unholy. Unnatural. *Wrong.*

"This is Calypso's doing. This is her curse." Avalon whispered to herself as she looked up at the sky. "She is the imbalance left... if she were to go..."

The world would be whole again.

Avalon stood and began to make her way inside the Citadel. She needed to make a plan. Yet as she entered the great halls all that hit her was the wretchedly familiar scent of sickness and death. A smell all too familiar to the royal scion from the days she had spent healing the sick with the church.

The sight was twisted. A funeral slab devoid of a body. Riches smashed and thrown about. A body — no, two bodies were strewn about the room. She squinted at one, desperately wanting to look at anything else. But wait... Was that the emperor?

Avalon began to run over to it. She tripped and fell onto hard gold and marble statues. Sharp bits pulled and tugged and her clothing as she fell. Avalon struggled to find places for her hands as she could hardly pull herself up Curling her lip in anger she spun around onto her knees to see what had made her fall.

"L...Lady Nephus?"

A face much like Ophelya's laid on the ground in a twisted position nearby. Was that what tripped her? The woman looked as though she had been crawling to the entrance... Who could have done this?

"Court members being killed, the emperor's body discarded like trash, the sky changing... Is this really the prophecy coming to?"

When Vasyla has over a thousand moons in its skies,
When the star of the white tern brings us a royal scion,
When the night outlasts the day, Vasyla will crumble
once more...

Avalon clenched a fist as a sound came from the entrance to the Citadel. A sudden feeling washed over her. Like a wave from the seas.

It was hard for her to describe, as it wasn't a thing she contemplated often. Anger. A violent delight as she felt herself wishing for combat all of a sudden.

This feeling... Calypso must be near. Why else would I feel the will of the Aspects through me now?

What else could this be?

Avalon knelt in the middle of the riches and the bodies and turned to look through the entrance back to the darkened skies. She slowly stood, eyes glazed over as she grabbed the a blunt object to use as a weapon. Slowly, she made her way to the Citadel entrance. A figure was coming through the gate.

"You've done enough here, *royal scion*." She said slowly. Words dripped from her mouth like poison. Slow, and concentrated.

"You took the words right out of my mouth." A deep voice echoed back. Avalon furrowed her brows as they stepped into the firelight of the great hall.

It was Adonys, yet Avalon's anger was unchanging. She felt horror as she looked upon her brother — the only brother she could truly claim as they shared all of their blood — and felt rage.

"What in the Aspect's... No! This can't be your will!" Avalon thought she spoke aloud, yet no words came from her lips as she watched her brother come towards her.

Just then, she remembered.

The curse.

They weren't lying.

Avalon clenched her jaw.

No! The Aspects could never allow such a thing! Never!

She struggled to focus on the figure before her. The world around her was spinning. It was shaking. Faster. Faster. Faster. Her hands shook along with it. Her head snapped to the side as chills ran up her neck.

"The challenge has begun sister." He said, his voice hoarse as though he was struggling to speak. "It's time to see which of us the Aspect's favor."

Avalon clutched a statue in her hands as he came closer. Unmoving. Still. Like the statue she held. The statue was once intended for a soul. Adonys continued to approach.

No! Run away! Go!

Can't you see I am not myself?!

Adonys stopped in front of her. She could see his eyes were bloodshot but he was still there. The veins on his arms stood out as he gripped his spear, yet he still showed some semblance of control. He was the younger, after all.

"Avalon?"

With one swift movement, the statue is raised and struck down.

The carvings of the Aspects watched on from the walls. The rain began to pour down even harder outside. Not from the magick that filled the air. But as they wept for their people.

For fate can be the cruelest of ironies.

30
THE WANT TO REMAIN
OPHELYA

It is in the nature of those grieving to wonder what if. To wonder if they could have done something different, to wonder if they could have avoided fate. Is fate something we control? Or is it predetermined by a power greater than ourselves? As Ophelya and Hectyr made their way to presumed safety — a similar train of thought filled both of their little minds. *What if I did something differently?*

What if I recognized sooner, could I have saved Maeve?

What if I had been there for Cal?

What if I hadn't let the curse get the better of me?

What if.

What if.

What if.

An endless cycle if ever there was one.

Ophelya leaned against Hectyr for support as he led the way out. Going from the main building in the Citadel and out the side entrance used primarily by servants running errands. Their goal was to find the safest passage out. It took a long time for Ophelya to even get enough energy to move, and when she finally could she was slow.

It was barren and dark, the only light looming overhead was from the blazing ring around the dark circle that once was the sun. The air felt thick with magick — a tingling sensation that provided a similar energy as the sun itself. It was felt even in the little raindrops that fell from the sky — as magick was a natural phenomenon... but this was different. Stronger. It almost would have been a nice feeling, like warm fleece on a cold winter night — if it weren't for the dark oddities that spilled forth from the heavens, that is. The saltwater smell hung heavy in the air.

"Where is everyone? Where are the servants? The guards?" Hectyr had a troubled expression on his face. "Where is Aneurin?"

"I... I'm not sure. There should have been... some sign of a fight at least." Ophelya paused to take a breath between words. The world was wobbly around her as she felt as though the energy had been sapped from her limb from limb.

There should even be sightings of cultists who got rid of the servants... right?

"Hectyr... you came from the Colosseum, right?" He nodded after a moment.

"Why did you come to the Citadel?"

Hectyr kept glancing ahead. "We were flushed out by cultists — I went after Calypso when I saw her."

The cultists have flooded the city?

A scream echoed throughout the courtyard of the Citadel. It was a primal grieving screech so shrill it made souls shiver within the body. Ophelya felt the hairs on her body stand straight.

"Avalon?" Ophelya and Hectyr look at each other horrified. She put her hands over her mouth as she realized.

She was looking for someone. Adonys.

She had found her brother.

The cries continued, and as the pair made their way around the courtyard they saw it. Avalon kneeling on the ground, clutching a body tightly. White hair stained red with blood — but not a bright red of a light strike. It was a deep maroon signaling a powerful and deep blow. Her eyes were wildly desperate as she clutched onto his head. Unblinking though tears spilled forth heavier than the rain from above. The blunt weapon which had done the job was thrown a few feet away from them. The statue was saturated in blood. Ophelya looked away.

"By the Aspects..."

"Hectyr?" She looked up at him. As he looked at his half-siblings there was no anger or rage in his eyes. Only a deep sadness for Avalon as she continued to wail. Did the curse lose it's affect on him now?

"Ophelya! Hectyr!" Avalon spotted them. Her teeth bared as she cried out. "It's Adonys! I — He—"

Before she could make out a complete thought, voices could be heard nearby. Coming through the gates were scraggly groups of upper-class lords and ladies with tattered robes clutching to broken jewels and riches. Chasing after them were more cultists dressed in feathered robes.

Ophelya clutched her blade with shaky hands as the two stood in plain sight. Hectyr only had a short sword with him.

Hectyr stepped in front of Ophelya. "Quickly, get to the servants' entrance and hide!"

She shook her head. "I can't move!"

Avalon hovered over the body of her brother, barring her teeth and cowering like a cornered animal. Yet none of the cultists went for her. She was already broken.

A few cultists continued to chase the rich into the Citadel.

Not all did.

Spotting Hectyr and Ophelya four stopped and turned their attention on them. After all, a royal and a court member's daughter? Excellent targets for those who despise the power which overthrew Cressyda and outlawed magick.

Hectyr held out his sword defensively as they all began to encircle the duo. Three held weapons and one seemingly prepared themselves to use magick. Hectyr held his arm out to protect Ophelya who stood back to back with him.

A spell began to gather above the combat, but it wasn't from the cultist who still struggled with their own magick.

Hectyr looked up. The rain was being gathered to a point, and as it did — a strange figure stepped out of the Citadel and under the safety of the spell. Keeping dry. Dragging Calypso with them.

Calypso!

Hectyr looked up at the rainwater collecting to a controlled area.

It's... similar to the spell over the arena. He felt chills up his spine. *But this is different... stronger.*

"It's Cressyda!"

"It must be her!"

"Lord Harkyn's mission was a success!" another yelled.

The stranger at the Citadel entrance curled their nose in disgust at the cultist's delight.

"I am sick and tired of being mistaken for that savage!"

Hectyr looked at the spell above the stranger — it was quivering and rippling with the caster's anger.

"Ophelya, run!"

As she tried to move her legs she realized she couldn't. There was no spell. She froze up. Looking at the collection above her, she felt her heart drop.

Is this really it? Bested by the waters?

She couldn't help but laugh.

I should have let the sirens take me.

"Ophelya!"

Hectyr rushed over to her and grabbed her, carrying her as fast as he could away from the spell as it erupted. She looked behind him just as it happened.

She watched the cultists below look up in awe — assuming it was Cressyda still — lost in unfathomable adoration for the greatest magick user in the empire, no, the world. That's when it was released.

A thousand tiny razors of rain shot out into its surroundings piercing many of the cultists. Death by a thousand cuts. Ophelya's eyes widened as some pierced Hectyr. He stopped and fell down, kneeling so he didn't drop her.

"Are you alright?!" she asked quickly, struggling to her feet.

"Yeah, I'll be fine."

Ophelya looked beyond Hectyr at the stranger coming down from the Citadel, they watched the pair's struggle with a bemused interest. They forced Cal to her feet, deep bags were visible beneath her eyes and she focused on nothing as she slipped in and out of consciousness.

"Is that another royal scion perhaps?" they asked her, holding her head to look at them. "Hmm, it seems I've been mimicking the wrong appearance after all."

They shoved Cal to the ground and gazed upon Hectyr. He felt himself grinding his teeth as he looked at her.

I can't let the curse get the better of me! Not now.

The stranger laughed as slowly their hair shifted to a white tone and their eyes gained a hint of blue to their dullness. As this happened, the sky shifted lighter for a moment, the spell weakening. Hectyr felt lighter for a moment as well, he felt his body relax slightly.

Did the curse... just weaken?

Hectyr narrowed his eyes at the stranger before him, he only had a dagger on him. Compared to a magick user — that wouldn't be enough to defeat them and get away unscathed. He held out the small blade defensively as he tried to stand in front of Ophelya. She stepped around him, wielding her own curved blade.

"Step away from her, *now,* "Ophelya demanded. Speaking in a low voice she glared through her brows at the stranger before them.

The loud clop of hooves on pavement echoed out as a figure stormed through the gates — spear in hand. They stop just a few feet before Avalon and quickly scan their surroundings.

Disheveled hair, tattered garb, and caked blood running down their sides. It was the last person Ophelya expected to see in such a state.

"Lord Harkyn?!"

The larger centaur glared back at them. It took them a moment to understand the state of things. From Avalon weeping over her brother to the dead cultists that surrounded them. The rainwater rinsed the pools of blood away slowly. He looked to the strange figure and curled his lip into a snarl.

"You... You aren't Cressyda." He held out a spear. "State your name," He commanded.

The figure laughed, throwing Calypso down as they flipped the half of blond hair that was left long over their shoulder. Their skin slowly gaining a natural glow to it as the dullness of death left it. Ophelya clenched a fist at her side as she looked at Calypso. She was on her last legs, and hardly moved from the ground.

Cal...

Hectyr grit his teeth. He wanted to charge in, to protect her — but he knew that would do more harm than good after what they just witnessed.

"Ah, someone direct and powerful. You must be one on the last emperor's council... Lord Harkyn was it?" When Harkyn looked taken aback the stranger let out a silvery laugh. "I've been around for quite some time now and I've done some research."

The centaur clenched his teeth and began to step forward spear in hand. "You're not Cressyda — yet I've seen those markings. That body isn't yours, and council... You are also an ancient soul." Lord Harkyn narrowed his eyes. "*Cronys*?"

"*Emperor* Cronys," the blond corrected him. "Though based on your reaction I believe you were hoping for a late Cressyda — were you not?"

When Lord Harkyn said nothing, Cronys continued. Walking towards him as he spoke in a sweetly disturbing tone. "I see. A council member desiring a higher position? How easy to read you are. You are parched and somehow — you saw my *dear* sister as a spring worthy of yourself, hm?"

"No, I wished to see the return of *Empress Cressyda*. The last great mage of Vasyla."

Cronys looked taken aback. Surprised by the boldness of the centaur before him. He laughed as Harkyn reared back with his spear. Cronys jumped away loftily, as though moving away from an insect as Harkyn's spear missed him by a hair.

Lord Harkyn leapt away as Cronys struck out with a blade of water magick. The rushed current in such a containing space sliced through him like nothing — leaving a thin scar across his chest as he narrowly avoided being cut open.

Ophelya watched as Lord Harkyn and Cronys exchanged blows. It was truly something to witness. Like a morbid dance with death. Lord Harkyn only managed to get surface-level scars upon Cronys.

Taking on more than he gave. Ophelya began to shake. The rain pouring down had drenched them all and washed the fresh blood down Lord Harkyn's body. Avalon watched their battle with a blank stare.

That's Lord Harkyn... And even he is struggling against such a foe.

Hectyr clutched his sword and began to step forward, but Ophelya stopped him.

"What are you doing?" She asked quickly.

Hectyr looked down, "He needs help! He cannot face Cronys alone!"

Ophelya grit her teeth, "Even if you help you will not defeat him!"

With a forceful blow, Lord Harkyn was thrown across the courtyard and onto the ground. He doesn't get up.

"Lord Harkyn!" Hectyr hurried over to him, and Ophelya slowly did too — keeping her eyes on Cronys who laughed nearby.

"She could have defeated him... Cressyda... Cressyda..." He was muttering to himself, eyes glued to the dark heavens above, reflecting its red glow.

"Lord Harkyn," Hectyr said as he kneeled beside his body. "You speak of Cressyda like she is near — You say she can defeat him?"

"If she wasn't in the armor then... The blade... That blasted guard pocketed it... I thought that would be Cronys —" Lord Harkyn coughed blood. A cut was seen in his chest, a lung was pierced. He wouldn't have long. "Make the mark, release Cressyda into a body. It's the only way now."

Guard? He means Leandre!

Ophelya and Hectyr exchanged a glance before looking to the Citadel.

Does he have the blade containing Cressyda?

Lord Harkyn laid his head down and his labored breathing slowed. He looked angry. Angry with the Aspects. Angry with the royals. Angry with his fate. But fate would not give him relief as his breathing stopped.

More people began filtering through the gate running to the Citadel for presumed safety of the royal guards — but none would be found. A few noticed the commotion of the stranger and Calypso near the edge of the entryway and slowed as they stared in horror.

"Lord Harkyn! He's... He's dead!" A woman screeched in terror as she looked upon the dead centaur. The bodies piled around them didn't look the best either. Cronys noticed this and flashed their teeth in a sickly smile.

"I will make sure it is known across the empire who was responsible for today," they hissed. Grabbing Calypso and lifting her up to her feet. "Calypso Pallas, royal scion who brings about the end times —"

Ophelya looked at Calypso, she was on the ground and hardly looking at anything. Their eyes met, and she could see the desperation in her friend's eyes,

"I, Cronys Pallas, will be the one to defeat her and I will claim the throne once more over a cursed scion!"

31
PROPHECY MISGUIDED
CRONYS

His eyes were darker than an abyss, as you look at him it was almost like nothing was looking back. He was unreadable. He was unknowable. He would make a powerful emperor. This is what the people of Vasyla used to sing of. Of a fine prince, next in line to rule. As the eldest child, there should have been no competition, no struggle. It was his birthright. The title, the crown, and the throne. *Emperor Cronys Pallas.* It had a charming ring to it, don't you think?

Yet there were whispers. Ideas — Foolish ones at that. Talk of an empress. Talk of his lesser sister, Cressyda Pallas.

For years the people had waited for the prophecy of one born under the white tern. The one to bring a turning point for the empire, and Cressyda fit the words like a silk robe made perfectly for a goddess. Not one piece fit wrong.

> *When Vasyla has over a thousand moons in its skies,*
> *When the star of the white tern brings us a royal scion,*
> *When the night outlasts the day, Vasyla will crum-*
> *ble once more, Returning brighter than before. As a*
> *phoenix from the ashes —So should Vasyla heal its*
> *gashes. To guard, a poet, and a royal scion, The Aspect's*
> *will lend their hand. Yet to return from death is no*
> *simple feat, A new world, A new life, The people must*
> *meet.*

From the star to the mentions of others, the people of Vasyla believed in Cressyda. From those she so foolishly called her allies — a guard and a poet of all things! To the most important aspect of it all. Her magick.

Cronys bared his teeth in a snarl as he bent over, panting in the training yard. A breeze made it's way through the hills of the capital city of Thooryn. The training yard was high on the hills near the capital. It was the perfect overlook of the city to train at without causing any trouble for the people. The mountain breeze brought with it the perfect weather for magick lessons. Yet as Cronys looked upon his sister, all he felt was greed.

She stood at the other side of the clearing. Her chestnut brown hair was pulled up into a tight ponytail, tanned skin glistening with sweat, and eyes wide with excitement. He scrunched his nose as he

looked at her. He took after their mother far more than father —
lacking the white hair of a royal scion. She wore men's armored pads
as she was far too burly to wear the woman's kind. Yet she paired it
with a feminine loose cream robe. She was scarcely out of breath, in
fact, this almost looked fun to her. The several magick teachers who
stood in the yard to watch looked pleased with her. Each teacher was
there to review their practice in magick — to ensure they were not
going too crazy in the amount they used to keep the royals from ever
experiencing Magick Hysteria. Yet as Cressyda showed proficiency
in wind, earth, water, and even lightning magicks — Cronys showed
signs of Magick Hysteria from just using a simple rain spell.

How can I have such a low energy for magick? Cronys pulled his
sleeve lower, hiding the markings he had made on his arm with
charcoal to cast even that one petty spell. It was seen as dishonorable
to rely on controlled magicks and not wild magicks. It showed a lack
of energy for the task. Yet still, even controlled magicks wore on the
elder royal.

"Prince Cronys," one of the teachers called out. "Are you alright?"

The elder scion glared up, pulled from his thoughts. The teachers
all were waiting on him while Cressyda stood aside. Two others
stood near the side of the arena and she strides over the them to chat.

The guard and the poet.

He glowered as he watched the two figures. Cressyda had a joyous
expression as she greeted the pair. The three began to speak —
casting glances his way every now and then. Cronys felt irritation at
her need to converse with two figures lower than them. It was almost
like she was *trying* to fulfill this prophecy.

Why else would one willingly befriend a guard and a poet of all things?

Even the cold winds couldn't cool his temper.

I can't escape that idiotic prophecy no matter where I go!

Cronys clenched his teeth and stood a little straighter. "I am just fine, thank you." He hissed out in as silvery a tone as he could muster. "Let's continue, and begin duels."

Cressyda stopped speaking with her *friends* and stared over at him. Pity was clear on her face as she looked at her brother.

"Duel? Are you certain, Prince Cronys?" The teachers all exchanged a look, making the prince's blood boil.

"Yes."

Cressyda said a few more words to her allies before making her way across the yard to stand a few feet away from her brother.

"Would you like me to lighten up today? You seem tired." Cressyda asked slowly. Worry laced in every word. Yet to Cronys, this was mocking and belittling to him. In front of their instructors no less!

Cronys said not a prayer, but a request to the Aspect that the markings on his arms would remain intact as he held out his hands in an aggressive position. It was hardly even a request, as he expected them to answer. To heed his words. To listen.

Cressyda gave him a forlorn look before slowly taking on the defensive.

Clenching his teeth, Cronys focused all of his mind onto the winds that surrounded them. The winds and the skies were the only magicks he could even *slightly* control without passing out. Yet he knew he was slowly improving. The winds began to whistle around them angrily, and whipped and lashed at his sister. If any were able to hit — they would most certainly tear through skin. The teachers nearby have to gather at a distance so as not to be harmed. Yet she showed no signs of harm, as before the wind could strike her she forced its flow to go around her form. A single bead of sweat dripped down her brow, while Cronys felt his whole neck soaking in it.

"Are you all right, masters?" Cressyda turned to their teachers for a moment and away from Cronys. As they dipped their heads at her she turned back to Cronys.

"Alright, my turn."

A dark gloom shone in Cressyda's eyes as the sky slowly went dark. Storm clouds gathered above covering the sun. A chill spread across. The hillside as raindrops began to spill from the heavens. They collected in one area where Cressyda's outstretched hand was. A wide disk of water gathered, one that would thrown at him. Yet she waited. Was she giving him a chance to defend?

Cronys grit his teeth and used the force of the wind to create a shield. He gasped out loud as she threw the disk at him — it broke through and soaked him but did not harm him. Cressyda was still moving. Her hands swayed in circular motions. Lofty and flowing motions mimic that of the water. The rain began to stream downhill, yet slowly lofted back into the air and returned into a new cloud form as the sun began to peek out once more. The instructors cheered. Cronys hardly stood his ground.

"I believe that is enough for today," Cressyda said with a glance at Cronys. "I apologize, but I am too worn to continue further. Is that alright with you, brother?"

Her words were meant with kindness as the teachers turned their focus from his bedraggled state after using very limited magick. Yet Cronys only felt contempt for the pity of his sister.

He watched as she hurried back over to her allies who greeted her with glee — the instructors were already making their way back down the hill, and soon Cressyda would follow with the guard and poet.

"Oboryn!" Cronys snapped at his guard nearby and they joined him for the trek down the hill.

I'm the one who is supposed to bring glory to the empire! To make conquest and gain more lands for our people.

How can I do that when I cannot even beat her in magick? Unless...

Perhaps magick is not such a good thing. Perhaps our people have been looking at it, and the prophecy in the wrong light for too long...

Cronys flashed his fangs in a grin as he watched the back of Cressyda with her allies.

Yes... You may have bested me in magick — but can you best me in influence?

32
THE NEED TO SURVIVE
LEANDRE

Fear was all that remained for Leandre as the minutes ticked by. Every second he sat there he could only hear his own voice screaming at him to move. To get up. To go after Calypso. The armor had turned its back on Leandre. Leaving the shard of the blade behind. The sounds of metallic clanking filled the halls as the possessed object collected its pieces — putting itself back together.

Why can't I get up!?

Leandre's hands shook as he slowly gained mobility - the shock from being thrown against the wall had left him temporarily frozen. Stuck. He had never been in such a situation. The armor had collected all its parts and began to walk away. In the direction Cal had been dragged just moments prior.

No! She won't be able to deal with both of them!

Clenching his teeth, Leandre looked for his weapon. The blade nearby still emit a faint glow from its hilt. Leandre grabbed it before struggling to his feet. Thunder echoed in the distance. Faint screams could be heard outside the Citadel's main building.

"Calypso!" Leandre called out, struggling to his feet. His legs were wobbly.

The armor let out a shrill laugh, "Oh no, you will not be going anywhere."

Oboryn lifted up Leandre and threw him across the hall. He hit a pillar with a thud and groaned. Limbs shaking as he struggled back to his feet.

I need to get past this thing!

I need to get to Cal!

Leandre glared up as the armor made its way over. Clutching the blade of Cressyda as tight as a talisman as they neared. He made himself look as small as possible. The armor laughed at the sight of him.

"You know, it's odd. I too was once a guard to a royal scion born under the white tern. Yet I broke free of that when I realized the doom she would bring on the empire - what stopped you from recognizing this?"

Leandre curled his lip in a snarl. "I'm no traitor, I'll stay by Calypso's side until the end."

"It's strange, I once said that myself. And yet... here I stand today." The armor began to lean down towards him, "The prophecy did speak of a poet and a guard... So why did that not happen I wonder?" They began to move forward, weapon in hand.

"There was a time, when that may have happened," Leandre spoke slowly - guilt lacing every word. "I am ashamed to even admit such a thing, but I was not myself. I now know that any bitterness I felt towards her, any semblance of doubt was manufactured with magick." Leandre smirked up at them. "So how can you be so sure that your actions were your own? Were you just a puppet in someone else's plan?"

Oboryn growled at this, taking a step forward and raising their weapon to attack.

As soon as they were within striking distance Leandre leapt to his feet and struck. Knocking the helmet off, as it landed he saw it. Two markings. Just like the one etched into the handle of the blade. One looked dull, yet the other had a faint... aura to it.

Is that what contains Oboryn's soul?

Leandre dodged just as a\the spear thrust in his direction — narrowly avoiding it as he grabbed the helmet. He took the broken blade and stabbed at the mark.

An otherworldly scream came from the hollow figure, Leandre began to stab again when the headless armor charged. Throwing aside its spear and using the blunt of its arm to block its body. It crashed into Leandre yet he held firm to the helmet. As the armor pushed Leandre through the halls and into a pillar he kept stabbing the mark. The armor shuddered and twitched with every strike. Oboryn stood back as Leandre fell down against the pillar and lifted both hands to strike down on him.

He grit his teeth and struck the mark one last time and the helmet cracked. Right through the mark. The armor fell the the ground, the clang echoed throughout the hall.

A chill surrounded Leandre as he slowly got to his feet watching the armor. Waiting for it to move. He didn't feel at ease with the silence.

He needed to get to Calypso.

As Leandre began to rush through the halls to the entrance of the Citadel a flash of feathers caught his eye.

What the —

33
SOULS THAT LINGER
OPHELYA

"Of course, the royal scions would be drawn here like moths to a flame. After all, the curse is carried in your very blood."

Ophelya stuck close to Hectyr as she watched the other royal scions enter the citadel. Avalon still sat over Adonys's body. Tears never stopped spilling from her eyes even as she turned to see the others. Deakon, Kyril, and Echo neared the paved clearing side by side – yet oddly enough their eyes were fixated upon the otherworldly man who stood on the steps of the Citadel. As though they had been lured there by this stranger.

The curse!

Cronys also carried the blood — and possibly the curse itself.

"Hectyr!" Ophelya looked up to the taller figure. "We need to defend Calypso and lure the others into attacking!"

"What?"

The other royal scions entering the courtyard had their eyes fixated on Cronys — yet none of them seemed too out of it. After all, they weren't fighting one another.

"The blood! Cronys is could be a target of the other royals as well, why else would they be lured here from a great distance?"

Cronys threw Calypso away from himself and down the stairs.

"Stand and face me, cursed scion! Or is the darkness you brought over Vasyla too much for you to handle?"

Deakon stepped forward, his hands were shaking and he looked exhausted. He saw Avalon, Adonys, and finally Lord Harkyn. His eyes go wide. He looked to Cronys.

"What have you done?"

"You are asking the wrong person, scion — it is Calypso who is to blame."

Ophelya pulled out her blade. She was still quite shaky but felt as adrenaline rushed through her veins. "No! It is you Cronys who brings about the end times! And you who will l fall!" She cast a glance at the other royal scions. They all looked horrified at the name mentioned. As Cronys focused on them they began to eye one another warily. *Can he control the strength of the curse?* Ophelya wondered.

"We need to distract him!" She said to Hectyr quickly. He nodded and the pair began their strike.

Calypso shakily was on her feet just as the pair neared. Hectyr grabbed a spear off a cultist and reared back, muscles tensed. He threw it with brute force straight for Cronys as Ophelya threw her blade at his shins. He avoided the knife, but the spear sliced through his thigh.

"Calypso!" Hectyr called out, throwing his blade to her. She caught it by the handle and quickly turned to Cronys. As soon as Cronys turned his attention off of the other royal scions and began to gather the rain once more, Deakon charged. An iron machaira in hand. Calypso dodged out of the way until she saw his goal. The two struck at Cronys together. Stopping him from having the time to prepare any incantations. Calypso aimed low, piercing his leg as Deakon slashed high for his head. Cronys narrowly avoided Deakon's strike, but Calypso's spear found flesh as he groaned in pain. The rainwater began to gather and form into daggers once more. Ophelya raised her arm to defend herself.

"Look out!"

The daggers flew everywhere within the courtyard. Several lords and ladies fell — leaving just the royal scions and Cronys. Ophelya grimaced as several struck her arm. It burned as it hit her despite being made of water - the lingering effects of magick.

Ophelya glared up at Cronys, she had no weapon - her body felt like it had been thrown around as well. Three people fought against one recently revived corpse and were getting nowhere.

Aspects, is this really what you wanted for us?

Ophelya curled her nose in disgust as she looked at the sky. *Will you really watch on and do nothing?!*

Cronys shouted in surprise. Ophelya looked over to see a small blurry shape moving quickly. It was feathered.

What the -

A small bird appeared from inside the Citadel. A white tern, it was carrying

The blade was dropped into Calypso's hand, she looked awestruck at the sight. A messenger delivered it to her. Leandre appeared from inside of the Citadel. Cronys, Calypso, and Deakon spun to face him.

"Calypso! That blade, it's Cressyda!"

Cronys growled before spinning back into combat — he struck for Calypso but she slipped and fell down the step, narrowly avoiding the attack.

"We need a body..." Ophelya recalled the markings her mother made from the statue to herself. She looked around. There were bodies all around them — but only one was in close enough of a state to be used. Adonys.

Ophelya hurried to his body. She had to make the mark on him fast. Avalon glared up at her and remained over the body. "I — I know what you want to do. You want to use him for something, but you can't! I can't let his body be disrespected, even if it helps us."

"Avalon! We have to do this!" Ophelya shouted as Calypso barely dodged another attack from Cronys. Deakon and Hectyr could only distract him for so long. Kyril shivered at the corner of the courtyard. Frozen in fear. Avalon pulled Adonys away.

"No! I won't allow it —"

Avalon fell back as someone tugged at her. A small figure. Ophelya looked up. Echo?

The small cyclops didn't meet Calypso's eyes as she pulled the larger girl off of the body. "Do what you have to." That was all she said.

Ophelya shut her eyes for a moment.

"I'm sorry Adonys."

She took her nails and dug into his skin, clawing the mark into his forearm. She struggled to not gag at the feeling.

The blade... Calypso can't do this part. She doesn't know the words.

Ophelya recalled her mother muttering over blood-stained pages. Memorizing the incantations quietly — but just loud enough that her daughter overheard it.

"Calypso! The blade! Give it to me!"

Except Calypso did not hand her the blade.

"Calypso, give her the blade!" Leandre shouted as he dodged a strike from Cronys. Ophelya looked up at her. Fresh blood welled up on Cal's arm forming a strange mark. She held out the blade. Ophelya already said the words, all that was left was...

"NO!" Ophelya screamed as she struggled to get to her in time.

Cronys struck Deakon aside and dodged a strike from Calypso. Glaring down at Ophelya with rage.

"Stop her! Stop her now!" He commanded as he watched in horror.

Calypso forced the shattered blade into her chest and through her heart. The air around them changed. She fell to the ground. Ophelya cried out and crawled across the ground to Calypso's side.

Her breathing was slowing down, and her eyes hardly focused on anything. Leandre fell down at her other side. Rain spilling down his face. Or were they tears?

"Calypso, no no no no *no*! Why would you do this?!" Ophelya bawled as she looked down at her friend.

She weakly smiled and shook her head, "This was the only way, Cressyda needs a body and we needed someone strong enough..." She let out one final breath before closing her eyes. Ophelya pressed her head to her chest. Her heart was still beating. Then it stopped, but only for a mere second.

The glow of the blade faded, and despite the rain around them. everyone went silent, watching the body with bated breath. Ophelya could only hear her own breathing as she watched the body for a sign. Suddenly, a heartbeat. Calypso's eyes opened and she gasped. Sitting up, she looked up to the skies.

"*Cressyda?*"

34

BODY AND SOUL
A BODY

A strange feeling. Like writhing and wriggling but deep inside of oneself filled her body. Her body, only whose body was it? Was it her own, or someone else's?

She stood slowly, looking down at the blade in her chest. Did she put that there? As she pulled it out, she couldn't help but feel this action was not her own.

"Cressyda?"

That name... Was it hers? It doesn't feel like it. It felt foreign, yet familiar.

She looked around. So many people, so much blood, so many... bodies. Even with the rain, the scent of fresh scarring and blood was pungent. Yet that was the last thing that filled her thoughts.

Did I not just die?

She jumped, putting her hands on her head and clutching it tight. Someone was in there.

"Cressyda?"

A quiet call came again from a woman on the ground. She was lithe, with deep sepia-colored skin. Her narrow eyes had dark marks beneath them, and tears spilled forth as she looked at her.

"You... Removed me from the blade?" The body spoke slowly and jumped. Startled by the voice that came with it. They looked baffled at this. As though they never believed such a thing could be done.

"Then why didn't I die?!" Another voice spoke from the body. It fell back onto the ground, eyes wide. It looked to the woman nearby.

"The incantation... who spoke it?!"

The dark woman slowly pointed to herself. "I... I did and then Cal.. she -"

Is anyone else there?

Silence for a moment, yet she could hear the other one thinking.

Yes... Cressyda?

Silence.

I heard your name spoken... Calypso?

"Ophelya... Leandre... I... lived?" The other spoke yet again. It was a gross feeling, submitting control to another inside oneself, but it was something she, no, *they* had little control over.

Cronys roared with anger, and Cressyda quickly got to their feet. Spinning around to face them. The color came back to them quickly as the body had not been dead for long. If dead at all.

"Cronys?" Cressyda asked as they looked at the other body. They clenched their jaw after a moment. "*How dare you*, we should be dead — You have defied the Aspects twice now! And pulled me into it!"

"Defied the aspects?" The body asked again. Leandre and Ophelya exchanged a glance.

"Calypso... and Cressyda?" Leandre asked slowly. The body nodded.

Cronys began to take a step back as Cressyda stood. Ophelya and Calypso exchanged a glance.

Does he fear her? Calypso thought as they looked at him.

My brother... Cronys and I... Last time things did not go the way I had planned.

Cronys howled in laughter as it clicked. "Is this what you throw at me Aspects? Two souls in one? Two under the white tern to fulfill a prophecy twice over?" He glared at the body. "You couldn't even do it the first time Cressyda - though I am surprised you had enough energy left to force your own soul into a weapon alone after pulling the capital into an abyss."

"The previous capital... so it was Cressyda," Leandre mumbled to himself.

The previous capital?

Cronys held out his hand, the rain formed a spear of water current.

Thooryn... We put the capital city into the ground in our battle. That was where I -

They barely dodged as he struck at them. He swept the spear across and the current struck their arm. Calypso went to strike back as Cressyda tried to pull away. The attack missed as they narrowly fell and avoided another attack.

Leandre grabbed a weapon from one of the fallen cultists and began to join the fight against Cronys. Deakon continued his strike as well. Despite having two other foes on him - the corpse figure managed to keep his focus set on the two in Calypso's body.

His eyes softened as he smirked - realizing how out of tune the pair were. A sick grin spread across his face as he reached tensed hands to the sky to pull another spear from the waters around them.

We need to work together. Aggressive. Who knows how long before we give out - I already used a lot of energy before putting you in my body. Calypso thought as she gripped the blade left.

Then let me take charge of magick, you handle the barbaric combat. Cressyda's thoughts seemed matter-of-fact.

But isn't magick barbaric?

Calypso grabbed a blade from the ground, it was better than what was left of Cressyda's old one. She held it with both hands as she raised both hands to strike at Cronys. He doesn't avoid the attack, taking the slash straight to the chest unflinching as he watched the skies in horror. Energy was draining from her body, but it wasn't as quick as before. Not as unfiltered, now it was as though sand grains were slowly falling through an hourglass. Calypso looked up.

By the Aspects...

Cressyda, is this your doing?

The stars had become visible in the bleak sky and seemed to all gather above them. Did they gather to the great sign of magick flowing through this? The rain had stopped, and any new drops that fell landed on an invisible sheet above the Citadel. It began to gather quickly, creating a lake above them. The earth began to shake beneath them as well.

Cronys's breath was shaky and loud at the sigh. He was panicked. Striking suddenly and aggressively he began to push forward against the body. Struggling to throw them off just enough for them to lose connection with the Wild Magick Cressyda was seamlessly linked to.

You'd best get your friends out of here, I can only focus on bringing Cronys down - I cannot also defend.

"Ophelya! Leandre! Hectyr! Get everyone else to safety now!" Calypso called out as she backed away slowly. Cracks began to form in the courtyard, splitting up through the Citadel's great hall itself. Any remaining royals or civilians were gone - all that remained were scions and allies of Calypso.

"We can't leave you!" Leandre shouted out as he struck at Cronys with a blade. It hit him yet still, he showed no signs of pain. No mere sharp blades or spears would cut it at this point.

Magick is the only way to beat someone so mired in it. Cressyda thought solemnly. Calypso felt confused at her tone, she could just grasp at a memory of it - yet she pulled it away.

"You have to!" Calypso shouted as she dodged beneath an attack. As the two clashed, they continued up the stairs of the citadel. Spears of water current began to strike out at Cronys from above, and the ground shaking beneath him shook his balance yet still he remained keen in combat. Calypso grit her teeth as she put all of herself into every strike. Playing as aggressively as she could - yet Cronys dodged or protected using his own Controlled Magick.

Ophelya grabbed Avalon and Leandre dodged around Cronys to help her get the other scion to her feed. She cried out as they pulled her away. Deakon and Echo began to hurry to the gates. The ground began to split open around them. Deep cracks split into small ravines that grew - shattering the gate of the Citadel and wrapping around them.

Hectyr grabbed another spear, clutching it with both hands as he rushed towards Cronys.

Calypso turned to look at him with wide eyes, "What are you doing Hectyr?!"

At her distraction, Cronys knocked the blade from her hands.

I need a little more time Calypso!

Hectyr was exhausted and heaving, yet Cronys raised his hands to strike again with his weapon. He leapt in the way, catching the magick weapon with his own.

"What?!" Cronys roared, "No one can be unharmed by Controlled Magick unless..." The corpse reared back in horror, "Accursed, an Ophiophor!"

Ophiophor? Perfect, he is resistant to Controlled Magicks - just as dragons once were.

Calypso's eyes widened, quickly grabbing up her weapon, the two fought together as Cressyda continued pulling the strings of the world around them.

This much for one man? Calypso looked around them. She was opening the heavens and the earth to defeat him.

I need your help with this, this body… it hasn't fully accepted me. You need to finish the spell.

"What?!" Calypso said aloud as she ducked beneath his strike. Hectyr struck him in the side with his spear before getting thrown aside. "Hectyr!"

Focus! Feel the water above you, and the ground below you. Think of it as an extension of your body, as your muscles through your arms…

But what are we going to -

Then it clicked. Suddenly Cressyda relinquished everything to Calypso. She clenched her jaw and shut her eyes.

This will fulfill the prophecy Cressyda.

It will.

The empire will fall… and it is my name they will remember this.

"The empire may fall," Cressyda said slowly. "But it will be rebuilt, and it will come back stronger than before."

Calypso felt tears as they filled her closed eyes. It was hard to imagine - her name in the history books for such a thing. The reasons were null for the actions that came with it. She could feel it now, Wild Magick couldn't be stopped once it got started. This would split the empire into many pieces. She felt the earth splitting across the continent. It was fast, uncontrollable. There was only one last thing she could direct.

The ground beneath Cronys opened up, he barely avoided it, teetering on the edge as he struggled to not slide in with the crumbling earth.

Now.

A lake's amount of water had gathered above, and it all began to pour in one place above him. Forcing him down into the earth. He grabbed at the edge and barely held on as the water torrent struck at him. Claws digging into concrete and breaking and pulling out as he tried to stay above.

"Cressyda! You can't do this to me! We're blood!"

She snarled as they stepped towards him, "You have given up the right to call me blood long ago, Cronys."

Snatching the spear from Hectyr, Cressyda pierced him through the chest. His grip loosened, and the water washed him deep into the heart of Vasyla. The water slowly stopped, but the earth still continued to split apart - and Calypso no longer felt a tether to the Wild Magick that continued to run rampant.

35

THE END OF AN EMPIRE

LEANDRE

Leandre's breathing was ragged as the world spun around them. He took a wide stance as he struggled to remain on his feet. Looking up, Calypso was the closest to the Citadel, everyone else was further away from it. The building above her was beginning to crumble.

"Cre - Calypso!" He leapt across the cracking ground towards the bulky woman - their gaze was still focused at the earth splitting open before them. He grabbed her arm, they looked up at him and for a moment confusion crossed their face.

"Leandre," they said slowly, as though telling someone else.

"We need to get out of here, now!" He said quickly, he looked her over. She was beginning to grow sluggish and weak. The Wild Magick had wreaked havoc on her body, and nobody knew what that would show to be as she recovered. Leandre put her arm over his shoulder. "Lean on me, you could give out at any moment."

"So could you!"

He grit his teeth as the pair struggled to safety as the world tore around them. The others were already finding the safest path out. The walls around the Citadel had crumbled.

"The shores - the Wild Magick will not spread to there." Calypso said through short breaths. Leandre nodded.

"Everyone! We have to get to the shore!"

As they made it to the streets, they were shocked to see many dead bodies. Cultists, upperclassmen, and some other civilians who had gotten in the way. The cracks made their way through the city, and the Colosseum was already caving in on itself as an Abyss opened up in its heart.

Leandre felt sick as they ran down through the city watching it crumble. He had never considered this place his home and yet watching it crumble around him brought about a strange feeling inside of him.

This feels wrong.

Is this really how this was meant to go down? With Lyreas crumbling?

Yet as Leandre looked out past the city buildings, he could see ravines and cracks continuing to split the lands even beyond the city. The skies above still swirled with dark colors, and the black hole where the sun once was still bled out into the heavens.

Is the whole continent going to be split into shards?

A Skorvian stood not far from the Colosseum, she pulled her spear out of a body adorned with feathers and cultist garb. Zagora!

"You're alive!" Calypso shouted out as they all raced towards her, she broke away from Leandre to try to hurry towards her. The woman looked up at them all. Exhausted and confused.

"Calypso? Why are you -" Her eyes went wide as Calypso stopped before her. "It isn't just you - Little bird, what have you done?"

Leandre nudged Calypso forward carefully, "We can discuss it later Zagora! We need to get out of the capital city!"

Zagora narrowed her eyes but dipped her head. The sounds of crumbling came from the Colosseum as the remnants of the walls began to fall inward into the ravine that opened in it. They were all slowly down by this point - but the Wild Magick was not. Deakon grimaced before grabbing Avalon and hoisting her up onto his back. Her gaze was still set on the Citadel where her brother's body remained.

"Let's keep moving!" Deakon shouted as he led to way towards the shore. They were close now - it was only a few more streets until they were near the docks. The ships swayed on uneasy waters - no crews were in sight.

The earth trembled beneath their feet, and cracks began to grow ahead of them. Deakon jumped across with ease, but it continued to grow wider and wider still. Leandre looked down inside. It looked a lot like the Abyss. Where the original capital had been. Was this what happened last time Cronys and Cressyda fought? Is this why magick was outlawed?

Leandre jumped across, and as Calypso did he grabbed her and pulled her away from the edge. Ophelya shook as she looked at the gap, it had grown too wide.

"Look out!"

Leandre spun around to find the other side of the path began to split as well - they were left on an island in the middle - buildings on either side began to slide into the ground below. Leandre looked across. Zagora, Ophelya, Hectyr, and Kyril were still further back.

Skorvians could only jump very short distances. Zagora froze and took a step back as the ground crumbled between them. Echo looked at her, eye widening. Did she recognize her?

"Hold on!" Echo shouted as the grounds continued to split in the streets ahead of them. She squinted her eye and grimaced as she began muttering words to herself - placing her hands on the ground before her. She glared at Calypso as rocks formed ahead building a narrow path across as well as one back to Zagora.

"Go!"

Kyril ran across first, Ophelya followed. She flinched with every crumbling sound as she rushed across. Hectyr followed. That left Zagora and Echo.

"Did you hear me, old woman? Go across! I can't hold this forever!"

Zagora shook her head, "I never thought I'd be helping any other royal scion!" She grabbed Echo and threw her over her shoulder. The bridge began to crumble.

The others ran across the other side as Zagora followed. Back claws slipped as the ground beneath her was breaking.

Calypso grabbed her claw with both hands to pull her across as the ground beneath her completely gave way. Kyril's eyes went wide at the strength behind her arms. Leandre couldn't help but smirk.

"We're almost there everyone!" Hectyr called out as they continued away from the crumbling city. They looked back as they reached the dock. A few ships had begun sailing away and could be seen in the distance - no sign of any life or any bodies.

One by one they stepped off of the docks and onto the sand. Zagora let Echo down onto the sand as well. Leandre joined Ophelya and Calypso as they all looked back to look at Lyreas as it continued to crumble.

"The prophecy is fulfilled, Vasyla has fallen." Calypso - no, Cressyda said after a moment. "I can feel the Wild Magick, though it is ever so slight of a connection now. It will continue to travel across the continent."

"When Vasyla has over a thousand moons in its skies, when the star of the white tern brings us a royal scion, when the night outlasts the day, Vasyla will crumble once more..." Avalon recited the prophecy absentmindedly as she fell to her knees on the sand. Calypso glared at her.

"That is not the whole prophecy." She snapped in a low tone. It was Cressyda speaking now.

"When Vasyla has over a thousand moons in its skies,
When the star of the white tern brings us a royal scion,
When the night outlasts the day, Vasyla will crumble once more, Returning brighter than before. As a

phoenix from the ashes —So should Vasyla heal its gashes. To guard, a poet, and a royal scion, The Aspect's will lend their hand. Yet to return from death is no simple feat, A new world, A new life, The people must meet."

Cressyda looked around at them all, "Is that really where you've all thought the prophecy ended? That Vasyla was destined to fall and not return?"

They all exchanged a glance.

Calypso shook her head, "No. The death of the empire is the rebirth of something new. That is what the prophecy spoke of. It should have been fulfilled long ago - but I died before I could complete the task."

"So if... If this is the rebirth of the empire - how do we return from this?"

They all looked at one another. Yet nobody had an answer. Royal scion looked fearfully at royal scion. Uncertainty hung in the air like a fog. Fear. Wild animals are seldom kind when cornered.

Leandre glared at them all as he stood close to Calypso and Ophelya. Whatever happened next – he would have no regrets. He would make his own choice – and he would defend them until the very end.

36
THE SHARDS LEFT BEHIND
OPHELYA

They sat on the shores for what felt like hours. Watching as the crumbling stopped, and the skies slowly lightened into the evening sun setting. It was over. The prophecy was fulfilled. So why did everything turn out so... wrong?

The smell of salt in the air was no longer calming as it filled the air with it's sickeningly strong smell. Not even sirens waited nearby for them after what just transpired. Ophelya trembled with her head resting on her hands as she watched Lyreas slowly stop crumbling.

"So... it really was a curse after all." Deakon looked down to the sands as she spoke. Breaking the long silence of royal scions warily glaring at one another. "That... violent urge I felt before towards you all. It's gone."

Leandre shook his head slowly, "Lord Harkyn was aware of it all along."

"He may have been the leader of the cult as well. This isn't over here, we may have killed Cronys - but Cressyda's soul remains as well as her followers." They all look to Calypso.

She frowned, "Cressyda is still here... with me, but perhaps... Perhaps we can get her out? Into another... Into the armor."

"It should still have a mark intact in it," Leandre said after a moment. "There were two, and I destroyed the one holding Oboryn."

Calypso looked grim at that name, or was it Cressyda's response?

Ophelya frowned as she looked around at the other royal scions. They were all there. Deakon, Hectyr, Avalon, Kyril, Echo, and Calypso. All that remained of the royals after Adonys's death. She narrowed her eyes.

The future of the empire rests in this moment.

"Now that you all understand that this was a curse... I believe one thing needs to be settled now."

They all looked to Calypso.

"Who will rule?" Deakon said grimly. She nodded.

Leandre furrowed his brow, "Ophelya, isn't it a bit too -"

"No Leandre, we cannot let this sit. The country is in ruins, multiple court members are dead. We need to have a plan and a royal on the throne if we are to rebuild. The prophecy may have meant the end of the empire, but we can spin it to be the rebirth of Vasyla." She glared around at the royals, looking at each one closely. "I believe the choice is obvious, and must be made now."

Deakon nodded in agreement. Echo clenched her teeth as she looked at another. Avalon was scarcely aware of the situation at hand - lost in the sea of her grief. Kyril? His opinion hardly mattered as the weakest of them all. Hectyr smiled sadly.

They all turned to Calypso.

They all bowed to her.

Cressyda remained silent as Calypso shook her head.

"No, I do not accept."

Ophelya remained silent, she smiled to herself. *Of course she wouldn't accept.*

But now the power of this conversation is in her hands.

"But if you don't.."

"It would be difficult to fix my name regardless, Hectyr."

The others all exchanged a glance before looking back to Calypso.

"Then what do you propose? Who should rule?"

Calypso smiled, "Hectyr." She stated simply.

"What?!" The lanky young man's eyes went wide as he looked up at her. "Are you sure?"

"I wouldn't pick anyone else. You truly understand the importance of social connections regardless of blood, class, or history. And... You treated me as a sister even when I was less than cordial towards you."

Ophelya and Leandre smiled at each other as she spoke. They looked exhausted, but proud of her words. The royal scions all looked shocked as they looked at the curly haired boy.

Deakon stepped forward. "It is a just choice, you haven't been in the capital as long - so your morals haven't been sullied by the opinions and nature of the ruling class."

So this is the nature of Deakon, no wonder the empire was so shocked by his outburst.

He was the first to dip his head to Hectyr. Avalon slowly did as well, a look of exhaustion filled her gaze as she didn't quite look at him. Echo narrowed her eye before bowing to him. Finally there was Kyril. They all looked at him.

He ducked his head, "Don't look at me, you hardly need my permission for anything after today." He slumped down and bowed to Hectyr.

Hectyr looked at Calypso with a worried expression, "Then... What will you do? The empire will blame you for this. How can we clear your name?"

She frowned and looked away, "We don't need to."

Leandre looked at Ophelya with wide eyes but she said nothing. Instead looking to Cal for her to continue.

"I never really was able to do that before now, there is no point in trying anymore." Calypso looked around her. "We can all live, the challenge does not need to continue in the new empire. And... now I will find my purpose."

"Was your purpose not the prophecy?" Kyril asked after a moment.

"My life does not end there," she said slowly. "But first... I must remove Cressyda from my body." She looked to Hectyr. "What will we do first, brother?"

He smiled at her, "We must make our way to the hills around the capital to help those who survived, but first - we must break the shard off of you." He looked to the Citadel. "Now that the magick has stopped, let us return to the Citadel to scavenge what we can and find the armor."

They had split up into groups to search through the Citadel for any survivors to take with them to the edge of the city. Calypso, Leandre, and Ophelya all traveled together as he knew right where to find it. Where he had last fought with Oboryn. When they finally found the armor, they were shocked to find it unscathed amidst the destroyed building. The pillars and ceiling above it are intact - covering it like a bird's wing.

"Do you really think you can use this incantation a second time Calypso?" Ophelya asked anxiously, biting her nails. "I know you said with Cressyda's soul you can handle magick better but -"

"I can do this. I did it once before as I lay dying to get my own soul into a blade - I can do it again to separate our souls from one another." Cressyda replied indignantly.

"She meant nothing harsh by it, Cressyda." Calypso chided.

"Please stop doing that, it's hard to tell when it's you and when it's Cressyda," Leandre said with a sigh. Calypso laughed. Ophelya smiled, she could tell the slightest difference of inflection in their voices when each one spoke.

"Calypso... Are you sure this can be done twice to the same body?" Leandre asked slowly as he looked between Calypso and the armor.

"There is only one way we can find out. It's that or be stuck with Cressyda taking control every now and then. And I don't particularly want to share it, no offense Cressyda."

"It should work, but we can only try once. Every incantation used on a body affects it - whether visibly or not. I don't believe your body could handle this anymore after this." Cressyda said in response from Calypso's body.

Leandre turned away, placing his hands on his head as he began to pace the ruins.

Calypso relinquished control to Cressyda, who began muttering the incantations as she held her hands over the armor in front of her. Leandre and Ophelya watched with bated breath as she performed the ritual of sorts. Until the body suddenly fell. Ophelya knelt by Calypso's body while Leandre continued pacing. She gnawed on her fingernails.

What if this doesn't work?

What if it can't be done twice?

What if we lose her this time?

Ophelya rested her head against Calypso's chest, listening as her heartbeat stopped. She held her breath.

Please, Aspects...

Ophelya looked up at Leandre and then back at Calypso.

You've kept them alive through this all – Please don't let me lose someone now.

Don't let this be the end.

The sound of metal being dragged filled the hall as the pieces began to pull together - forming as though someone were putting them on, piece by piece. Ophelya sat up to watch.

The Aspects had heard her prayer.

As the armor slowly pieced itself back together, the body's eyes opened.

"Calypso?" Ophelya asked slowly.

The body turned to her, eyes wide. She smiled, a wide grin with teeth flashing like fangs. Ophelya reared back and looked to Leandre. His hands were over his mouth.

"Yes, Ophelya?"

The armor responded. Calypso's voice was dull as it echoed from shiny metal.

"I... I made a mistake." Cressyda lifted her arms to look down at the form below her. Large cream-colored arms and a plump round figure in tattered light armor. This was not what she had intended.

Ophelya slammed her fist on the ground while Leandre blankly stared from Calypso to Cressyda. They had flipped a coin on whether or not the incantation would work on a body with two souls.

The coin had landed, and Calypso had ended up on the wrong side.

Epilogue
THE OTHER SIDE OF THE COIN
CALYPSO

At first, a feeling of dread filled Calypso. The scene slowly unfolded before her. She sat, so close to herself yet she was no longer in her body. Dread. Yet like a wave striking the shore, it slowly receded. She lifted her arm, and then the other. Where milky pale skin should have been, metal shone back at her like sunlight. She laughed, as she moved around. No restraints of muscle or skin. Nothing holding her back like energy or weight. She felt new. She felt free. More free than she ever had in her entire life.

She was a royal scion cut from the strongest of metals, worn from the years of strong service to those it had adorned; the scars and marks on it would never heal, and would forever show the battles she and others had survived.

This armor has already built a reputation – through me and Oboryn. A far better one than the Pallas name ever did for me.

Calypso looked up at her friends, a warm feeling filled her until she saw their faces. Her friends, mortified. The body she had shed slowly got to its feet, and Calypso slowly did the same. The clang of metal armor never felt so... exhilarating.

"By the Aspects," Ophelya looked between Calypso and her old body with wide eyes. "How did this happen?"

Calypso – no Cressyda sighed, "I was worried it could go wrong. The magick of this spell is closer to Wild Magick than Controlled Magick – I suppose trying it that many times on two souls kept me from controlling it's flow."

Ophelya looked at the armor with wide eyes, she chewed on her nails anxiously as she approached it. "Calypso? Are you... Alright in there?"

"Of course I am! I've never been better!"

"But don't you understand?"

Ophelya and Leandre exchanged a glance.

"I am finally free! No more Calypso Pallas – I can be whoever I want to be now!"

Ophelya's gaze faltered, "But... your body..."

She looked at her old form, Cressyda resided inside it now.

Cressyda looked down at the mark, frowning.

"What's the matter?" Calypso asked, following her gaze.

The mark on her arm was different. Changed. Three scars ran across it like that of a bird's talons. They were dull like the mark – despite the rest of the mark being freshly made and still oozing red – the three marks looked as though they had been there for years.

"I don't think what we have done today can ever be undone, young scion."

"No, don't call me that. Not anymore." Calypso began moving in place. Stretching out her arms, and moving her legs. She scarcely felt anything. She understood the movement like it was a ghost of what she should feel but beyond that - there wasn't any cold, pain, or discomfort of any kind. She looked up at the rubble around them. A bird sat perched on the broken pillar nearby. Watching.

Aspects... Had you been listening to my prayers all these years?

Is this the freedom I earned for fulfilling the prophecy?

"Perhaps this was meant to happen." She said slowly, pointing at the bird nearby. The others spun to look at it immediately. It was a white tern.

It spread its wings and flew away from them, a few feathers left in its place. Leandre rested a hand on his head.

"Then, you're happy, Cal?" Leandre asked slowly.

She nodded, "We've fulfilled the prophecy – but it didn't mean the end! Think about it Leandre! The empire is going to change, it will be better this time. And this time, I can be the warrior I always wanted to be."

Leandre rubbed at the nape of his neck and let out a sigh, "Then nothing more needs to be said."

Ophelya said nothing as she looked between Calypso and Cressyda. She looked... Mildly perturbed.

"Ophelya?"

"the prophecy... Never spoke of multiple born under the white tern so... Is it really fine for her to continue to live as you?"

Cressyda looked down at herself, her eyes narrowed as she scanned her figure.

"I have lived as a royal scion before, I can do it again." She looked up at Calypso. "I will take on the role you despised so you may take on one that will bring you joy – after all, it was my failure to succeed in the original prophecy that led you to this."

Moonlight shone on the metal of Calypso's new form and a cool breeze filtered over the rubble of the citadel. *This place, this wretched place is destroyed.*

Calypso pulled Cressyda into a hug, though she felt nothing she still felt warm and comforted. "Thank you, you've given me the rest of my life."

It feels like a weight has been lifted off of my shoulders...

"Something new, and something better will be built on what is left of Vasyla." Calypso pulled away from hugging Cressyda. She looked at her old form for a moment, briefly startled to see herself from an outside view. She shook her head before turning back to Leandre and Ophelya. "And we can finally choose how we affect that."

The empire was in ruins around them, who knew how far the cracks had stretched across the continent? Yet the worst of it should have been over. Next was the rebirth of Vasyla, and Calypso intended to make the most of it.

Acknowledgments

I have to start by thanking my dogs. Starting with Cooper. Without you, I never would have come up with the title of *The Final Born*, and while you are no longer the youngest dog in the house – you are still the biggest baby here.

Bailey – thank you for cuddling next to me while I worked, you were distractingly adorable but I appreciate the attempt to support me.

Darcy, you challenge my patience – but at least you're cute.

To my very first beta reader, Kaitlin Sclafani – I loved reading your comments throughout my story, seeing you fangirl over certain characters and your excitement for what was to come helped me finish this project – and your feedback was out of this world! Thank you so much!

To the rest of the beta readers involved in the project: Ann, Jennell Brown, Rebekka Alvie, and the rest of my beta reader team – your feedback was incredibly valuable! Each one of your perspectives on the book made me see it in a new light and made the revision process much less of a struggle. Thank you all for your time and effort in reading and commenting on my book!

To all of the artists involved in this project: Miriam Schwardt, Okaykois, Senrouk, the team at Etheric Tales, and Saumya Singh –

you all absolutely blew it out of the park with your extraordinary work!

To my three favorite literature professors: Dane Galloway, David Ball, and Darcy Lewis. You all helped me not only enjoy classical literature but to learn how to become a better writer by studying it. Thank you all!

To my family. Mom, if you ever make it this far in the final copy I will be so proud. Thank you for reading so many early editions of this and being willing to help me edit.

To my brother, Tristan, thank you for listening to me ramble about random ideas and helping me refine them. Also for listening to music from *Ghost* with me while I would rant about how *"That's so Leandre!"*

To my dad, thank you for listening to all of my ideas even though you aren't the biggest fan of fantasy – and for helping me come up with the best idea for the ending.

Finally, to those who are no longer with me but supported my work wholeheartedly. I always write with you in mind and will be forever grateful for your support of my wanting to become an author.

About the Author

Mason Monteith is a self-proclaimed champion daydreamer. From getting lost in a simple idea at the grocery store to zoning out while doing homework to envision the most fantastical of fantasy worlds. She has been writing fantasy for over a decade now – though she only recently got into self-publishing her works. She is a book fanatic, a movie nut, a freelance writer/editor, an avid *Soulsborne* fan, and for fun photographer. She does her best writing at a cafe, in the woods, or on the couch with her three dogs Bailey, Cooper, and Darcy all piled on top of her. Mason loves to get into the nitty-gritty of the lore of her favorite stories and games and loves to piece bits of hidden stories together. There is a story in everything after all! From the obvious stories of strangers on the street to the smallest hidden ring forgotten on the back of a shelf. Stories are everywhere – and she intends to find and make the most of them.

www.ingramcontent.com/pod-product-compliance
Lightning Source LLC
Chambersburg PA
CBHW031201010826
48971CB00013B/1177